CELESTIAL SILENCE: THE DEADLY SECRET

CELESTIAL SILENCE: THE DEADLY SECRET

DAVID LINGARD

Prologue

In the year 2028, Earth's leaders made a momentous decision that could change the direction of the human race for generations to come: humanity would finally begin colonising the moon. The Lunar Settlement Initiative, or LSI, was an ambitious project that aimed to establish a permanent human presence on our celestial neighbour. The mission demanded precise calculations, coordination, and the utmost in human ingenuity to achieve its goals of becoming not only self-sufficient, but also expandable.

Dr Alice Mendez, a brilliant astrophysicist who had worked with teams from around the world for a number of years, was chosen to head the LSI. She had spent her entire career studying lunar colonisation and was well-versed in the intricacies and the difficulties of the task ahead. Alongside her was a team of skilled engineers, scientists, and astronauts, all focused on overcoming the challenges that lay before them. The mission not only relied upon the pioneers that would relocate to the lunar settlement themselves, but also on the Earth-based team led by Dr Mendez.

The team's first objective was to place a manned shuttle on the moon. The shuttle, dubbed 'Lunar Pioneer I,' was designed to transport the small initial crew of scientists and engineers. These pioneers would be tasked with laying the groundwork for a permanent lunar settlement so that the following teams and future inhabitants would have a solid foundation on which to build.

To ensure the Lunar Pioneer I's safe arrival, Dr Mendez and her team had to account for a myriad of factors. They needed to calculate the optimal launch window, taking into account the distance, the alignment of Earth and the moon, and the orbital mechanics that would allow the shuttle to use as little fuel as possible. The calculations were painstakingly detailed, with little room for error and everyone involved was meticulously chosen for their skill and expertise.

Meanwhile, a separate team of engineers was responsible for designing the habitat modules and supply shuttles that would be sent to the moon ahead of the crew. These unmanned shuttles, known as 'Lunar Cargo Carriers,' would transport the materials needed to build the settlement and sustain its inhabitants.

The engineers designed the habitat modules to be modular and easy to assemble, ensuring that the crew could quickly set up a base upon arrival. The modules included living quarters, research facilities, large capacity batteries, solar arrays and life-support systems, all designed to withstand the harsh lunar environment and provide a sustainable living arrangement for the entire project.

As the launch date approached, Dr Mendez and her team carefully monitored every variable. They scrutinised the weather on Earth, the solar radiation levels in space, and the stability of the lunar landing site. Any small deviation could jeopardise the entire mission.

Finally, the day arrived. The Lunar Pioneer I and the Lunar Cargo Carriers were ready for launch. Millions of people around the world held their breath as the countdown began.

"Ten, nine, eight..."

The rocket engines roared to life, and the Lunar Pioneer I soared into the sky, followed closely by the speedier Lunar Cargo Carriers. As the vehicles disappeared into the vastness of space, the world as one celebrated this historic achievement.

Once in space, the Lunar Pioneer I and the Cargo Carriers began their carefully calculated journey to the moon. The team on Earth, led by Dr Mendez, monitored their progress around the clock. They kept a close eye on the spacecraft's trajectories, ensuring they remained on course and adjusting their paths as needed.

After just days of travel, the Lunar Cargo Carriers reached the moon ahead of the Lunar Pioneer I, as planned. They successfully deployed the habitat modules and supplies, paving the way for the manned shuttle's arrival. Everything went without a hitch.

Finally, the Lunar Pioneer I approached its destination. The crew, led by Captain Jack Armstrong, prepared for the descent onto the lunar surface. Every detail of the descent had been meticulously planned, and the stakes were higher than ever, given that this time there were human lives on board.

The descent was tense, with Captain Armstrong and his crew carefully following Dr Mendez's instructions. The Lunar Pioneer I's engines fired in precise bursts, slowing the shuttle down for a soft landing.

As the dust settled, the Lunar Pioneer I touched down on the moon's surface, marking a new era for humanity. The crew disembarked, and they stood on the lunar soil, staring at the blue marble that was Earth in the distance, filled with awe and a sense of accomplishment. They had made history, becoming the first humans to establish a foothold on the moon. But their mission had only just begun.

Under the guidance of Dr Mendez and the team back on Earth, the crew began to assemble the habitat modules. The process was slow and laborious as the astronauts adapted to the moon's reduced gravity and the challenges of working in their bulky spacesuits. But they pressed on, fuelled by the knowledge that they were paving the way for generations to come.

As the habitat took shape, Captain Armstrong and his team encountered unexpected difficulties. The lunar regolith proved more challenging to work with than anticipated, and the crew had to improvise new techniques to stabilise the foundation of the settlement.

Back on Earth, Dr Mendez and her team analysed the data from the lunar pioneers, learning from their struggles and adapting the mission plan accordingly. With each passing day, the lunar settlement grew stronger and more stable, a testament to human ingenuity and resilience.

Once the habitat was complete, the crew turned their attention to the life-support systems. They needed to ensure that the settlement could generate power, recycle air and water, and maintain a stable temperature. The team worked tirelessly, testing and refining the systems, all the while relying on the expertise of Dr Mendez and her colleagues on Earth.

As the weeks passed, the lunar pioneers began to acclimate to their new home and surroundings. They conducted experiments, studied the lunar environment, and documented their experiences for future generations. It was a time of discovery and learning, as humanity took its first steps toward a permanent presence on the moon.

Meanwhile, back on Earth, the success of the Lunar Settlement Initiative captivated the world. News outlets covered every development, inspiring a renewed interest in space exploration and igniting the imaginations of millions. Young people around the globe aspired to become astronauts, engineers, and scientists, eager to contribute to the next phase of human exploration and as far afield as the human race would dare to travel.

As the months turned into years, the lunar settlement continued to grow and evolve. New modules were added, expanding the living and research quarters, and additional supply shuttles brought advanced technology and resources from Earth. The pioneers conducted groundbreaking research, uncovering new insights into the moon's geology, the effects of long-term space habitation on the human body, and the potential for utilising lunar resources to further humanity's reach into the cosmos. All in all, the mission lurched from success to success.

The Lunar Settlement Initiative was not without its challenges, but through the dedication and perseverance of countless individuals, humanity had once and for all, successfully colonised the moon. Earth's first lunar settlement stood as a shining beacon of human achievement, a testament to our potential as a species, and the beginning of a new chapter in the story of our exploration of the universe.

As the lunar settlement grew, its inhabitants predictably formed a tight-knit community, though this community was led by a small group of individuals. These pioneers hailed from diverse backgrounds, each with their unique skills and personalities. Together, they overcame the challenges of life on the moon and created a home away from Earth.

Captain Jack Armstrong, a seasoned astronaut and the leader of the pioneers, was known for his calm demeanour and unwavering focus. He inspired confidence in his crew and maintained a strong rapport with Dr Mendez and her team on Earth.

Dr Priya Nair, a geologist and the settlement's lead scientist, was passionate about understanding the moon's geological history. Her enthusiasm was infectious, and she often led the crew on expeditions to explore lunar craters, caves, and other interesting areas of the lunar landscape.

Grace Thompson, a skilled engineer, had a knack for fixing and maintaining the settlement's equipment. Her resourcefulness and quick thinking were invaluable, as she frequently improvised solutions to unexpected issues that arose in the harsh lunar environment and as the equipment they had brought with them aged.

Leo Martinez, the crew's botanist, was responsible for cultivating plants in the settlement's hydroponic garden. This quiet and introspective man took pride in providing fresh vegetables and herbs to the crew, knowing how essential they were for both nutrition and morale.

Dr Adrian Whittaker, an expert geologist was tasked with sampling sections of the moon's surface to test for their mineral content. It was only with the dedicated human eye, rather than precise machinery could it be determined where crops could potentially grow, or what minerals of value could be extracted from the surface of the planet.

Daily life in the lunar settlement was both exciting and demanding. The pioneers followed a strict schedule, with time allotted for work, exercise, meals, and sleep. Due to the moon's weaker gravity, the crew had to perform daily exercise routines to maintain their muscle strength and bone density.

Breakfast was a time for the pioneers to come together and share a meal, often consisting of rehydrated or freeze-dried foods brought from Earth, supplemented with fresh produce from the hydroponic garden.

The crew would discuss their plans for the day and exchange information about ongoing projects.

During the workday, a strict rota was adhered to. Workgroups of three would work in rotating shift patterns of between six and eight hours so that at no point was anyone ever alone. This rule of course did not come into play for the heads of departments, Jack, Priya, Grace, Leo and Adrian.

The pioneers performed a variety of tasks, from conducting experiments and maintaining equipment to exploring the lunar surface and tending to the garden. They always had to work efficiently, knowing that their time outside the habitat was limited by their spacesuits' life support systems. All except for Leo Martinez, who could carry out all of his duties from inside the habs.

In the evenings, groups would gather in the common areas, taking a moment to relax and unwind. They shared stories from their lives on Earth, played games, and watched movies from the extensive digital library that Dr Mendez had curated. These shared moments of camaraderie were deemed vital in maintaining their mental health, as they were isolated from friends, family, and the comforts of Earth.

Despite the harsh conditions and isolation, the pioneers found solace in their shared mission and the support of their fellow crew members. The lunar settlement was not just a collection of habitat modules and equipment; it was a home built on the foundation of trust, friendship, and human resilience. And as they gazed upon the Earth, shining like a beacon in the darkness of space, the pioneers knew that they were writing a new chapter in the story of humanity.

Evidence: Statement - Captain Jack Armstrong

I, Captain Jack Armstrong, leader of the Lunar Settlement Expedition, submit this official statement regarding the tragic death of Dr Adrian Whitaker. The following account is based on my personal observations, as well as information gathered from my team members during the course of our investigation.

On February 16th, 2043, at approximately 09:45 Lunar Standard Time, I was alerted by Dr Priya Nair, our lead scientist, that Dr Whitaker had not reported to his scheduled shift at the geological laboratory.

Concerned about his absence, and knowing that Dr Whitaker took pride in his punctuality and dedication to his work, I decided to go and check on his living quarters.

Upon reaching Dr Whitaker's quarters, I found his door locked. Repeated knocks and attempts to communicate with him bore no response. Given the circumstances, I made the decision to override the door's security protocols and enter his room. As Captain I was within my rights to do so as I believed that the wellbeing of one of my crew could've been in danger.

Inside, I discovered that Dr Whitaker's living quarters were in disarray, with various items scattered across the floor. It appeared as if someone had broken in to the place to try to find something. I do not know if they found what they were looking for.

However, Dr Whitaker himself was not in the room. Immediately after this discovery, I initiated a full-scale search for Dr Whitaker, enlisting the help of the entire settlement's crew. We began a systematic search of all modules within the habitat, as well as the surrounding lunar surface within a reasonable radius, taking into consideration the limitations of our life support systems. We also continuously broadcast a radio signal in the hope that Dr Whittaker would hear it and make his presence known.

During the search, I interviewed several crew members who had interacted with Dr Whitaker in the days leading up to his disappearance. According to their testimonies, Dr Whitaker had been exhibiting some signs of stress and had become increasingly distant in the days prior, though during this expedition I note that most people do experience such issues.

In addition, Dr Whittaker was overheard having hushed conversations on his communication device, seemingly with someone back on Earth though the subject of these calls was not clear. Despite his unusual behaviour, no one reported witnessing any altercations or conflicts involving Dr Whitaker.

On February 18th, 2043, after nearly two full days of searching, one of our engineers, Grace Thompson, discovered Dr Whitaker's lifeless body in a remote and distant section of the lunar surface, approximately three kilometres from the settlement. This section had not been designated as an area of interest, nor was it on any schedule to be assessed for mineral composition, according to my conversations with Dr Nair.

Dr Whittaker's suit appeared to be damaged, with a puncture in the torso area, which had caused a catastrophic loss of oxygen.

Grace then, under instruction from Dr Nair carefully transported Dr Whitaker's body back to the settlement for further examination. Dr Nair, who has some experience in forensic pathology, performed an initial assessment of Dr Whitaker's injuries. She determined that the puncture to his suit was not accidental but rather appeared to have been inflicted by a sharp, pointed object, likely wielded by another person.

The unsettling realisation that Dr Whitaker's death was likely a result of foul play sent shockwaves throughout our small community. It was difficult to accept that one of our own could be responsible for such a heinous act. Nonetheless, I made it my priority to ensure the safety of my team and to discover the truth behind Dr Whitaker's untimely demise. Whatever it would take.

In the days following the discovery of Dr Whitaker's body, I conducted thorough interviews with each crew member, attempting to piece together a timeline of events and identify any potential suspects. During these interviews, I focused on gathering information about Dr Whitaker's recent activities, as well as any possible conflicts or altercations he may have had with other crew members.

Despite my efforts, establishing a clear timeline proved to be challenging, as many crew members had only limited interactions with Dr Whitaker in the days leading up to his death. However, it was again reinforced that he seemed to have been under an unusually large amount of stress, and sometimes his conversations seemed shallow or distant with other crew members. I tried to find out more information regarding the hushed or secretive communications that he was having with somebody back on Earth, but again my investigations led to a dead end.

As I continued my investigation, I paid close attention to the alibis provided by each crew member. While some had seemingly solid alibis, others were more difficult to verify due to the nature of their work or the absence of witnesses during the time of Dr Whitaker's disappearance and subsequent murder. The fact that the crew always worked in strict rotations did narrow the possible pool of perpetrators though. This fact is what saddens me the most; one of my most trusted heads of departments could have done this.

Despite my efforts, no concrete evidence emerged that would implicate any specific individual in the crime.

Ultimately, my investigation hit a brick wall. With no solid leads or evidence pointing to the identity of Dr Whitaker's killer, I was forced to make the difficult decision to request assistance from Earth-based authorities. It is my hope that the additional resources and expertise available on Earth will help to solve this tragic case and bring the responsible party to justice.

In the meantime, I have implemented additional security measures within the settlement to ensure the safety of the remaining crew members, though I am unable to carry out any specific security measures as each member of the team is mission critical, and vital to our ongoing success.

We all mourn the loss of Dr Whitaker, and we are determined to see justice served, no matter how long it takes or how difficult the path to uncovering the truth may be.

This concludes my account of the events surrounding Dr Adrian Whitaker's death. I solemnly affirm that the details provided in this statement are true and accurate to the best of my knowledge.

Signed,

Captain Jack Armstrong Lunar Settlement Expedition

The News that Shook the World

Breaking news: it has been brought to our attention here at Live News Today, that the Lunar Settlement Initiative has been rocked by the loss of one of its key members: Geologist Dr Adrian Whittaker who has been a part of the initiative for many years.

Dr Whittaker, a respected scientist and integral part of the Lunar Settlement Expedition, was found dead on the surface of the moon, on the morning of February 18th. His death is being investigated as a potential homicide, and the remaining members of the settlement have been placed on high alert. As yet, no formal accusations or allegations have been made.

The Lunar Settlement Initiative, a joint venture between various space agencies from around the world, has been at the forefront of scientific research on the moon for the past decade. The settlement, which consists of a team of five lead scientists and engineers, as well as a crew numbering in the sixties has been tasked with conducting experiments and research into various fields including geology, botany, and astronomy. This initiative has been widely touted as the very future of human existence, and the first real step towards the human race colonising anything other than planet Earth.

Dr Whittaker, the lead geologist on the team had been on the moon since the first landing, studying the unique geological features of the lunar surface. His work was considered vital to the success of the settlement's mission, and his loss has come as a devastating blow to the team and the wider scientific community.

The circumstances surrounding Dr Whittaker's death remain unclear, but early reports suggest that foul play may have been involved. Only very few members of the expedition were capable of carrying out such a crime, and there were apparently signs of a struggle. The remaining members of the team, including the settlement's lead scientists, are being questioned by Captain Jack Armstrong in an effort to determine what happened to Dr Whittaker. It is unclear how effective this investigation can be within the tight-knit settlement, and authorities around the globe are doing what they can to try and aid in the process.

The news of Dr Whittaker's death has sent shockwaves through the scientific community, with many expressing their condolences to his family and colleagues. Dr Karen Patel, a professor of planetary science at the University of Edinburgh, described Dr Whittaker as "a brilliant scientist and a kind and generous person who will be missed not only for his scientific contributions to the world, but also as a loving and devoted father and husband."

The investigation into Dr Whittaker's death is ongoing, and The Lunar Settlement Initiative has released a statement assuring the world that they are fully cooperating with the investigation, and that the safety of the remaining team members is their top priority.

The loss of Dr Whittaker is a reminder of the dangers that come with exploring the universe beyond our small blue planet. The Lunar Settlement Initiative and other space agencies around the world, will no doubt use this tragedy as a catalyst to improve safety measures and protocols for future missions. But for now, the focus remains on finding out what happened to Dr Whittaker and bringing those responsible to justice.

The scientific community has been left reeling from the loss of one of its most esteemed members, and the world waits with bated breath for answers to the many questions surrounding Dr Whittaker's untimely death. As investigations continue on the lunar settlement, experts from around the globe will undoubtedly join forces to try and piece together the puzzle of what happened to Dr Whittaker and ensure that justice is served. The future of space exploration hangs in the balance, and only time will tell how this tragedy will shape our understanding of what it means to explore the vast expanse beyond our planet.

In the wake of Dr Whittaker's death, the Lunar Settlement Initiative remains on high alert. The remaining members of the team are all suspects in the investigation, and tensions must already be running high in the tightly-knit settlement.

~

Reports from the moon were limited, as communication with the settlement was disrupted by the ongoing investigation. The world watched and waited for updates on the case, as experts speculated on what might have happened on the lunar surface.

Vince Callahan, a renowned investigator with a track record of solving high-profile cases was inevitably brought in to assist in the investigation. With his expertise and experience, it was hoped that he could provide fresh insights into the case and help bring the killer to justice.

Vince had immediately set to work as soon as he had been given the task that the entire world was watching, slowly working through all of the information that was available from the lunar surface. He knew that the devil was always in the details, though not being able to visualise the actual place where the crime was committed was always going to be an issue.

Chapter 1: Vincent "Vince" Callahan

Vince Callahan carefully read Captain Jack Armstrong's official statement on the screen in front of him. His keen eyes darted back and forth, taking in every word and detail about the tragic death of Dr Adrian Whitaker. Even though the account seemed thorough and sincere, Vince couldn't shake the nagging feeling that something was amiss.

As he read, Vince mentally dissected each section of the statement, searching for discrepancies or inconsistencies. He couldn't help but wonder if Captain Armstrong had truly revealed everything he knew, or if there were pieces of information deliberately left out to protect someone, or to maintain the illusion of control over the situation. After all, if there was anyone that should've been in control on the lunar surface, it was the Captain. If anything had happened that shouldn't have, or was happening that shouldn't, then there was always the possibility of a cover up.

Vince paid particular attention to the accounts of Dr Whitaker's unusual behaviour prior to his disappearance and the hushed conversations with someone back on Earth caught Vince's attention. He internally questioned why Captain Armstrong didn't mention any attempts to identify or contact the person Dr Whitaker was communicating with. Surely, that person could provide valuable insights into Dr Whitaker's state of mind and any potential motives of his killer.

The Detective also scrutinised the alibis of all of the crew members. He wondered whether Captain Armstrong's own assessment of their alibis might have been influenced by personal relationships, given the close-knit nature of the lunar settlement. As a seasoned investigator, Vince knew that it was not uncommon for people to be blind to the guilt of those close to them. The dynamic of the lunar settlement though, pointed his mind in only a few directions; if the crew worked in rotating shift patterns and only the heads of departments were allowed to work alone, then it reduced the pool of suspects down dramatically.

Vince leaned back in his chair and placed his hands behind his head, taking a moment to ponder the situation. He knew that to truly understand the events surrounding Dr Whitaker's death, he would need to delve deeper into the lives of the crew members, their relationships, and the overall dynamics of the lunar settlement. There were likely hidden tensions, rivalries, and secrets that could shed light on the case, and it would be his job to uncover them.

As he continued to analyse the statement, Vince felt a surge of determination swell within him. He knew that his unique perspective and expertise as a Detective could make all the difference in solving this case and as usual, he vowed to bring justice to those who had passed.

However, he also knew that it wouldn't be easy. The Lunar Settlement Expedition was like a family, and the crew members had been living and working together for months. Any investigation would likely be met with suspicion and resistance. Additionally, the unique challenges of conducting an investigation in a lunar environment, with limited resources and communication capabilities, would make the process even more difficult.

But Vince wasn't deterred. He had a reputation for being thorough and relentless in his pursuit of justice, and he was determined to uncover the truth behind Dr Whitaker's death, no matter what obstacles he faced.

Vince Callahan had built a reputation as one of the most sought-after private Detectives in the world. Over the years, he had taken on countless cases that had stumped government agencies and law enforcement, earning him the respect and admiration of his peers in the industry. From solving complex financial fraud cases to uncovering high-profile political scandals, there was no challenge too great for Vince to tackle.

So when the news broke that the first murder outside of Earth's atmosphere had occurred, it was no surprise that Vince's phone began to ring off the hook. Everyone from government officials to private companies were eager to hire him to solve the case. However, Vince was not one to be swayed by the promise of fame or fortune. He carefully considered his position before ultimately accepting the contract from the Lunar Settlement Initiative.

As Vince began to delve into the details of the case that the LSI had provided, he couldn't help but feel a sense of excitement mixed with apprehension. This was a case like nothing he had ever worked on before. The sheer fact that a murder had occurred on the moon was unprecedented, and he knew that the eyes of the world would be on him to solve it. It was a daunting task, but Vince had confidence in his abilities as a Detective, and again, he felt he owed it to the victim and the family he left behind to solve the case.

As he began his process, Vince reviewed the official statement provided by Captain Jack Armstrong. While the statement was thorough, Vince couldn't shake the feeling that there was more to the story than what was being presented. He knew that in cases like these, people often had something to hide or protect, and he was determined to uncover any hidden truths.

Vince's first step was always to gather as much information as possible, and in this case, it was predominantly about the Lunar Settlement Expedition and its crew members. He conducted extensive background research on each crew member, including their personal and professional histories, relationships, and any potential motives for harming Dr Whitaker. Vince knew that the key to solving any case was to understand the people involved and the dynamics at play, and this case was no different.

He also made his list of potential suspects, taking into consideration any suspicious behaviours or alibis provided by the crew members.

Vince knew that he needed to remain objective and unbiased in his investigation, but he couldn't help but feel a sense of unease about how short his list was.

In order to gather more information, Vince began to research the technology and procedures used in the Lunar Settlement Expedition. He studied the design and layout of the settlement, the equipment and tools used by the crew, and the protocols for communication and emergency situations. He also familiarised himself with the limitations and challenges of life on the moon, such as the harsh environmental conditions and the reliance on technology for survival.

As he dug deeper into the details, Vince began to piece together a timeline of events leading up to Dr Whitaker's death. He studied the official statement and cross-referenced it with other reports and testimonies from the crew members. He noted any discrepancies or inconsistencies and made a list of questions that he would need to ask when the time came.

Vince also made connections with experts in relevant fields such as forensic pathology, lunar geology, and space technology. He knew that he could then lean on their expertise and guidance as he delved deeper into the investigation, though he knew that sometimes involving more people than necessary in a case could be dangerous.

As he worked tirelessly to gather information and piece together the puzzle, Vince's sense of determination grew stronger. He knew that he was on the right track and that he would eventually uncover the truth behind Dr Whitaker's death, he could sense it. He also knew that he would need to be prepared for the unexpected, as this case was like no other he had ever encountered.

Evidence: Statement –
Grace Thompson

I, Grace Thompson, engineer of the Lunar Settlement Expedition, submit this official statement regarding the tragic death of Dr Adrian Whitaker. The following account is based on my personal observations, as well as information gathered from my team members during the course of our investigation.

On February 16th, 2043, at approximately 09:45 Lunar Standard Time, I was in the main engineering bay working on routine maintenance of our life support systems when I heard that Dr Whitaker had not reported to his scheduled shift at the geological laboratory. Given the urgency of the situation, I immediately volunteered to join the search for Dr Whitaker, hoping that my knowledge of the settlement's infrastructure and the lunar surface could be of assistance. Unfortunately I found nothing that pointed to the whereabouts of Dr Whittaker.

For the next two days, the entire crew searched tirelessly for Dr Whitaker, both inside and outside the habitat. During this time, I mainly focused on the external search, using my engineering background to search areas that might be difficult for others to access or even recognise as potential hiding places. I checked the solar arrays and the battery storage compounds as these are places that are potentially dangerous for people who don't know what they're doing, but also large enough to hide someone from view if they get trapped.

On February 18th, 2043, while searching a barren section of the lunar surface approximately 3 kilometres from the settlement, I discovered Dr

Whitaker's lifeless body. His suit was damaged, with a clear puncture in the torso area that had caused a catastrophic loss of oxygen. It was a horrifying sight, and one that I'll never forget. I checked to see if Dr Whittaker was responsive but it was clear that he had been out of oxygen for a long time.

After alerting the rest of the crew and receiving instructions from Captain Armstrong and Dr Nair, I carefully transported Dr Whitaker's body back to the settlement for further examination. Dr Priya Nair, our lead scientist, performed an initial assessment of his injuries and concluded that the puncture to his suit was not accidental, but rather, appeared to have been inflicted by a sharp, pointed object. I can't honestly comment on this because I had no involvement in the assessment of the Doctor's body.

I was shocked at the fact that Dr Nair determined that the damage to Dr Whittaker's suit wasn't accidental because it could only mean one thing: that somebody up here had killed him and on purpose. I don't know what to think or who to trust, but I can say truthfully that I have no idea who to suspect.

After the determination by Dr Nair, I cooperated fully with Captain Armstrong's investigation, providing any information and assistance that I could, in hopes of finding the person responsible for Dr Whitaker's death.

In the days following the discovery of Dr Whitaker's body, I continued to work on the settlement's engineering systems while also assisting with the ongoing investigation whenever possible. Like the rest of the crew, I was interviewed by Captain Armstrong, during which I provided details about my interactions with Dr Whitaker, as well as any observations I had made regarding his behaviour in the days leading up to his disappearance.

Despite my own efforts, I had no ideas or insights into who might have been responsible for Dr Whitaker's death. It was a deeply troubling and unsettling situation that weighed heavily on all of us. I, like everyone else, mourn the loss of Dr Whitaker and hope that the truth behind his untimely demise will eventually be uncovered.

As time has passed, I can't help but feel a sense of unease, knowing that the killer is still among us. It was a sobering reminder of the fragility of our small community on the lunar surface, and the importance of trust among our team. I was and am still determined to do everything in my power to help bring justice to Dr Whitaker and restore a sense of security to the settlement.

In my statement, I have provided all the information that I can recall regarding the events surrounding Dr Whitaker's disappearance and death. I solemnly affirm that the details provided in this statement are true and accurate to the best of my knowledge.

Signed,

Grace Thompson

Lunar Settlement Expedition

Chapter 2: Pioneer

Vince Callahan sighed as he glanced at the stack of reports and audio recordings on his desk. There was only so much information one could glean from written statements and voices over the radio. No matter how hard he tried to analyse the available data, he simply couldn't shake the feeling that something was missing, a piece of the puzzle that remained elusive. He needed to be there, on the lunar surface, to get a true sense of what had transpired. Only then would he be able to place all of the pieces of the puzzle together and get a clear image of what happened up there.

He leaned back in his chair and rubbed his temples, feeling the tension in his muscles where he had been holding his shoulders so high as he worked. The murder of Dr Adrian Whitaker was a high-profile case, and the pressure to solve it was immense. With the Lunar Settlement Expedition rapidly expanding, new habitats being built, and more people joining the colony, the stakes were higher than ever. But of course, what had already happened was never going to change. The thought of a murderer running loose on the lunar surface, though, was a chilling prospect, and Vince knew he had to act fast to ensure the safety of everyone on the expedition.

His decision made, Vince drafted a request to the LSI stating that it was his intent to personally visit the moon. He explained that he needed to be physically present at the crime scene to conduct a thorough investigation, and that he wished to travel on the next shuttle heading to the moon. Shuttles were of course infrequent, and manned shuttles even less so, but he knew that coincidentally there was a staffing rotation soon to happen on the lunar settlement, and he could therefore travel up and back in a short space of time, but also be in a better position to conduct his investigation.

Vince was no stranger to challenging cases, but this one was different. With each new bit of information, it seemed as if the case became more complicated, the threads intertwining and diverging in unexpected ways and it was his physical distance from the case that seemed to be fuelling these difficulties. As a seasoned private investigator, Vince had a knack for getting to the heart of a mystery, but this one already felt like it was slipping through his fingers.

Days passed and Vince grew increasingly restless, waiting for the LSI's response but hearing nothing either way. In the meantime, he continued to pour over the evidence, searching for patterns and connections that might provide a breakthrough. He listened to the recorded interviews and read the written statements from Captain Jack Armstrong and engineer Grace Thompson multiple times, trying to discern any inconsistencies or hidden clues.

Finally, the response he'd been waiting for arrived and it wasn't a moment too soon. The LSI – and Dr Mendez - granted Vince's request and in doing so gave him permission to travel to the moon as part of the upcoming shuttle mission. He would be joining a group of scientists, engineers, and other specialists all bound for the lunar surface to contribute to the ongoing expansion of the colony.

A mixture of excitement and trepidation washed over Vince as he began to prepare for his journey. He had never been to space before, let alone the moon, and he knew the experience would be unlike anything he'd ever encountered. But he was determined to uncover the truth behind Dr Whitaker's death, no matter how far he had to travel or what challenges he might face.

As the days counted down to his departure, Vince immersed himself in training for his lunar mission under the expert tutelage of the seasoned pro's from the LSI. He learned about the specific challenges of working in a low-gravity environment, the intricacies of the life support systems, and the basics of lunar geology. He wanted to be as prepared as possible when he arrived, ready to hit the ground running in his search for the truth, and the LSI did everything within their power to ensure Vince had all the tools he would need in his arsenal when dealing with such a mission.

Finally, when the day of the launch arrived, Vince knew that he was ready. He found himself clad in a sleek spacesuit, his heart pounding in his chest. Everything felt tight, but he knew that once they had launched and the shuttle had breached the Earth's atmosphere, he could remove much of the bulky suit and walk freely around the shuttle.

The shuttle loomed before Vince, a gleaming testament to human ingenuity and ambition. He took a deep breath, steadying himself as he slowly walked the boarding ramp, the eyes of the world upon him and the others.

Vince quickly took his seat along with the others and as the shuttle roared to life to begin its ascent, Vince felt a rush of adrenaline unlike anything he'd ever experienced. The shuttle began to move and he watched the Earth recede in the window, quickly becoming a distant blue orb suspended in the void of space. His destination loomed ahead, the barren, cold, silvery surface of the moon beckoning.

The shuttle that Vince was now free to move about in was a marvel of modern engineering, the result of decades of research and development. The vessel, "Luna's Promise," was designed not only for safety and efficiency, but also for comfort and in some cases even luxury, a far cry from the cramped, utilitarian spacecraft of the past. Its sleek, stream-lined exterior seemed almost sculpted from advanced materials, making it both lightweight and incredibly durable.

Once Vince had stretched his legs, removed some layers and settled into his seat, he was immediately struck by how smooth and quiet the ride was. Gone were the days of deafening rocket engines and bone-shaking vibrations and G-forces. Instead, the shuttle glided effortlessly through the space, propelled by an array of state-of-the-art powerful ion thrusters. There was still the feel of immense acceleration of course, but it was nothing like what he had been expecting.

The interior of Luna's Promise was luxuriously appointed, with soft lighting, plush seating, and an array of amenities designed to make the journey as pleasant as possible. Vince couldn't help but marvel at the high-resolution display panels that lined the walls, showing real-time views of the Earth and the Moon as they travelled along their path.

The Earth as seen from the shuttle, was a breath-taking sight. The vibrant blues, greens, and browns of the planet's surface were juxtaposed against the inky blackness of space, creating a stunning visual tapestry that Vince found himself staring at for hours on end. He felt a pang of nostalgia and a deep sense of awe as he watched his home planet recede into the distance, a testament to the ingenuity and determination of the human spirit. Vince had never left Earth before, and although it was expected to become quite normal to do so now, he still felt the slight twang of trepidation at the experience.

As the Moon drew nearer and the viewscreens shifted to images of the lunar surface, Vince was struck by its stark, otherworldly beauty. The barren, grey landscape was a mesmerising contrast to the vibrant Earth he had left behind. Craters and mountains stretched across the regolith, a testament to the violent history of the celestial body. As the shuttle continued to approach its destination, Vince found himself captivated by the desolate beauty of the Moon.

The journey from Earth to the Moon took approximately three days, giving Vince ample time to familiarise himself with the shuttle and his fellow passengers. In addition to the crew and scientists bound for the lunar settlement, there were a few other passengers, each with their own reasons for making the voyage. Among them, Vince happened across a woman named Eleanor Whittaker, who, as Vince would immediately realise, was the wife of the late Dr Adrian Whitaker.

Eleanor was an attractive woman in her early forties, with a kind face and a quiet, introspective demeanour. She was an accomplished geologist in her own right and had been working back on Earth studying the composition of soils that could help plants grow in the harsh environments on the moon. She didn't work for the LSI, but it was apparent that she had been doing her best to do what she could to help her husband with his work. Vince wondered how difficult it must've been to live apart from her spouse for so many years.

It was during one of the group meals in the shuttle's dining area that Vince struck up a conversation with her.

"Excuse me, is this seat taken?" Vince asked politely, gesturing to the empty seat beside Eleanor.

She glanced up from her meal and offered a warm smile. "No, please, have a seat."

And then they began to chat. Eleanor revealed her connection to the victim. "Adrian was my husband," she explained, a note of sadness creeping into her voice. "He was a brilliant geologist, and his work on the moon was incredibly important to him. He loved the excitement and the challenges of living and working in such a unique environment."

Vince offered his condolences, genuinely moved by her loss. "I'm so sorry for your loss, Eleanor. I can't imagine how difficult this must be for you."

She nodded, her eyes glistening with unshed tears. "Thank you, Mr Callahan. It's been a terrible shock, and I still find it hard to believe that he's gone. But I hope that by coming here, I can find some answers and give him the send-off that he deserves."

Throughout their conversation, Eleanor shared more about her husband's life and work, painting a vivid picture of the man Vince was investigating. Adrian had been passionate about his research, dedicated to uncovering the secrets of the lunar surface and its potential to provide valuable resources for Earth. He had been enthusiastic about the possibilities of lunar colonisation and the opportunities it presented for scientific advancement.

Eleanor also spoke of their life together on Earth, of their love for each other, and the mutual support they provided in their respective careers. "We were a team," she said, her voice filled with pride. "We both believed in the importance of space exploration, and we wanted to contribute to the progress of humanity in any way we could."

In addition to their shared love for space exploration, Eleanor also revealed that they had a shared love for art. Adrian had a particular interest in photography, and he had taken stunning images of the lunar landscape during his time on the Moon. She showed Vince some of his work, and he was struck by the beauty and intricacy of the photos. It was clear that Adrian had a unique eye for capturing the essence of the lunar environment.

As they continued to chat, Vince couldn't help but notice that Eleanor seemed to be holding something back. There was a tension in her body language and a guardedness in her tone that suggested she was not completely comfortable discussing certain aspects of her husband's life, and Vince wondered if there was something she was not telling him, some piece of information that could shed light on the mystery of Adrian's death.

But Vince knew that it would be crass to begin his investigation early. Eleanor's demeanour could simply be that of a woman mourning the loss of her husband, caught in limbo between not having seen him for a long time, and journeying to visit his lifeless body. Vince could only imagine the pain that the woman must have been experiencing.

Eventually, as the time passed and the lunar settlement came into view, the shuttle's intercom crackled to life, and the Captain's voice boomed through the speakers. "Attention, all passengers. We are approaching the lunar settlement, and we will begin the landing procedure in approximately fifteen minutes. Please ensure that your belongings are stowed and that you are seated with your seatbelts fastened."

As the shuttle began its descent towards the lunar surface, Vince felt a flutter of excitement and anticipation. It was morbid, but he was eager to begin his investigation. He glanced over at Eleanor and saw that she was staring out of the window, her expression pensive and contemplative.

As they landed softly at the settlement, Vince could feel the tension in the air. The other passengers and crew members were quiet and subdued, their thoughts no doubt turning to the tragedy that had occurred there that had become widespread knowledge back on Earth.

Vince gathered his belongings and made his way to the exit, where he was met by a team of security personnel.

They escorted him into the first of a series of white habitats that, up close, seemed so much larger than he would have guessed. On the TV, when they'd shown the lunar settlement placed against the backdrop of vast, grey nothingness, these habitats always seemed so tiny and insignificant. Now though, Vince could see that they spanned up high and away from the shuttle as he peered out of the clear glass tube that connected the shuttle to the hab.

Captain Jack Armstrong greeted Vince upon his arrival at the main control hub. This was the man in charge of the colony and the person who had been leading the investigation into Dr Whitaker's death. With a firm handshake, the Captain welcomed Vince to the settlement and expressed his gratitude for the investigator's involvement in the case.

"You have no idea how relieved we are to have you here, Mr Callahan," Captain Armstrong said earnestly. "We've done our best to investigate, but we're certainly not experts in this field. We need someone with your skills and experience to help us find out what really happened here."

Vince nodded, understanding the gravity of the situation. "I'll do everything I can to solve this case, Captain. I'm committed to finding out what happened to Dr Whitaker and bringing the person responsible to justice."

As they walked through the lunar settlement, Captain Armstrong began introducing Vince to the key members of the crew. Each of them, in turn, would be a potential suspect in Dr Whitaker's death, and Vince knew he needed to get a feel for their personalities and motivations if he was to solve this case.

First, they met Grace Thompson, the engineer Vince had already read about in her written statement. She was Asian and an average though slender woman with a serious expression and an air of not quite knowing if she was truly in the right place. "I hope you can help us, Mr Callahan," she said, her voice quiet and sounding rather tired. "We're all on edge, and we need answers."

Vince nodded and gave Ms Thompson a warm handshake.

Next, Captain Armstrong introduced Vince to Dr Priya Nair, the lead scientist who had performed the initial assessment of Dr Whitaker's injuries. Dr Nair was a petite woman with dark, intelligent eyes and a warm smile. She shook Vince's hand and said, "I trust you'll do your best to find the truth, Mr Callahan. We all want to see justice done."

Again Vince politely made his introduction and offered the Doctor a warm smile.

The last introduction to make, was that of Leo Martinez, the settlement's botanist. Vince knew that he had a quick wit and a seemingly endless supply of anecdotes about his life on Earth. He greeted Vince with a hearty laugh, clapping him on the back as he said, "Welcome to our humble abode, Mr Callahan! I hope you can bring us some peace."

As Vince met each crew member, he carefully observed their reactions and body language, already looking for any signs that might indicate guilt or deception. While it was too early to make any definitive judgments, he knew that establishing a rapport with each of them would be essential to his investigation.

With the introductions complete, Captain Armstrong led Vince to a small, spartan room that would serve as his temporary quarters during his stay. "Make yourself at home, Mr Callahan," the Captain said, giving him a reassuring pat on the shoulder. "And if you need anything, don't hesitate to ask. We're all here to help."

The Captain left Vince to unpack and become accustomed to his new surroundings and as he settled into his new yet temporary home, Vince reflected on the task that lay ahead. The lunar settlement, with its tight-knit crew and isolated location, was unlike any crime scene he had ever encountered. But he was determined to find the truth behind Dr Whitaker's death and bring the murderer to justice, no matter where the investigation led him.

With a deep breath, Vince began to unpack his belongings, preparing himself for the long, difficult search for answers that awaited him on the lunar surface.

Just as Vince finished unpacking his belongings, there was an immediate knock at the door. Vince called out, "Come in," and the door slid open to reveal Captain Armstrong standing in the doorway again, with a smile on his face.

"Mr Callahan, I hope I'm not interrupting," the Captain said, taking a step into the room. "I know you haven't had much of a chance to properly begin yet... but I was just wondering if you had any thoughts about the case so far. Anything that stands out to you? You've read all the notes I take it?"

Vince looked at the Captain, noting the eagerness in his eyes. It was clear that Captain Armstrong was desperate for answers, and Vince couldn't blame him.

"Well, Captain, it's still too early for me to draw any concrete conclusions, but I do have some thoughts."

He gestured for the Captain to take a seat and proceeded to share some of his initial impressions. "From what I've gathered, it seems that Dr Whitaker was respected by his colleagues. However, that doesn't mean there couldn't have been some underlying tensions or conflicts that we're not yet aware of."

Captain Armstrong nodded, his brow furrowed. "Yes, I've considered that as well. Everyone here is under a lot of pressure, and it's possible that personal and professional lines may have been blurred. But who would have had a motive to murder him?"

Vince leaned back in his chair, crossing his arms. "That's the million-dollar question, Captain. I have a few potential leads, but I need to investigate further before I can be sure. I plan to spend some more time with the crew, get to know them better, and see if I can detect any inconsistencies or signs of deception. I'll also need to visit the crime scene and examine it for any clues that may have been overlooked."

Captain Armstrong nodded, his expression serious. "I understand, and I'll make sure you have full access to the crime scene and any other areas you need to investigate. But, Mr Callahan, I have to ask – do you have any suspicions at this point? Even if they're just hunches, I'd like to know what you think."

Vince hesitated for a moment, weighing his words carefully. "Captain, it's far too early for me to point fingers or name suspects. But there are a few things that have caught my attention. For example, I'd like to know more about the nature of Dr Whitaker's work and whether it could have played a role in his death. From what I understand, he was a respected geologist here in the settlement?"

Captain Armstrong nodded. "Yes, Dr Whitaker was a geologist, and his work focused primarily on the composition and distribution of lunar minerals. He was also part of a team exploring the possibility of extracting valuable resources from beneath the surface. This research has the potential to provide valuable resources for both the settlement and Earth. I can't see that his work might have made him a target, but it's hard to say for certain at this point."

Vince considered this information, his mind racing with possibilities. "In addition to his research, I'm also interested in learning more about Dr Whitaker's personal life. Were there any known conflicts or issues that might have contributed to his murder? Did he have any close friends or enemies among the crew?"

Captain Armstrong sighed, rubbing his temples. "Dr Whitaker was a private man, so I can't say anyone really knew him well on a personal level. However, I never observed any open conflicts or issues with other crew members. Still, I'll make sure you have access to his personnel file, as well as any communication records we have. Perhaps there's something there that could provide more insight into his relationships and motivations."

Vince nodded, making a mental note to review the files. "Thank you, Captain. I appreciate your cooperation in this investigation. Rest assured that I will do everything in my power to get to the bottom of this and find the person responsible for Dr Whitaker's death, one way or another."

Captain Armstrong offered a solemn nod. "I have full confidence in your abilities, Mr Callahan. The crew and I will assist you in any way we can. It's crucial that we bring his killer to justice and restore a sense of safety and stability to the settlement."

"There is one more thing though, Captain," Vince said. "During my research into the lunar settlement, it was noted that there were sixty-five members of the expedition at the time of Dr Whittaker's death."

"That's correct," Armstrong replied.

"And of these, sixty members were never allowed to be alone, due to their working patterns?"

"Yes," the Captain replied.

"Except for yourself, Grace Thompson, Dr Nair, Leo Martinez and Dr Whittaker himself, correct?"

"Yes, that is correct. Due to our protocols here regarding crew safety and mission viability, our crew work in rotating shift patterns, except for those you've already mentioned, of course."

"And this is how you negated most of the crew's involvements in this case?"

"It is," the Captain replied. "Because most people were together in groups of three, then it was easy to corroborate stories and alibis. I understand what you are saying, Mr Callahan, and I can't say that I didn't have the same thought: our pool of suspects, in this case, is rather small, and even I am not exempt from scrutiny here."

Vince nodded. "I appreciate your honesty, Captain. As part of my investigation, I will need to speak with each of the individuals you mentioned, including yourself, to establish their whereabouts and actions at the time of Dr Whitaker's death. I understand that this may be difficult or uncomfortable, but it's necessary for me to be thorough in my work."

"I understand," Armstrong said with a nod. "And I will ensure that everyone cooperates fully with your investigation."

Vince stood up, ready to leave the Captain's office. "Thank you for your time, Captain. I will be in touch as soon as I have any updates or further questions."

"Of course, Mr Callahan. Good luck with your investigation."

With their conversation concluded, Vince and Captain Armstrong left the quarters, and Vince began to lay out all of the information he had in front of him.

In the centre of his desk, Vince began to build a likely timeline of events, based upon the testimony that he had reviewed so far.

Timeline based on the testimonies of Captain Jack Armstrong and Grace Thompson:

- February 16th, 2043, 09:45 Lunar Standard Time: Dr Whitaker is reported missing by Dr Priya Nair after failing to show up for his shift at the geological laboratory.
- Captain Armstrong checks Dr Whitaker's living quarters, finding the quarters in a mess, but no trace of Dr Whitaker.
- Captain Armstrong initiates a full-scale search for Dr Whitaker involving the entire settlement crew.
- Interviews with crew members reveal that Dr Whitaker had been stressed and distant in the days leading up to his disappearance, engaging in secretive conversations with someone on Earth.
- February 18th, 2043: Engineer Grace Thompson discovers Dr Whitaker's lifeless body three kilometres from the settlement, with a punctured spacesuit.
- Dr Whitaker's body is transported back to the settlement for examination by Dr Nair, who determines the puncture in his suit was inflicted by a sharp object and probably not accidental.
- Captain Armstrong conducts thorough interviews with each crew member to gather information and establish a timeline.
- Despite the interviews, no concrete evidence emerges to implicate any specific individual in the crime.
- Additional security measures are implemented in the settlement by Captain Armstrong.
- The investigation ultimately hits a dead end, leading Captain Armstrong to request assistance from Earth-based authorities.

No matter how Vince looked at the timeline and the testimonies, there seemed to be no inconsistencies or anything particularly out of the ordinary.

Some minor differences between the two statements, he could see lay in the focus of each individual's account: Captain Armstrong's statement clearly focused more on his role as the leader of the Lunar Settlement Expedition and the investigation process, while Grace Thompson's statement was centred on her discovery of Dr Whitaker's body and her engineering background, which helped during the search.

Vince scratched the top of his head as he thought. It was a habit he'd picked up a long time ago, but these kinds of habits, he found, always helped place him in the correct mindset for the task that lay before him.

Chapter 3: The Scene of the Crime

As Vince continued to review the evidence, he couldn't help but wonder if there was something that had been overlooked, some detail that had been missed that would blow the case wide open. But in the end, he knew that he needed to take a closer look at the crime scene so that he could place his mindset on location. Then he would need to conduct more thorough interviews with each crew member if he was to have any hope of solving the case.

With a deep breath, Vince stood up and headed out of his quarters, determined to begin his investigation in earnest. He knew that the road ahead would certainly be long and difficult as it had a way of being, but he owed it to Adrian's wife, the lunar settlement and all the people who this affected to solve this case. Plus the eyes of the world would be watching and the results of his investigations would no doubt be on show once all of this was said and done.

As Vince walked through the narrow corridors of the lunar settlement, he could feel the weight of the artificial gravity pulling him down. Every step felt heavy and laboured as he adjusted to this new environment. He slowly made his way towards the airlock, where he was met by a team of security personnel and the engineer, Grace Thompson, who would be accompanying him to the crime scene.

"Mr. Callahan," Grace said, greeting him with a nod. "Are you ready to go?"

Vince nodded, his mouth dry with anticipation. Visiting the lunar surface was no doubt normal for all of the engineers and scientists up here, but to him this was completely different. And this was no sight-seeing trip. This was a mission to uncover the truth behind a man's death, and he knew that the stakes were high. He wondered if the circumstances were different whether he would be able to enjoy such an excursion. Perhaps one day he would find out.

"I'm ready," Vince said, trying to sound confident though there was a slight hesitation to his voice.

Grace then led him to a small room where a spacesuit was waiting for him. The suit was sleek and white, with a domed helmet that covered his entire head. Vince had worn spacesuits before and even one on the launch from Earth, but he knew that this one was different. This suit would be his lifeline as he ventured out into the harsh lunar environment and the more he thought about it, the flimsier it looked.

"Is this the kind of suit that Dr Whitaker was wearing when he died?" Vince asked, unable to shift his gaze from the point in the space suit that he had read had been torn on Dr Whittaker's suit.

Grace gave him a sort of awkward, half smile though didn't reply.

Vince took a deep breath and stepped into the suit, sealing it up with all of the clips and fasteners that lined up so perfectly. It was a slow and meticulous process, with each layer of the suit carefully checked and secured to ensure there were no leaks or vulnerabilities. Once he was fully sealed, he felt the suit's cooling system kick in, and he was immediately relieved to feel the chill on his skin.

Grace helped Vince into the vehicle that would take them to the crime scene. The rover was a small, open-top, wheeled vehicle that looked like a larger version of the Mars rovers. It had four wheels and a high suspension that allowed it to easily navigate the uneven and rocky terrain of the moon's surface. The rover was not only used for transportation, but also had a key function in boosting the communications array of the somewhat limited spacesuits that Vince and Eleanor were wearing. The rover had an external antenna array that could transmit and receive signals from the habs, allowing them to maintain constant communication with their base and relay information back and forth. This was especially important in a situation where every moment and detail counted, and time and communication could mean the difference between life and death.

Vince noticed that the rover also had sturdy-looking bull-bars on the front that looked as though they could easily smash through large rocks. It was clear that the vehicle was built to withstand the harsh conditions of the moon's surface, and to ensure the safety of those who operated it.

As they began to drive towards the crime scene, Grace made small talk about life in the settlement. She spoke about the challenges of living in such a confined space, the pressure of constantly being in a life-or-death situation, and the camaraderie that had developed among the crew members.

Vince listened intently, taking mental notes about the dynamics between the crew members. He wanted to know everything he could about the people who lived and worked in the settlement, as he knew that it could be a valuable source of information when it came to identifying a suspect.

As they approached the crime scene, Vince could feel his heart rate quickening again. He knew that this was where the real work would begin. Once the rover came to a halt, the pair exited the vehicle and Vince could clearly see the poorly etched outline of Dr Whitaker's body still lying on the lunar surface. He knew that Grace had been the one to find the body, and she had been told to make this outline so that in the future, his final resting position could be documented. Not that it really made a difference to Vince, but it was something at least.

Vince's first steps had been tentative, nervous almost as he adjusted to the reduced gravity again. He could feel the crunch of the lunar regolith beneath his boots as he made his way towards the place where the body had lain before it was taken back to the habs.

The scene was eerie and quiet, with no sounds other than the sound of their breathing and the hum of the rover's engines. Vince could feel a sense of isolation and vulnerability as he approached the outline, knowing that he was alone with a potential killer on the loose.

Standing over the outline, Vince made a point to look around in all directions, searching for any signs of struggle or any potential evidence that might have been missed during the initial investigation and the recovery of the body by the engineer. The surface of the Moon was unforgiving, and Vince knew that any clues would need to be carefully preserved and documented if they were to be of any use. There was a plus though, without wind to ruin footprints or anything of the like, it meant that any evidence would be preserved, just like the outline had been.

As he examined the area, he could see that there were no obvious signs of a struggle. There were no footprints or scuff marks on the lunar surface, and the body had appeared to be lying in a relatively undisturbed area. It was possibly a little too undisturbed, though, to Vince's mind, like it had just been dropped there, seemingly without disturbing anything else in the area.

Vince took out his camera and began to document the scene, taking pictures from different angles to capture every detail. He photographed the outline, the area around it, and the general landscape to provide context. He took close-up shots of the lunar surface, looking for any unusual marks or indentations that might provide a clue.

As he was taking pictures, he noticed something unusual on the ground that seemed to reflect the light. There was a small object, only a few feet away from the outline. He walked over to investigate and saw that it was a small metallic fragment. It was about the size of a fingernail and had an irregular curved shape, as though it had been torn or cut from a larger piece of metal.

Vince carefully picked up the fragment with his gloved hand and examined it closely. It was made of a shiny, grey metal that he didn't recognise, but he could see that it had been scored and scratched in a way that suggested it had been in contact with another object.

He took a series of pictures of the fragment and then showed it to Grace. "Do you know what this is?" he asked her.

Grace examined the fragment and shook her head. "I'm not sure. It doesn't look like anything from the settlement. Maybe it's from a piece of equipment that Whittaker had been using?"

Vince nodded, his mind racing with possibilities. This fragment could be a vital clue in the investigation, but he needed to find out where it came from and what it was used for. He carefully put the fragment into a specimen bag and sealed it up, making a note to try to figure out exactly what it was.

As Vince continued to investigate the crime scene, he began to get a sense of the scale of the challenge ahead of him. The lunar environment was expansive, hostile and unforgiving, and every piece of evidence would need to be carefully collected and analysed to build a complete picture of what had happened. He knew that this would take time and effort, but he was still determined to see it through.

After documenting the crime scene and collecting the fragment, Vince decided that he had seen enough, and the pair made their way back to the settlement in the rover. The ride back was quiet, with both of them lost in their own thoughts. Vince was thinking about the investigation and the fragment he had found, while Grace seemed lost in her own world, staring out at the desolate lunar landscape.

As they approached the settlement, Vince finally broke the silence. "Thanks for coming out there with me, Grace. Your help was much appreciated."

Grace turned to him and smiled. "No problem, Mr Callahan. I'm happy to help in any way I can." It seemed to Vince as though this small amount of praise meant quite a lot to the engineer, who was now clearly smiling.

Vince nodded appreciatively. "I'll be in touch if I need anything else. But for now, you should probably get some rest."

Grace nodded and stepped out of the rover, making her way back to the hab. Vince watched her go, grateful for her assistance and eager to get back to work on the case.

As he made his way out of his spacesuit and back to his own quarters, Vince couldn't help but think about the fragment. It was an unusual piece of evidence, and he knew that it could be a crucial piece of the puzzle. He needed to find out where it had come from and what it was used for. It was strange too, that it had either been left or ignored by either the killer, or Grace herself – who had brought the body back to the settlement.

He made a note to contact some of the other crew members and see if they had any knowledge of the fragment or what it could be a part of.

As he settled back into his quarters, Vince pulled out his laptop and began to review the photos he had taken at the crime scene. He zoomed in on the fragment, examining it closely for any clues or identifying features. He was determined to find out what it was and how it fit into the bigger picture of the investigation.

When that turned out to reveal nothing more exciting than he had already ascertained from it, he turned to some of the video tapes that he now had access to as he had been logged into the settlement's computer network.

Evidence: Video Tapes

Captain Armstrong: "Another productive day, team. Priya, how's the research on those lunar rock samples coming along?"

Dr Nair: "It's fascinating, Jack. We found some evidence of ancient volcanic activity. I can't wait to analyse the samples further and see what secrets they might reveal."

Grace: "That's great, Priya. By the way, I noticed the oxygen generator has been making some strange noises lately. I'll take a look at it tomorrow if nobody minds me taking a few hours. It's probably just a minor issue, but better safe than sorry."

Leo: "Speaking of tomorrow, I'll be harvesting some tomatoes from the garden. We should have enough for a nice salad at dinner."

Dr Nair: "That sounds delicious, Leo! It's amazing how something as simple as a fresh tomato can lift our spirits."

Captain Armstrong: "Indeed. Your work in the garden is invaluable, Leo. I'm glad we can rely on you to provide us with fresh produce."

Leo: "It's my pleasure, Jack. It's rewarding to see the fruits of my labour, literally. Plus, the team is really pulling out all the stops to work together down there. I couldn't have asked for a better bunch."

Grace: "Hey, I have an idea! Why don't we have a movie night tomorrow? We haven't had one in a while, and it might be a nice way to unwind."

Dr Nair: "That sounds like a fantastic idea, Grace. What movie should we watch?"

Grace: "How about something light and funny? We could all use a good laugh."

Captain Armstrong: "I'm on board with that. Laughter is the best medicine, after all. What do you suggest?"

Grace: "Well, I saw 'The Martian' in our digital library. It's a bit ironic, considering our situation, but I've heard it's both funny and inspiring."

Dr Nair: "I love that movie! It's a great choice, Grace."

Captain Armstrong: "Alright, it's settled. Movie night tomorrow, after dinner. For now, let's get some rest. We have another busy day ahead."

~

Captain Armstrong: "Good morning team, how is everyone doing today?"

Grace: "Good morning Jack. I'm doing well, thanks. Just finished the maintenance check on the life support systems. A few tweaks here and there but nothing major to report."

Dr Nair: "I'm feeling great, Jack. I've been analysing the lunar samples all morning and those things never cease to amaze me."

Leo: "Hey Jack, morning. I've been tending to the garden as usual. Everything's looking good."

Captain Armstrong: "Glad to hear it. Say, I received an email from Earth this morning with some news. They're sending a new crew member to join us here on the Moon. Her name is Dr Ava Patel, and she's a geologist."

Grace: "That's great news! We could use some more expertise in the research team."

Dr Nair: "Absolutely. And it'll be nice to have a new face around here too. When is she arriving?"

Captain Armstrong: "In a few days. Until then, we need to make sure everything is in order for her arrival. Grace, can you show her around and make sure she's settled in?"

Grace: "Of course, Jack. I'll make sure everything is ready for her when she gets here."

Dr Nair: "And I can show her the research lab and get her up to speed on our findings so far."

Captain Armstrong: "Excellent. We'll all do our part to make Dr Patel feel welcome here on the Moon. Now, let's get back to work. We have a lot to do before her arrival."

~

Captain Armstrong: "Doctor Whittaker, what have you been working on lately?"

Dr Whittaker: "Well, Captain, I've been conducting a survey of the ancient mineral deposits in the region. It's been slow going, but we're making progress."

Captain Armstrong: "Mineral deposits, huh? Sounds fascinating."

Dr Whittaker: "I'm afraid it's not the most exciting work, Captain. It's mostly just collecting data and running simulations."

Captain Armstrong: "I see. And what do you hope to learn from this survey?"

Dr Whittaker: "We're hoping to gain a better understanding of the geological history of the Moon, Captain. By studying these mineral deposits, we can learn more about the formation of the Moon and its composition."

Captain Armstrong: "I see. Well, keep up the good work, Doctor."

Dr Whittaker: "Thank you, Captain. I'll be sure to keep you updated on our progress."

Chapter 4: First Interview with Captain Jack Armstrong

Of course, the crew knew that the famous Vince Callahan would be interviewing them one at a time, so they weren't surprised when it was announced that the Detective had been given a small office, table and chairs so that he could sit and gain a first-hand insight into the happenings of the lunar settlement in the days leading up to the murder of Dr Adrian Whittaker.

The first person that Vince had asked to join him in his little office was of course the Captain. Captain Armstrong had taken such a hands-on approach to the investigation, and seemed to know everything about the happenings in the settlement that there was honestly nowhere else that Vince could begin.

"Thank you for taking the time to meet with me, Captain Armstrong," Vince said, adjusting his notebook on the table in front of him.

"Not a problem, Mr Callahan," Armstrong replied, clasping his hands together on the table. "What can I do for you?"

Vince decided to take the most formal approach he could. "I'm conducting an investigation into Dr Whittaker's death, and I was hoping you could shed some light on his relationships with the other crew members," Vince said, looking at the Captain intently.

Armstrong sighed heavily, his face drawn with concern. "It's a difficult situation, Mr Callahan. We're a small crew, living and working in close quarters for years on end. We were like a family, for better or for worse."

"I understand," Vince said, making a note in his notebook. "Can you tell me about Dr Whittaker specifically? How did he get along with the rest of the crew?"

Armstrong paused for a moment, as if searching for the right words. "Adrian was a brilliant scientist, there's no doubt about that. But it was no secret that he could be... well let's say difficult to work with at times. He was a perfectionist, and he expected the same level of dedication from his colleagues."

Vince nodded, writing down the Captain's words. "Did he have any close relationships with anyone on the crew?"

Armstrong hesitated for a moment before answering. "He was closest with Dr Nair, I would say. They shared a love of geology and spent a lot of time working together on various projects. But even that relationship could be strained at times. As I have said, Whittaker could be a bit strong willed. If he thought his way was the right way, then there was no other way."

"Any conflicts, specifically?" Vince asked, but the Captain shook his head. Vince made another note, though he wasn't sure if the Captain was being entirely truthful.

"What about Grace Thompson or Leo Martinez, the other heads of departments here in the settlement? Did he get along with them?" Vince asked, referring to the settlement's engineer and botanist, respectively.

"Grace and Adrian had their differences, but they respected each other's expertise as far as I am aware. As for Leo, he and Adrian didn't have much interaction as their fields of work didn't overlap much," Armstrong said, leaning back in his chair.

"Can you tell me more about the kind of person Dr Whittaker was? Did he have any notable habits or behaviours?"

Armstrong thought for a moment before responding. "He was a bit of a busy... well you could call us a workaholic, to be more accurate. He would spend hours poring over data, running simulations, making sure everything worked the way it was supposed to. He also had a tendency to be, I wouldn't say abrasive, more difficult, I suppose you could say. He didn't suffer fools gladly and could be very direct in his communication style."

Vince nodded again, taking note of Armstrong's observations and assuming that he was playing them down somewhat. The Captain was clearly filtering his responses, but. Vince couldn't decide if it was because of his normal position of keeping things running smoothly or not.

"Did he have any known enemies or grudges against anyone on the crew?"

Armstrong shook his head. "Not that I'm aware of. We all had our disagreements from time to time, but nothing that rose to the level of animosity or resentment. Dr Whittaker was a respected member of the team, and we all valued his contributions to the mission."

"Right, that's understandable," Vince said, nodding as he scribbled yet more notes into his notebook. "Were there any specific recent incidents or events you can recall that may have caused tension between Dr Whittaker and any other crew members? Anything at all could be helpful so please don't feel the need to overlook anything you might see as par for the course."

Armstrong paused for a moment, looking thoughtful. "There was an incident a few weeks ago involving a disagreement between Dr Whittaker and Grace over the allocation of resources. Adrian believed that more resources should be dedicated to his research, while Grace argued that the settlement's infrastructure needed more attention. It was a tense discussion, but ultimately we were able to come to a compromise."

"What was the compromise?" Vince asked.

"We agreed to allocate resources evenly between Adrian's research and the settlement's infrastructure. It wasn't ideal for either side, but it was a fair compromise," Armstrong explained.

Vince nodded, writing down the information. "And how did Dr Whittaker react to the compromise?"

"He was... dissatisfied, to say the least. But he understood the importance of maintaining the settlement's systems, and he didn't make an issue out of it," Armstrong replied.

"What kind of resources were they?" Vince asked. He didn't have a great idea of what would be required to be shared sparingly on the settlement, but information was always good to have, even if he potentially wouldn't understand it. Thankfully though, it was something he understood.

"Power," Captain Armstrong replied simply. "Our solar arrays only provide so much power and there's always going to be compromise between the settlement's internal systems and structures, and the allocation to research facilities. It's actually what Grace has been working on long-term: upgrading the number and efficiency of our solar collectors."

"It seems like it could be difficult to balance," Vince replied. "But how can you share something like that?"

"In short, blackouts," Captain Armstrong said. "We keep the minimum possible systems running, like life support, but beyond that for a few hours every day, we go dark. The lights, your coffee maker, everything goes offline while research does its thing."

"So I suppose that would mean surveillance cameras too, then?" Vince asked, peering up at the Captain.

Armstrong nodded. "Yes, unfortunately. We have a limited amount of power, and we need to prioritise where it goes. During blackouts, our surveillance systems are shut down along with everything else. Usually, we'd have twenty-four-hour surveillance of all common areas as well as a full three-sixty-degree showing of the lunar surface. You couldn't go to the toilet without being caught on camera in the hallways. Kind of ironic, really; If the cameras had been rolling, we might've had a good idea about what happened to Whittaker. Bet he wouldn't advocate for the power share if he had the chance now."

Vince frowned. "That's unfortunate. It would have been helpful to have surveillance footage during the time of the murder."

Armstrong nodded in agreement. "Yes, it's frustrating, but it's a reality of our situation up here on the moon. We have to make difficult choices with the resources we have."

Vince made a note in his notebook. "I understand. Moving on, can you tell me more about Dr Whittaker's state of mind in the days leading up to his death? Did he seem troubled or agitated?"

Armstrong thought for a moment before responding. "I wouldn't say troubled or agitated, per se. But he did seem maybe a little preoccupied. Like his mind was elsewhere. He spent a lot of time in his lab, running experiments and analysing data. He didn't socialise much."

Vince scribbled down the information. "Did he confide in anyone about what was bothering him?"

"Not that I'm aware of. Whittaker was a private person, and he didn't tend to share his personal problems with others," Armstrong said. "Personally I think he would see that as a sign of weakness, you know: letting people in and all that?"

Vince nodded, making another note. "And did he have any enemies, either on the crew or outside of it?"

Armstrong shook his head. "Again, not that I know of. Adrian could be difficult to work with, but he was a respected member of the team. We all valued his contributions."

Vince looked up from his notebook and met the Captain's eyes. "Thank you, Captain Armstrong. You've been very helpful. Is there anything else you think I should know?"

Armstrong thought for a moment before responding. "There is one thing. I know that Adrian had been in regular contact with someone back on Earth. It didn't seem like his usual communication style and he seemed pretty secretive about it. I know he spoke with his wife frequently, but this seemed different. It's possible that it could be related to his death."

Vince's interest was piqued. "Do you have any information on who he was calling, or why?"

Armstrong shook his head. "No, I'm afraid I don't. Adrian kept personal details very close to the chest."

"Do you have phone records I could have a look at?"

"I'll get them sent to your quarters. Honestly, we didn't think they would come in handy for something that was happening up here – it's not like anyone could get to him anyway. If Whittaker was killed, then the sad fact of the matter is that it happened up here, and it was one of us that committed the crime."

Thank you, Captain. That would be very helpful," Vince said. "And you're right, it would be impossible for this to have been the doing of someone thousands of miles away. But tell me, is there anyone else on the crew who might have more information about Dr Whittaker's contacts back on Earth?"

Armstrong thought for a moment before answering. "Dr Nair might know something. She and Adrian spent the most time together as they worked together on their projects. It's possible that he confided in her about his communication with Earth, but I couldn't be sure."

Vince made a note of this information. "Thank you, I'll be sure to speak with her next. Is there anything else you can think of that might be relevant to the investigation?"

Armstrong leaned back in his chair, deep in thought. "There is one other thing. I don't know if it's relevant, but it's been bothering me since Whittaker's death."

"What is it?" Vince asked, looking up at the Captain.

Armstrong hesitated for a moment before speaking. "The day before Adrian died, he and I had a conversation about the future of the mission. He seemed... preoccupied? He kept talking about how important it was that we succeed here on the moon, that we make significant progress in our research."

Vince furrowed his brow. "That doesn't seem too unusual, given the nature of the mission."

"I know, but it was the way he said it. It was almost as if he was afraid of something, or felt like time was running out," Armstrong explained.

"Do you have any idea what he might have been afraid of?" Vince asked.

The Captain shook his head. "I'm sorry, I don't. But it's been weighing on my mind since he died. I can't help but wonder if there was something he knew, something he was trying to warn us about."

Vince nodded, taking in the Captain's words. "Thank you, Captain Armstrong. I appreciate your time and your help with this investigation."

Armstrong stood up from the table and extended his hand. "Of course, Mr Callahan. Anything to help find out what happened to Adrian."

Vince shook the Captain's hand. "Thank you, Captain. I'll be in touch."

"If there's anything else I can do to assist in your investigation, please don't hesitate to ask," the Captain added with a smile.

"Thank you, Captain. I appreciate your cooperation. I know how difficult this must be for all of you."

Chapter 5: Phone Calls

When Vince returned to his room to gather himself before he went to the mess hall to find some lunch, sitting in the mailbox attached to his door were a few folded pieces of paper and that could only mean one thing: the call records from Dr Whittaker to Earth had arrived. He didn't know if it was normal for them to have arrived so quickly, given the hoops the team must've had to jump through to get their hands on them, but he certainly wasn't going to complain.

Vince picked up the paper and scanned through the records. There were several numbers that Dr Whittaker had called frequently, but one in particular caught his eye - a number that had been dialled over a dozen times in the past month. The number was unfamiliar to Vince, but he shrugged, typed it into his phone and decided to give it a call. He wasn't sure what he was hoping to achieve, but any lead was worth pursuing at this point.

Vince dialled the number and waited as it rang. After a few rings, there was no answer. He hung up and tried again, but still no answer. It was frustrating, but Vince didn't give up. He tried the number a few more times over the next hour, but still, no one answered. He did think about moving down the list and trying another of the numbers, but something was telling him that he needed to remain methodical. He wouldn't move on until he'd at least tried a few more times.

Feeling defeated, Vince decided to take a break and headed down to the mess hall for some lunch. As he was making his way through the cafeteria line, his phone rang. It was the number he'd been trying and he rushed to answer it before the caller could hang up the line.

"Detective Callahan speaking," Vince said, trying to sound professional despite the din of the mess hall around him.

"Hey there Detective. I saw you called my number a few times," a sultry female voice purred on the other end. It was clear right away that this was not a voice suitable for anyone under eighteen.

Vince was taken aback. "I'm sorry, who is this?"

"It's Veronica. You called me a few times today and somebody who calls that many times knows what they're looking for in my experience."

Vince felt his cheeks turn red. "I apologise, Veronica. I must have dialled the wrong number."

"No worries, Detective. Is there anything I can help *you* with? Sometimes the *wrong* number can lead to something very, very *right*," Veronica said, her voice dripping with suggestion.

Vince cleared his throat. "Actually, could you tell me who you are?" he asked.

"Well, my name's Veronica, and I know exactly what to say to get you in the mood," Veronica said. "I can be whoever you want, so why don't we drop these formalities and..."

Vince hung up the phone and shook his head. He'd never been one to indulge in those kinds of activities, but it was apparent now, that Dr Whittaker was. It seemed so out of character for what he thought of the man already though. A family man? And what would he get out of calling such a person?

As he hung up the phone, Vince couldn't help but feel a bit embarrassed, but at least he could rule that particular number out as a potential suspect.

But Vince wasn't ready to give up just yet. He held the phone in his outstretched hand, retrieved the call list from his pocket and decided to try another number on the list - one that had been dialled several times in the past week.

He dialled the number and waited as it rang. After a few rings, a woman answered.

"Gambling helpline, how may I assist you?" she said, in a professional voice.

"Hi, my name is Detective Vince Callahan. I'm calling because I noticed that this number was called several times by a Dr Adrian Whittaker in the past week," Vince explained.

"I see. Well, I can tell you that we don't provide any personal information about our clients. But if you're concerned about someone you know who may have a gambling problem, we can certainly offer resources and support," the woman said.

Vince felt frustrated. He knew he had to do what he could to talk this woman around, but from her tone he already knew what a task that was going to be.

"I don't need any details, but you're familiar with the Whittaker case, aren't you? It's all over the news."

The line was silent for a long moment, then the woman finally spoke. "I am familiar with the case, yes."

"Then could you please confirm if you have previously spoken to Dr Whittaker, and when?"

The line was silent again, but eventually the woman apparently decided that her best course of action was to fall back on her previous statement. "We don't provide any personal information about our clients. But if you're concerned about someone you know who may have a gambling problem, we can certainly offer resources and support," the woman said.

"So Dr Whittaker *was* a client?" Vince asked.

"Listen sir," the woman replied curtly. "You could be a reporter for all I know, or a member of the investigating board into personal data in our organisation. I'm sorry, but I have to terminate this call right now." And with that, the phone clicked, and the line went dead. Vince stared at the handset for a moment before turning back to the call logs. This one was a dead end plain and simple.

Undeterred by his lack of progress, he decided to try one more number on the list - a number that had been dialled just a few times less than the first two. It had a different area code to the first two, but Vince dialled it anyway.

"Hello?" a gruff voice answered on the other end.

"Hi, my name is Detective Vince Callahan. I'm calling because I noticed that this number was called repeatedly by a Dr Adrian Whittaker in the past month. Do you know him?" Vince said, trying to sound confident.

There was a pause on the other end of the line before the man spoke again. "No idea what you're talking about, pal. And if that 'Alan' guy has any problems then I suggest he takes it up with his local representative."

"His name was Dr Adrian Whittaker," Vince replied, somewhat taken aback. I'm investigating Dr Whittaker's death. I was hoping to speak with anyone who knew him," Vince explained.

"I think you got the wrong guy here, pal," the man replied with somewhat of a waver to his voice. "All I do here is take a few bets over the phone on the football, or the tennis you know? I don't know nothing about no deaths," and with those words, the phone clicked off and Vince was left sitting alone again with nothing but the call logs and a handful of new information that he couldn't seem to put together.

'So the three most called numbers were to an escort, a gambling addiction hotline, and some illegitimate bookie?' Vince thought to himself. *'Who the hell was this guy?'*

Then Vince spotted someone he knew, also sat alone. It was Dr Whittaker's wife and as Vince watched, she twirled around her food, chasing it about the shiny metal tray though she didn't take a single bite from it. She looked both confused and upset. Standing up, Vince moved to sit himself opposite her and as she looked up to see who it was, he offered her a warm smile.

"It's kind of just become all so real, I... I don't know what I'm supposed to do next," Eleanor said.

"I know," Vince replied softly. "But it gets easier, trust me, I know."

Eleanor looked back down to her food but made no move to eat anything at all.

"Tell me Detective, have you got any ideas about what might've happened? Do you have any suspects so that when I bury my husband, I'll at least be able to know the reasons why I'll never be able to speak to him again?" she trailed off as the tears welled in her eyes and she begun to sob. Vince moved around the table to sit by her, and Eleanor buried her face into his shoulder. He had questions he wanted to ask her, but they could wait for later. It would do no good to upset the woman any further.

Vince wrapped his arm around Eleanor and let her cry. He felt a sense of guilt that he didn't have any answers for her, and that he was no closer to finding out what had happened to her husband. If anything he had even more questions than answers right now. But he knew that he had to keep trying.

Eventually, Eleanor composed herself and pulled away from Vince. "I'm sorry," she said, wiping her eyes.

"No need to apologise," Vince replied.

Eleanor nodded. "It's just so hard to accept that he's gone. We had so many plans for the future, he never even got to say goodbye to Helen... and now...," she trailed off, her voice breaking.

Vince placed a comforting hand on her shoulder. "I promise you, we will find out what happened to him. And whoever is responsible will be caught and tried."

Eleanor looked at Vince, her eyes filled with a mixture of grief and gratitude. "Thank you, Detective. I really do appreciate everything you're doing."

Vince nodded, his mind already back on the case. He needed to find some more leads or this case would turn as cold as the lunar surface. As he got up to leave, he made a mental note to check who 'Helen' was, but in context, he could only assume that it was their daughter.

As he walked back to his room, Vince couldn't help but think about the people he'd spoken to on the phone. It was an odd mixture, but if he had to make an assessment of the late Dr Whittaker now, then it could only have been that he was antisocial, argumentative, and a cheat with a gambling addiction. These were all things that would lead to motives in most cases, after all it's common knowledge that murders are usually charged by either love or money. All of a sudden, this case had both.

Vince entered his room and sat down at his desk. He pulled out his notebook and began to jot down notes, trying to piece together the information he had gathered so far by rewriting the information in and out of order to try to find common links and themes. He had a feeling that the key to solving the case lay in Dr Whittaker's phone records, but he didn't know why he felt that way, and didn't know what more he could do with them.

He decided to take a closer look at the numbers he had called frequently. The first number was the escort. It seemed unlikely that this would be related to his death, but Vince made a note to follow it up again to see if he could talk to the woman. It also opened up the door to the possibility of spousal jealousy – if Dr Whittaker's wife had found out he'd been calling an escort, then perhaps she'd have killed him. The problem with that of course being the fact that Eleanor was on Earth during his murder, *'though she could've paid someone up here to do it',* Vince thought. It was seriously farfetched though, and Eleanor's reactions had seemed genuine so far, so Vince filed that one away as a 'long shot'.

The second number was the gambling addiction hotline. This one intrigued Vince. Nobody had mentioned that Dr Whittaker had a gambling problem, but if he was seeking help from such an organisation, then he wondered if it was possible that he had gotten into some kind of trouble with a bookie or had accumulated some debts. That of course led onto the last number Vince had called. Dr Whittaker had phoned the bookie several times, presumably to place bets on whatever took his fancy. In this case, it seemed that location hadn't been an issue, and even if you lived on the moon, then you could place bets as and when you wanted.

But that in itself would create more logistical issues, wouldn't it? If he had to pay a bookie then there would be a paper trail, wouldn't there? Bank transfers or at least something that showed that Dr Whittaker had been either paying the bookie or had been receiving his winnings. Vince made a note and circled it in his notebook, which simply read: 'Find the money'. It seemed that all the most common cause for murder had finally revealed itself in full. And there it was, all laid out right there in front of Vince in black and white, Love, jealousy and money.

'If only there was someone up here who Whittaker had beaten to the top job. Then maybe we could add revenge to the list,' Vince thought as he leant back in his chair again.

Evidence: Statement – Dr Priya Nair

I, Dr Priya Nair, lead scientist of the Lunar Settlement Expedition, hereby submit this official statement regarding the tragic death of Dr Whittaker. The following account is based on my personal observations, as well as information gathered from my team members during the course of our investigation.

On February 16th, 2043, at approximately 09:45 Lunar Standard Time, I was informed by Captain Jack Armstrong that Dr Whittaker had not reported to his scheduled shift at the geological laboratory. Concerned about his absence, I immediately began to search for him, checking his living quarters and laboratory. Upon finding no sign of him in either location, I requested assistance from the rest of the crew and we began a full-scale search of the habitats and surrounding lunar surface.

During the search, I was interviewed by Captain Armstrong, who asked me about Dr Whittaker's recent behaviour and interactions with other crew members. Based on my observations and conversations with Dr Whittaker, I reported that he had been exhibiting signs of stress and anxiety in the weeks leading up to his disappearance. He had become increasingly withdrawn and had been spending more time alone in his quarters or in the laboratory, neglecting his personal hygiene and appearance.

Furthermore, I also reported that I had overheard Dr Whittaker having hushed conversations on his communication device, which led me to believe that he was having some sort of personal or professional conflict with someone back on Earth. Despite these concerns, however, I did not witness any altercations or conflicts between Dr Whittaker and other crew members during this time.

On February 18th, 2043, after nearly two full days of searching, one of our engineers, Grace Thompson, discovered Dr Whittaker's lifeless body in a remote and seldom-visited section of the lunar surface, approximately three kilometres from the settlement. His suit appeared to be damaged, with a puncture in the torso area, which had caused a catastrophic loss of oxygen.

I performed an initial assessment of Dr Whittaker's injuries and concluded that the puncture to his suit was not accidental, but rather, appeared to have been inflicted by a sharp, pointed object, likely wielded by another person. It was a shocking and deeply troubling realisation that Dr Whittaker had been the victim of foul play.

Following the discovery of Dr Whittaker's body, I continued to work closely with Captain Armstrong to assist in the investigation. I provided any information and assistance that I could in hopes of finding the person responsible for Dr Whittaker's death.

During this time, I also observed the reactions and behaviours of the other crew members. It was clear that Dr Whittaker's death had a profound impact on everyone in the settlement, and many were understandably shaken and upset. However, I did notice some suspicious behaviours from certain individuals, such as avoiding eye contact or being evasive when asked about their whereabouts during the time of Dr Whittaker's disappearance.

As the investigation progressed, I remained vigilant and observant, hoping to uncover any clues that would lead us to the killer. However, despite our best efforts, no concrete evidence emerged that would implicate any specific individual in the crime.

In the days and weeks following Dr Whittaker's death, I struggled to come to terms with the loss of a colleague and friend. It was difficult to comprehend that one of our own could be responsible for such a heinous act, and I found myself constantly looking over my shoulder and questioning the motives of those around me.

Overall, the loss of Dr Whitaker was a tragic event that deeply affected all of us on the Lunar Settlement Expedition. He was a valued member of our team, and his contributions to our research will not be forgotten. I am hopeful that one day the truth behind his untimely demise will be uncovered and justice will be served.

Signed,

Dr Priya Nair

Lunar Settlement Expedition

Chapter 6: First Interview with Dr Priya Nair

"I have a couple of questions that I would like to ask you, Doctor," Vince said as he stared across the table at Dr Priya Nair.

"You can ask me anything and I would of course be happy to help," the scientist replied. "And please, you may call me Priya."

"OK," Vince said, "Priya. I've read through your statement of accounts of what happened before and after Dr Whittaker's death, and there are a few things that I'd like you to clarify, if that's OK?"

"Of course," Priya replied immediately, interlocking her fingers on the table in front of her.

Vince cleared his throat and leaned forward, pulling out a small notebook and pen from his pocket. "Firstly, can you elaborate on Dr Whittaker's behaviour in the weeks leading up to his disappearance? You mentioned that he had become increasingly withdrawn and neglectful of his personal hygiene. Was there anything specific that could have caused this change in behaviour?"

Priya paused for a moment, clearly thinking back to that time. "Well, as you know, living on the lunar surface can be extremely stressful, both physically and mentally. We are isolated from the rest of the world and have to rely on each other for support. I believe that the constant pressure and isolation could have contributed to Dr Whittaker's decline in mental health, and therefore had a knock-on effect on his attention to his physical appearance."

Vince nodded, jotting down notes as she spoke. "And what about the hushed conversations you overheard on his communication device?"

Priya's brow furrowed slightly. "Yes, I did overhear some conversations, but I couldn't make out much of what was being said. It sounded like Dr Whittaker was speaking to someone back on Earth, and it seemed like they were arguing about something. I never got the impression that the person he was speaking with posed any physical threat to him, though."

Vince nodded thoughtfully, scribbling down notes. "Understood. And finally, can you tell me if you noticed any suspicious behaviour from any of the crew members during the search for Dr Whittaker?"

Priya hesitated for a moment, clearly thinking back to that time. "Well, everyone was obviously upset and shaken by Dr Whittaker's disappearance, but there was one person in particular who seemed to be acting a bit odd. I don't want to name any names, but they were avoiding eye contact and seemed to be evasive when asked about their whereabouts during the time of Dr Whittaker's disappearance."

"I'm afraid I must press you for a name, Priya, you understand that, right?" Vince said.

Priya nodded slowly. "Yes, I understand. It was Leo Martinez, the lead botanist. He didn't seem to be acting like himself during the search, and I just had a feeling that something wasn't right. He didn't want to even search the area surrounding the habitats, he said he wanted to make sure everyone was safe inside, and that he would act as internal security. It just seemed to me as though if you think someone is in trouble, you'd do everything you can to try to find them, and help them, no?"

Vince scribbled down the name in his notebook next to a reminder to himself of what the Doctor had said, then looked up and smiled. "Thank you, Priya. This information will be helpful in my investigation."

Priya nodded, looking slightly relieved to have shared her concerns with someone outside of the crew. "Is there anything else you need from me, Detective?"

"Yes, just a couple cursory questions, if I may?" he said.

Priya nodded to allow him to continue.

"When Dr Whittaker's body was brought back to the habs, was he brought directly to you?"

"He was," Priya replied. "As the lead scientist for the expedition and settlement, Whittaker's body was brought to me for examination. As I mentioned in my statement, I determined that his cause of death was a loss of oxygen through the puncture wound in his suit, something that nobody would have been able to survive."

"And you were able to determine that this puncture wound was caused by another individual?" Vince asked.

"Well unless you are suggesting that Whittaker had purposefully travelled three kilometres away from the settlement, and then decided to damage his suit in a way that would surely cause his death, then yes, that is what I determined from the facts that I had available."

Vince looked down at his notes for a moment. He knew what he was going to ask, though he found that people often offered up more information when pressed by moments of silence.

"Are you suggesting that he could have killed himself, Mr Callahan?" Priya asked.

Vince looked back up after feigning finding what it was in his notes that he was looking for.

"Are you aware that Adrian had called a gambling helpline on a number of occasions over the last few months?" He didn't want to divulge the rest of what he had found in the call logs, but decided to go with something that he would be able to gauge a reaction with.

"No," Priya replied simply. "I had no idea. I mean... how would someone even be able to gamble up here? And what with?" she seemed genuinely perplexed by the information she'd been given and Vince didn't detect any falsehoods in her reaction.

"I can't say that I know the answer to either of those questions yet," Vince said. "But I presume that I can have access to his financial records at some point?"

Priya nodded. "I would assume so, but that would have to come from the Captain. But if it helps, then I don't see why it would be an issue."

"Please," Vince said. Then looked down at his notes and paused again. "I've looked through your personnel file," he flipped pages as though he was looking at it at that very moment, "could you tell me where it discloses your background in forensic pathology?"

Priya sat ever so slightly more upright, appearing to lean over to see what Vince was looking at, but he quickly dropped the papers down flat.

"I uh..." she started, but offered nothing more.

"I only ask because in the Captain's statement, he said that you conducted the initial assessment of Adrian's body, and that was because you have a background in forensic pathology. And you yourself confirmed that when the body was brought back to the habs, that it was brought directly to you. You are a geologist, are you not, Priya?"

"It is true that geology is my field of expertise, but I am a scientist first and foremost..."

"But it does not say anywhere in your personnel file that you have a background in forensic pathology, so my question is: how did they know to bring the body straight to you, if your talents are undocumented?"

Priya looked slightly taken aback by Vince's line of questioning. "Well, it's not something that I've had much formal training in, but I have worked with autopsies before in a research capacity," she explained. "And as the lead scientist on the expedition, I was the most qualified person available to conduct the initial assessment of Dr Whittaker's injuries, so I told Grace to bring Whittaker straight to me."

Vince nodded slowly, appearing to consider her response. "I see," he said finally. "And can you describe in more detail the injuries you observed on Dr Whittaker's body?"

Priya hesitated for a moment before continuing. "There was a puncture in the torso area of his suit, which had caused a loss of oxygen and ultimately led to his death," she said. "Upon further examination, I determined that the puncture was not accidental, but rather appeared to have been inflicted by a sharp, pointed object. It's possible that Dr Whittaker was stabbed with some sort of improvised weapon."

Vince scribbled down notes, his mind turning over the information Priya had provided. "Thank you, Priya. That's all for now," he said, closing his notebook. "I may need to follow up with you at a later time."

"Of course," Priya replied, appearing relieved that the questioning was over. "Please let me know if there's anything else I can do to assist with the investigation."

"I'm sorry Dr Nair," Vince said, shaking his head as Priya stood up to leave.

"Yes?" Priya replied, stopping.

"I just don't understand. There are protocols in place for when something like this happens, are there not? The mission did have a guidance on what you should have done with a body, who should have investigated and how, right?"

Priya nodded. "Yes, there are protocols in place. But given the circumstances and the urgency of the situation, we had to act quickly. We couldn't afford to wait for a full investigative team to arrive from Earth, so we had to do the best we could with the resources we had available."

Vince nodded slowly, his expression thoughtful. "I understand. And I appreciate your willingness to cooperate with this investigation. We will do everything in our power to find out what happened to Dr Whittaker and bring his killer to justice."

Priya offered a small smile. "Thank you, Mr Callahan. I hope we can get to the bottom of this soon and bring some closure to everyone involved."

Chapter 7: Past Fragments

The day had drawn on as Vince had conducted a walk-around of the lunar settlement and the habs. It was much larger than he'd ever have imagined, and now housed over one hundred people who had all been chosen because of some expertise they had that would help the settlement to both grow and flourish. He had returned to his room once he had familiarised himself with the corridors, the security cameras, the mess hall and the entertainment sections – everywhere people would go to be away from their work and catch that well-earned downtime. After all, if Whittaker had been killed up here, then there were two very real possibilities – it was either because of his work, or because of what he did with his free time.

The metallic fragment had been a bit of a mystery to Vince though, and as he sat pondering the case, he turned it over and over in his hand. It was about half the length of his finger, and had a half point, half scoop at the end. It looked like it had been snapped, but Vince hadn't ever seen anything like it before, so he couldn't figure out what it was supposed to be a part of. It was clearly sharp enough to pierce a spacesuit though, and almost certainly at least a part of the murder weapon.

Vince was lost in peering down at the scratches on the surface of the fragment, when a gentle knock on his door startled him.

"Come in," he called, not taking his eyes off the fragment as he tried his best to fit it to something larger with his mind's eye.

The door opened slowly, and Dr Whittaker's widow, Eleanor walked in and remained stood by the door.

"Good evening, Mrs Whittaker," Vince said with a genuine smile. "Is there anything that I can help you with?"

Eleanor linked her fingers together in a gesture that Vince recognised as a sign of unease or anxiety.

"I... I guess I just wanted to see if you've gotten anywhere with the case yet? The crew are having a memorial for Adrian tomorrow, and I'd really like to know... you know..." she trailed off, but Vince caught her meaning.

"I'm afraid I don't have anything concrete as of yet, Mrs Whittaker," he said. "It's a very complicated case and the more I work it seems like the more there is to examine."

Eleanor's shoulders slumped slightly, and Vince could tell that she had been hoping for more positive news. He didn't want to leave her feeling completely hopeless, though, so he added, "But I can assure you that I'm working tirelessly to uncover the truth. I'm following every lead and exploring every possibility, no matter how small. It may take some time, but I won't rest until we have answers."

Eleanor nodded, and Vince could see a flicker of gratitude in her eyes. "Thank you, Mr Callahan. I appreciate everything you're doing, I know I must seem impatient, but I just want all this done with..."

Vince smiled warmly. "Please, call me Vince. And if there's anything else I can do to help or if you remember anything that might be relevant to the case, don't hesitate to contact me."

Eleanor nodded again and turned to leave the room.

"Actually, you may be able to help me out with a few things," Vince said. "Now I know it may be a bit difficult and some of the things I have to ask may very well be upsetting, but..."

"I don't mind," Eleanor said quickly. "We shared everything with each other, and we spoke on the phone all the time. If there's any questions that I can answer that could help find who did this, then I'd be more than willing."

Vince looked at Mrs Whittaker, trying to make an assessment on whether or not the widow was in the right state of mind to be answering questions, but eventually he decided that it was going to be a risk worth taking.

"Dr Whittaker made several phone calls to a selection of numbers down on Earth," he started.

Eleanor nodded her head silently.

He paused for a long moment, almost long enough for Eleanor to prompt him to continue, but then he said: "One of the places he would call, was a gambling addiction hotline. Did you know anything about that?"

Eleanor remained silent, though slowly shook her head. Her expression was blank and Vince couldn't decide if it was because she was in shock at the call itself, or if she was hiding something from him.

"Adrian wasn't the sort to have addictions, and I'd never seen him gamble, not on anything, ever..." she said with a confused expression that Vince could only assume was genuine.

"Do you think that it could've been a deep secret of his, one that you'd never have been told?" Vince asked.

Eleanor remained silent again for another short pause. Eventually she shook her head.

"Listen... Mr Callahan... Adrian would never jeopardise what money we had between us. I suppose you'll find out in your investigation, but we have a daughter who requires constant and expensive care. We make ends meet with what we take combined, we don't spend anything on luxuries because we simply can't afford it. Adrian wouldn't risk anything before we pay what we need to for our Helen..."

Vince could see the pain and worry etched on Eleanor's face, and he immediately regretted bringing up the gambling hotline. He hadn't considered the financial strain that the Whittaker family might be under, and he made a mental note to be more sensitive in the future. The problem was though, that he knew that financial worries like this were exactly the thing that could lead someone to gamble.

"I'm sorry, Mrs Whittaker," Vince said sincerely. "I didn't mean to upset you. I understand that this is a difficult time for you and your family, and I'll do everything I can to be respectful of your situation."

Eleanor looked up at him, her eyes searching his face for any sign of insincerity. After a moment, she nodded her head. "Thank you, Vince. I appreciate that."

Vince took a deep breath, and then asked, "Is there anything else that you can tell me about Adrian that might help with the investigation? Any strange behaviours or interactions with crew members that you knew about?"

Eleanor thought for a moment, and then said, "There was one thing that struck me as odd. A few days before his death, Adrian mentioned that he had found something on one of his rock-collecting missions that he thought was significant. He wouldn't tell me what it was, just that he needed to study it more closely. He seemed excited and a little bit scared at the same time, if that makes sense."

Vince's interest was piqued. "Do you have any idea what it could have been?"

Eleanor shook her head. "I don't, I'm sorry. Adrian was always very passionate about his work, but he rarely shared the specifics with me."

Vince jotted down a few notes, and then said, "Thank you, Mrs Whittaker. Let's move onto something else."

Eleanor nodded.

"It's... not easy, but I have more calls to go through. Is that something that you could help me with?" Vince asked. "I'm afraid I think I started with the easiest to talk about..."

"Listen, Mr Callahan," Eleanor interrupted him before he could continue.

"Mr Callahan... if you could just show me the call log or whatever it is, rather than run this awkward commentary on it, it may be a little bit more comfortable for us both, no?"

Vince peered at Eleanor for a second, trying to figure out just how annoyed she was, but in her expression, he saw less annoyance and more of a desire to get to the bottom of all this. Then he picked up the bundle of papers from his desk and passed them to Eleanor without another word.

Eleanor looked down at the list for a long while, turned the page to look at the next, then turned them both over in her hands with a smirk.

"What is it?" Vince asked.

She paused for a moment before replying "I don't want to tell you how to do your job, Mr Callahan, but these aren't Adrian's call records."

"What?" Vince asked incredulously, snapping the paper back from Eleanor. "What do you mean?"

"Exactly what I said," Eleanor replied. "These aren't my husband's call logs."

"... how do you know?" Vince asked slowly, trying to see if there was a name at the top that he had missed or something.

"It's simple really," she replied. "Vince and I spoke almost every single day and in most cases, multiple times in a day."

"Right," Vince said.

"Well, Mr Callahan," Eleanor said. "My number isn't in these logs. Not even once."

Vince furrowed his brow at the revelation. It was such a silly oversight, but now that he had been told, it was glaring at him right there from the paper. If these had been Vince's call logs, then Eleanor's number would indeed have been on the list, appearing over and over, probably above most others.

Vince felt his cheeks flush with embarrassment. He couldn't believe he had overlooked something so basic. "I'm so sorry, Mrs Whittaker. I don't know how I missed that. I'll have to go back and check the records again."

Eleanor smiled understandingly. "It's all right, Vince. I'm sure you have a lot on your plate right now. Just let me know if you need any more information from me."

Vince nodded, feeling a mixture of frustration and gratitude towards Eleanor. Frustration at his mistake, but gratitude for her patience and willingness to help. "Thank you, Mrs Whittaker."

He'd already begun thinking about how the logs had been wrong – whether they were the incorrect logs entirely, or if these were indeed the correct logs, only they'd been doctored at some point. Whatever the reason, someone had given him the wrong information either by accident or on purpose, though he felt like this wasn't something that was easily mistaken.

"Vince," Eleanor asked while he was deep in thought as apparently she'd not yet entirely left the room.

Vince nodded silently in response.

"Can I ask you a question?"

"Anything, go ahead."

"I don't understand why you seem to be carrying out this process backwards. You seem to be looking into motives, suspects, their stories and their alibis, but you don't seem to be focussing too much on what actually happened to Adrian, or why. Wouldn't it be logical to figure out these details first, and then see who could even have been able to commit this crime in the method and timeframe allowed?"

Vince smiled. "Mrs Whittaker, I've been doing this for a very long time, and while I admit that my processes aren't infallible, and will sometimes lead me to places that are unnecessary or tedious, but it is the best way that I have found, for me. For instance, are you aware of a phenomenon called 'confirmation bias'?"

"I am," Eleanor replied.

"Well if I were to create an entire scenario surrounding *what* happened here, then I could get bogged down in the nitty-gritty of a million minute details, all of which could be skewed ever so slightly to fit different individuals, motives et cetera. The sad fact of the matter is that your husband has passed. The events that caused his death – regardless of what they were – will not change. What has happened has happened and these facts are constants, not variables. Now the people that remain - lets call them our pool of suspects because in essence, that is what they are – are variables. Their behaviour is current and ongoing, and throughout the course of my investigation, those behaviours will change and adapt. In addition, these variables will change in the future, where the constants will not."

"So you're saying that your process is to create a background for the victim, and then once you are sure of the kind of person he or she was, then you start to build your case? Mr Callahan, I can't help but say that seems so illogical, that I can't even begin to see how that would work."

Vince smiled. "Well let me put it this way. I have interviewed three of the four heads of departments on this settlement so far, with one still remaining, and what I have learnt has indeed shed a lot of light on how things are run, and how interpersonal relationships were during the time your husband was alive. This is all information that has not been tainted by any murder investigation, thoughts into what actually happened or my own personal bias. I begin my work in facts, to create a solid foundation and after that, I will work to solve the murder that has been committed."

Eleanor thought about Vince's explanation for a moment before nodding. "I see your point," she said slowly. "Starting with the victim's background and the relationships between the people involved could provide a clearer understanding of the potential motives and suspects. I suppose I just want to know what happened to my husband as soon as possible, and it feels like we're not making much progress on that front."

"I understand how you feel, Mrs Whittaker," Vince said sympathetically. "But I assure you, we are making progress. It's just a slow and methodical process. We need to be thorough and gather as much information as possible before we can start piecing everything together. I promise you that I will do everything in our power to find out what happened to your husband and shine a light on this entire mess."

Eleanor nodded, looking slightly comforted by Vince's words. "Thank you, Mr Callahan. I do appreciate your dedication to this case," then she paused for a moment and added quietly: "Do you think my husband suffered? I mean do you think it hurt, when he died?"

Vince's expression softened as he leaned forward slightly. "I can't say for certain, Mrs Whittaker. But I can tell you that he was no doubt unconscious when he passed away, so he wouldn't have felt any pain. From what we know, it seems that his oxygen supply was cut off quickly and he would have lost consciousness within a few seconds."

Eleanor's face relaxed slightly at the reassurance. "Thank you for telling me that, Mr Callahan," she said quietly. "It's comforting to know that he didn't suffer."

Vince nodded in understanding. "Of course, Mrs Whittaker. If you have any other questions or concerns, please don't hesitate to ask."

"Just one, actually," Eleanor replied. "Why do you have a broken mineral scoop on your desk?"

Vince looked down at his desk, not entirely sure what the woman was talking about, when his gaze fell upon the broken metallic fragment that he had found at the scene of the crime. He picked it up and handed it to Eleanor.

Mrs Whittaker turned it over and over as she peered down at it, then started speaking again almost absent mindedly. "Looks like it's seen a fair amount of use. I've never actually seen one break before. These ones were made specifically for the lunar mission. I remember Adrian showing me one before he left. Lightweight and strong, and…" She peered down at the fragment, looking closely at it. "The scores here along the shaft… for something to have scratched the tool this deep, it would have to be at least a seven on the Mohs Hardness scale. If memory serves, Quartz at least. It looks like…" she trailed off and didn't finish her sentence.

"What?" Vince asked eventually.

Eleanor composed herself. "It looks like this scoop must have been used on something very hard, though what that is up here I don't know."

Vince raised an eyebrow. "That's an interesting observation, Mrs Whittaker. Thank you for bringing it to my attention." He made a mental note to examine the scoop more closely and see if he could determine what it had been used for. "Is there anything else you can remember that might be helpful for the investigation?"

Eleanor shook her head and Vince couldn't help but notice the slight change of tone in her voice. "No, I can't think of anything else at the moment. But I'll let you know if I do."

"Thank you, Mrs Whittaker. Please don't hesitate to contact me if you think of anything else."

Eleanor nodded, turning to leave. "I will. Thank you again, Mr Callahan."

Vince watched as she left the room, the broken mineral scoop again in his hand. He couldn't shake the feeling that there was more to it than just a broken tool, and he made a note to investigate further.

Evidence: Statement – Leo Martinez

I, Leo Martinez, the lead botanist of the Lunar Settlement Expedition, submit this official statement regarding the tragic death of Dr Whittaker. The following account is based on my personal observations during the investigation.

On February 16th, 2043, at approximately 09:45 Lunar Standard Time, I, along with the rest of the team I was working with, was informed that Dr Whittaker had not reported to his scheduled shift at the geological laboratory. As the lead botanist, I was not directly involved in the search and rescue operation and honestly I had no idea where Whittaker might have gone. However, I did assist in any way that I could, providing any information about the layout of the habitat and the surrounding lunar surface that might be helpful in locating Dr Whittaker. I don't spend much time outside the habs, but I am quite familiar with the area immediately around the settlement.

During the search, I was interviewed by Captain Armstrong, who asked me about my interactions with Dr Whittaker in the weeks leading up to his disappearance. While I did not observe any specific behaviours or interactions that would suggest a motive for Dr Whittaker's murder, I did note that he had become increasingly withdrawn and distant in the weeks prior. He had missed several scheduled meetings that I had been a part of, and had not been responding to emails or messages in a timely manner – according to the Captain.

I also overheard him having hushed conversations on his communication device on a few occasions, which led me to believe that he was dealing with some sort of personal or professional conflict. However, I did not witness any altercations or conflicts between Dr Whittaker and other crew members during this time.

Following the discovery of Dr Whittaker's body, I assisted in securing the habitat and ensuring the safety of the remaining crew members. I continued to work on my botany experiments and assisted in any way that I could with the ongoing investigation, but there was not much for me to do in any case. Since the death of Dr Whittaker, not much has changed for me and my team, so I can only apologise for the frankness of this statement.

In my statement, I have provided all the information that I can recall regarding the events surrounding Dr Whittaker's disappearance and death. I solemnly affirm that the details provided in this statement are true and accurate to the best of my knowledge.

Signed,
Leo Martinez
Lunar Settlement Expedition

Chapter 8: First Interview with Leo Martinez

Vince sat across from Leo Martinez in his small interview room, a notebook and pen in hand. Leo fidgeted nervously in his seat, looking around the room as if he was trying to find a way out.

"Thank you for agreeing to speak with me, Mr Martinez," Vince said, breaking the awkward silence. "I'd like to start by asking you about your interactions with Dr Whittaker in the weeks leading up to his death. Can you tell me about any conversations or interactions that stood out to you?"

Leo cleared his throat before responding. "Well, as the lead botanist, I didn't work closely with Dr Whittaker on a day-to-day basis," he said. "But I did notice that he had become more withdrawn and distant in the weeks before his disappearance. He was missing the lead's scheduled meetings and not responding to messages in a timely manner according to some of the others."

Vince nodded, jotting down notes. "Did you notice anything else that seemed unusual or out of character for Dr Whittaker during this time?"

Leo thought for a moment before responding. "I overheard him having some hushed conversations on his phone every now and then," he said. "I couldn't make out what he was saying, but it sounded like he was dealing with some sort of personal or professional conflict. I tried not to pry, but he seemed stressed."

Vince leaned forward, intrigued. "Do you have any idea what that conflict might have been about?"

Leo shook his head. "I'm sorry, I don't. I wish I could be more helpful."

Vince didn't seem discouraged. "No need to apologise, Mr Martinez. Every bit of information is helpful in an investigation like this. Can you tell me about your relationship with Dr Whittaker? Did you ever notice any tension or conflict between the two of you?"

Leo shook his head again. "No, not really. Like I said, we didn't work closely together. We were both scientists, but in different fields. Our interactions were mostly professional and cordial. We spoke in the meeting between department heads, but not much crossed between both of us."

Vince made a note of this before continuing. "What about Dr Whittaker's interactions with other crew members? Did you ever observe any conflicts or issues between him and anyone else?"

Leo hesitated before answering. "I didn't witness any altercations or conflicts between Dr Whittaker and other crew members, but there were a few people who seemed to rub him the wrong way," he said. "Dr Nair, for example. They had very different approaches to their work, and Dr Whittaker wasn't shy about expressing his opinions on the matter."

Vince made another note. "And how about Captain Armstrong or Grace Thompson?"

Leo shook his head. "No, not that I noticed. They all seemed to work well together. But again, my time with all of them was limited, so I could be wrong about that."

Vince paused for a moment, flipping through his notes. "You mentioned that you didn't work closely with Dr Whittaker. Do you have any insight into his personal life or background?"

Leo thought for a moment before answering. "Not really. We didn't socialise much outside of work. I know he was married, but that's about it."

Vince nodded, making another note. "Thank you for your time, Mr Martinez. Is there anything else you can think of that might be helpful for me to know?"

Leo shook his head. "No, that's all I can think of."

Vince paused for a moment before changing tact to more direct questions.

"Did you know about the argument between Dr Whittaker and Grace Thompson regarding the sharing of power so that he could run his experiments?"

Leo looked surprised at the question. "No, I didn't know about that argument," he said slowly. "I mostly keep to myself and focus on my work in the botany lab. And I don't really have much of a requirement for power in there."

Vince nodded. "I see. And what about Dr Nair? Did you witness any real arguments or disagreements between her and Dr Whittaker?"

Leo paused for a moment, appearing to consider his response carefully. "There was a bit of tension there, yeah," he said finally. "Dr Nair is very focused on her research, and I think Dr Whittaker may have felt like she wasn't giving him enough attention or support for his own experiments. But it was mostly just small disagreements, nothing serious."

Vince made a note of this. "And what about Captain Armstrong? Did you notice anything unusual in his behaviour around the time of Dr Whittaker's death?"

Leo shook his head. "No, I didn't notice anything out of the ordinary. Captain Armstrong is very professional and keeps a tight ship, so to speak."

Vince nodded, making another note. "Thank you, Mr Martinez. That's all for now. I may need to follow up with you at a later time."

Leo nodded, standing up to leave. "Of course, let me know if there's anything else I can do to help. I'll no doubt be tending to the crops if you need me."

Vince watched as Leo left the room. The botanist had been the third of the initial interviews that he'd wanted to conduct, though there was still something that just wasn't clicking for him and he wondered if his upcoming interview with Grace Thompson would put some things into perspective.

After a short while as Vince tried again to organise his notes, a light knock on the door brought his attention back to the room, and a second later, Captain Armstrong entered.

"Mr Callahan," the Captain announced politely.

"Good morning Captain," Vince replied.

"Please, call me Jack."

"Alright, good morning Jack," Vince replied.

"It's good to see that you're already up and on the case again. Have you found anything that might point to a suspect?" the Captain asked.

Vince looked down at his notes and frowned. "There are a few things that I am yet to understand, though I think I'll get there in the end. Your settlement is very tightly knit, and it's still a wonder to me how something like this could actually happen."

"I'm still not sure myself actually," the Captain agreed, folding his arms across his chest.

"But seriously, on a settlement where the eyes of the world are always watching, and where the entire crew is buddied up in a rotational working system... it's almost as though it is unfathomable that such a huge oversight has been made."

"Oversight?" the Captain asked, perplexed.

"Well, it can be nothing other, can it? The way this investigation has panned out we have been left with an effective suspect pool of just four individuals, all of whom are able to work alone, though all of whom should have had their comings and goings recorded at every given moment. It can only be sheer dumb luck, or lack thereof that Dr Whittaker would find himself in a situation where he could be killed – if that is indeed what has happened here – and nobody on this entire planet, or Earth for that matter, knows a thing about it."

"And that is why you are here, the famous Vince Callahan, isn't it?" the Captain asked with a smile. "If anyone can get to the bottom of all of this, its you."

"I do know that my reputation somewhat precedes me, Captain, but I'm nothing more than someone who takes the information given to them and presents it in a way that reveals the truth. If the information doesn't exist, then I will end up as stumped as the next man."

Captain Armstrong nodded thoughtfully. "Well, let's hope that's not the case here, Detective."

Vince gave a small smile. "I'll certainly do my best."

There was a brief pause before the Captain spoke again. "I understand you'll be interviewing Grace Thompson next?"

"Yes, that's correct," Vince replied. "I hope to gain some insight into her relationship with Dr Whittaker and any potential conflicts that may have arisen between them."

The Captain nodded. "Grace is a good engineer and a valuable member of the team. I hope your questioning doesn't cause her too much stress."

Vince reassured him. "I'll be professional and respectful in my questioning, Captain. I have no intention of causing undue stress to any of the crew members. My goal is simply to gather as much information as possible to solve this case."

"I appreciate that," the Captain said. "If there's anything else I can do to assist with your investigation, please don't hesitate to ask."

Vince thanked him before the Captain took his leave. Then he sat back in his chair, taking a deep breath before standing up to stretch his legs. He knew the upcoming interview with Grace Thompson would be a crucial one, and he needed to be fully prepared. He spent the next few moments reviewing his notes and formulating his questions before finally calling Grace into the interview room.

Chapter 9: First Interview with Grace Thompson

"Tell me about the falling out you had with Dr Whittaker," Vince said immediately as the engineer sat down opposite him. It was a tactic he didn't always like to employ, but he felt that he had been using a soft touch for far too long in this investigation already.

Grace looked taken aback by the directness of the question, but she quickly composed himself and cleared her throat. "I'm not sure I would call it a falling out," she said carefully. "We had a disagreement, but it wasn't anything major."

"Can you tell me what it was about?" Vince asked, noticing that the engineer was already having trouble figuring out what to do with her hands.

Grace hesitated for a moment before finally speaking. "It was about power distribution," she said. "Dr Whittaker needed more power to run his mineral sample tests, but Captain Armstrong ordered a power share to prevent widespread blackouts. Dr Whittaker wasn't happy about it, and we had a heated discussion. He was a fool who didn't understand the need for following safety protocols up here and if he hadn't have wanted to run his experiments at the expense of the security systems, then perhaps your presence wouldn't even be needed up here, Detective."

Vince nodded, jotting down notes, though he didn't take the bait, remaining calm and collected. "And how did that argument end?"

"We agreed to disagree," Grace said. "But I could tell that he was still upset about it." Her eyes were angry and Vince could see that no matter how much she tried to hide it, her emotional response was winning out.

"And did you notice any changes in his behaviour after that?"

Grace thought for a moment before answering and visibly composed herself, taking deep breaths. "He became more withdrawn," she said. "He stopped coming to some of the team meetings and wasn't responding to emails or messages requesting his presence at certain times and places."

"Did you witness any altercations between him and other crew members during this time?" Vince asked.

"No, I didn't," Grace said. "But I did hear him having hushed conversations on his phone, which made me think that he was dealing with something or other. Maybe that's why he was so short with people – like something was finally getting to him... it's not easy up here I can tell you..."

Vince gave Grace a warm smile, sensing that he had finally arrived at a raw and unedited answer. "Thank you for your honesty, Ms Thompson. But please understand that I am here to help. With that in mind, is there anything else you can think of that might be helpful for me to know?"

Grace thought for a moment before answering. "I've been working on upgrading the efficiency of power transfer and the solar arrays," she said. "I believe that this could have prevented the power distribution issue that Dr Whittaker was so upset about."

Vince nodded, taking note of this information. It wasn't particularly relevant to his case, but it was helpful to know. "That's certainly something to consider. But with regards to our investigation, have you noticed anything unusual or out of the ordinary happening around the time of Dr Whittaker's death? Anything at all?"

Grace shook her head. "No, nothing that I'm aware of. The days leading up to his death were just like any other, as far as I could tell."

Vince nodded. "Thank you, Ms Thompson. That's all for now. I may need to follow up with you at a later time but for now you have been most helpful."

Grace nodded, standing up to leave. "Of course, let me know if there's anything else I can do to help. I'll probably be somewhere nose-deep in some system or other so just call out if you can't find me."

Vince watched as she left the room, pondering over the information he had just gathered. The argument between Grace and Dr Whittaker certainly seemed like a plausible motive for murder, but he couldn't shake off the feeling that there was still something missing from the puzzle.

As Vince sat alone in the small interview room, he couldn't help but feel like he was still missing a crucial piece of information that would tie everything together. He had interviewed all the suspects that had plausible opportunity and had gathered as much information as possible about Dr Whittaker's background and the circumstances surrounding his death. But despite all of that, he still couldn't quite grasp the motive behind the murder, or even any real reasons why anyone would actively dislike the man beyond an average working argument or two.

He looked down at his notes, scanning through them once again. He had a list of potential suspects, but each of them had no clear motive. He had considered the possibility of an outside party being responsible, but the tight security measures and working arrangements in place made that unlikely.

Vince let out a frustrated sigh and leaned back in his chair. He needed a fresh perspective, something that would help him see the case in a different light. He knew that he now needed to approach the case from a more traditional perspective.

He immediately got up from his chair and headed towards Whitaker's room. As he walked, he thought about the evidence he had gathered so far - the broken mineral scoop, the damage to Dr Whittaker's suit, and the state of Whittaker's quarters. Perhaps a closer examination of the physical evidence would provide him with the missing piece of the puzzle.

Chapter 10: Investigation

When Vince arrived at Dr Whitaker's private quarters, he was greeted by three members of the expedition standing guard at the door, which stood firmly closed. The men weren't particularly security-esque, it stood to reason that the expedition didn't have security personnel as that would simply take up valuable space and resources, though the three at least looked like they had been taking their jobs seriously.

"Good morning," Vince said to the group en masse.

"Good morning, Detective," each of the group replied. Then one man stepped forward and asked: "Is there anything we can help you with today?"

"Well I came by to have a look in Dr Whitaker's private room, but now you've piqued my curiosity. If the corridors, hallways and communal sections of the habs are back under twenty-four-hour surveillance, then why is there a need for three guards on the door, no less?"

The group exchanged quick nervous glances with each other before the same man replied.

"We're not really security. I'm a botanist and Hobbs and Sinclair are engineers. We've had this post included within our standard rotation of duties and since the passing of Dr Whittaker, this door has been guarded all day, every day. I don't know if it's because of the possibility of more blackouts, or just a cover your ass kind of thing, but this is what we've been told to do, so it's what we do."

"Oh? Who ordered this rotation?" Vince asked.

"The Captain of course. All changes to rotations get signed off by him and nobody else has the authority to make them."

"I see," Vince said. "Can I go in and have a look around?"

The man hesitated for a moment. "I... I've been told not to let anyone in without the Captain's say-so. Do you mind waiting for just a moment so I can ask him?"

Vince nodded. "Take your time," he said. "I'll wait."

The guard turned away from Vince to speak to the Captain on his communicator, leaving Vince to take the opportunity to glance around the hallway and notice any details he might have missed before. The corridor was narrow and well lit, with a few doors leading off to different parts of the hab. The walls were made of sheet metal, with various pipes and cables running along them. The air was cool and dry, with a faint smell that Vince could only assume was the telltale sign of recycled air.

A few moments later, the guard turned back to Vince and smiled.

"You're good to go in, Detective," he said. "Captain Armstrong said you can have a look around."

"Thank you," Vince said, stepping forward towards the door. The guard stepped aside to let him pass and Vince stepped into the room. The first thing he noticed was just how large it was compared to the room that Vince had been given. Dr Whittaker's quarters were sparsely decorated, but also had a few things that looked as though Whittaker would be using them for his work. There was a bed, a desk, and a few shelves on the walls. Only a few personal items were scattered around - a photo of Dr Whittaker with his wife along with some other photographs, an array of books on lunar geology, textbooks and other scientific tomes, and a small potted plant.

The place, though, looked as though it had indeed been ransacked.

Vince surveyed the room, taking note of the disarray. Drawers had been pulled out and their contents were scattered haphazardly around the room. Papers and books had been tossed onto the floor, and the bed looked as though someone had rummaged through it. Vince made his way over to the desk and began to sift through the papers that had been strewn about.

As he flipped through the papers, Vince could see that most of them were related to Dr Whittaker's work with the LSI. There were geological surveys, reports on mineral samples, charts and graphs that meant absolutely nothing to Vince, and notes on experiments that the Doctor had been conducting.

It took a short while of flicking through the papers for Vince to realise that they had been shuffled. At first glance it wasn't obvious because of the nature of the documents, but he managed to separate the printouts of various different projects and was eventually left with four neat piles and one of these piles was not like the others.

The pile contained detailed schematics of the power systems within the hab and handwritten notes on possible upgrades that could be made to improve efficiency. It appeared that even though Whittaker wasn't an engineer, he had some of his own ideas on how the settlement's power network should've been handled. Vince could only assume that this little side project was related to the power-sharing argument between Whittaker and Grace Thompson.

Just as he was about to continue his search, Vince heard a knock on the door. He placed the tablet back down on the table and made his way to the door to see who was there. It was one of the guards from outside.

"Detective," the guard said, "Captain Armstrong would like to speak with you."

Vince nodded, took a single look over his shoulder and followed the guard out of the room. As far as he was concerned, he felt like the room had told him everything he needed to know, and the fact that the guards remained meant that the room would probably remain unmolested as it was.

As they made their way down the hallway, Vince tried to align all of the new information that he had discovered. The ransacked room, the shuffled paperwork, and the sudden summoning to speak with the Captain all seemed to be connected somehow.

When he arrived at the Captain's quarters, Vince was surprised to see that Grace Thompson was also present. The Captain gestured for Vince to take a seat, and then he and Grace exchanged a meaningful glance. It was clear to Vince that they had been discussing something important before he arrived. Whatever it was, Vince felt that it wasn't going to be good.

"Detective," the Captain said, "I wanted to speak with you about the investigation. I know that you've been working hard, but I wanted to remind you that we need to find out what happened to Dr Whittaker as soon as possible. We don't want this to impact our mission any more than it already has."

"Of course, Captain," Vince said. "I'm doing everything I can to find out what happened."

"I'm glad to hear that," the Captain said. "But I also wanted to let you know that we have some concerns about your methods. We've received reports from some of the crew that you've been asking a lot of questions and that it's making them uncomfortable. I can't have my people wandering around worried that they may be accused of something they didn't do."

Vince was taken aback. "I'm just doing my job, Captain," he said. "I need to ask questions to get to the bottom of this, and I'm afraid that some of them are going to be difficult. You must understand..."

"I understand," the Captain interrupted. "But we need to maintain order and discipline on this mission. We can't have crew members feeling like they're under suspicion or being harassed."

Vince could tell that there was more to this conversation than just concerns about his methods.

"Understood, Captain," Vince said. "I'll be sure to be more discreet in my questioning. But just to be clear with you, the people that I have spoken to so far... are all suspects, as you may imagine. Yourself included."

The Captain's expression hardened. "I understand your position, Detective, but please be mindful of how your questioning may be perceived by the crew. We don't want to create unnecessary tension or mistrust among us."

"Of course, Captain," Vince said. He couldn't help but feel frustrated by the conversation. It seemed that the Captain was more concerned with maintaining the status quo than getting to the truth of what had happened to Dr Whittaker and that was something that could become very obstructive in the long run.

"Good," the Captain said as though to draw a line under this difficult conversation. "Now, Grace here has some concerns of her own to voice with you too." The Captain nodded to Grace to let her know that it was her turn to speak.

Grace cleared her throat and spoke up. "Yes, Detective. I'm concerned that you're not considering all of the possibilities in this case. You seem to be fixated on the idea that someone on this mission is responsible for Dr Whittaker's death, but there are other possibilities that need to be considered."

"Such as?" Vince asked.

"Well, for one thing, there's the possibility of an accident," Grace said. "Dr Whittaker was often conducting experiments with volatile materials and sometimes he would even invent his own ways of doing things that weren't particularly orthodox, and it's possible that something went wrong and caused an explosion or some other accident that led to his death."

"I see," Vince said, considering her words. "That's certainly a possibility, but I still believe that foul play is the most likely explanation."

"We understand your perspective, Detective," the Captain said. "But we need to consider all possibilities. It's important for the morale and safety of the crew."

"Tell me, Ms Thompson," Vince said. "Let us suppose that Dr Whittaker's death was indeed an accident. Could you theorise why his lifeless body was then found three kilometres away from the settlement with a puncture wound to the torso of his suit?"

"OK, if you want a theory straight off the top of my head," Grace paused for a moment, considering Vince's question as though it was a challenge. "I suppose it's possible that the force of an accident propelled him that far away, and the puncture wound could have been caused by debris or shrapnel from the explosion in an experiment that went wrong. But that's just one theory off the top of my head, and we won't know for sure until we have more evidence. Tell me, what are your theories?" The engineer folded her arms across her chest, awaiting Vince's answer.

Vince could detect a large amount of sarcasm in the engineer's voice, though he chose to ignore it. This community had been very small for a long time and it would only be normal for at least some social niceties to be lost.

He thought for a moment before answering. "My theory is that someone on this mission had a motive to kill Dr Whittaker and acted on it. I've been interviewing everyone on the crew and investigating any possible leads."

Grace raised an eyebrow. "And have you found any solid leads yet?"

Vince shook his head. "Not yet, but I'm still gathering evidence and piecing everything together. There are a few things that I have noted thus far though."

"Such as?" Grace replied before the Captain could insert himself back into the conversation.

"Well, I don't think there's any harm in telling you both this right now," Vince replied, internally screening what he was about to say. "But during my investigation and my conversations with the crew here, it struck me as odd that although you all spoke of friendships and camaraderie, not a single one of Dr Nair, Leo Martinez, yourself, Captain, or indeed you, Ms Thompson referred to Dr Whittaker by his first name. In fact, on a number of occasions, you even thought it prudent to drop his title of 'Doctor', and simply called him by his surname. Tell me, does that sound like a fried to you?"

Grace's face reddened, and she stood up from her seat. "Are you accusing us of something, Detective? Because it certainly sounds like it," she said, her voice rising in anger.

Vince raised his hands in a placating gesture. "No, not at all. I'm just observing a pattern, and I wanted to bring it to your attention."

"Well, I don't appreciate the insinuation," Grace said, still standing. "I think I should leave now before I say something that I regret."

The Captain spoke up, trying to diffuse the situation. "Grace, let's all just calm down. Detective, we appreciate your efforts, but Grace, perhaps it's best if you leave us alone for a moment now."

Grace shot a glare at Vince before storming out of the room, slamming the door behind her. The Captain let out a sigh and ran a hand through his hair. "I apologise for that, Detective. Grace can be a bit hot-headed sometimes. She's a great engineer..." then the Captain stopped speaking and Vince wondered if there was about to be a comment on her temper. He didn't need the comment though, he'd just witnessed it first-hand.

"It's all right, Captain," Vince said. "I understand that tensions can run high in situations like this."

The Captain nodded before continuing and sighed. "To be honest, there has been some tension between some of the crew members, including Dr Whittaker. But we've been trying to keep it under wraps for the sake of the mission. We're supposed to be a beacon of hope for humanity, and if people see us squabbling like school kids, they might not look up to us anymore."

"I understand," Vince said. "But do you think this tension could have played a role in Dr Whittaker's death?"

"I didn't think so before, but saying it out loud... it's certainly possible," the Captain said, looking thoughtful. "We've had some disagreements about the direction of the mission, and Dr Whittaker was known for being very passionate about his work. But again, we need to be careful about how we handle this. We don't want to cause panic or mistrust among the crew."

"I understand, Captain," Vince said. "But I need to follow every lead I can and I need the people who I speak to to be entirely truthful with me, not least of all yourself, Captain."

The Captain nodded. "I understand, Detective. And I can assure you that I am being truthful with you. We want to get to the bottom of this just as much as you do, but we also need to handle it carefully and with discretion."

Vince nodded. "I appreciate your honesty, Captain. I'll continue with my investigation and keep you updated on any developments."

"Thank you, Detective," the Captain said. "And please keep us informed. We're all in this together, and we need to work as a team to find out what happened to Dr Whittaker... Adrian," he corrected himself with a smile that didn't reach his eyes.

Chapter 11: Power Failures

The heated conversation with Grace had been the first time that Vince had ever felt any sense of danger while he had been on the lunar settlement. It wasn't the sense that he was in immediate danger, but rather the fact that he was on a settlement that had pretended to be so tightly-knit and absent issues, and it was proven to be of the contrary in such an obvious way. It just didn't sit right with him; surely they would know that he would uncover such things in the course of his investigation? Why would they have even tried to hide such a fact?

As he left the Captain's quarters, Vince couldn't shake off the feeling that something was off about the settlement and its crew. He wondered if there were more secrets that they were trying to hide, and if they were willing to go to great lengths to keep them hidden.

He made his way back to his own quarters, deep in thought about his next move. He needed to continue his investigation, but he also needed to be careful to keep a low profile while doing so. If one of these people truly was a murder, he couldn't let them know he had any strong suspicions of any of them.

Vince sat down in his chair and realised that on his desk, he still had some of the papers that he had been looking at from Dr Whittaker's floor strewn about. He didn't understand most of them, but they had been there for a reason, and he made it his mission to read them through to see what the late Doctor had thought about the rolling blackouts, and the power situation.

The first few pages Vince rifled through looked as though they were just notes or the working out of whatever it was the Doctor was thinking, though the more Vince looked at them, the more he somehow knew they were pertinent to his current line of enquiry.

He didn't have the engineering background to decipher the calculations, though there was at least one person he knew would be able to help him. The problem though, was that she wasn't present in the lunar settlement.

Dr Alice Mendez was head of the Earth-side of the Lunar Settlement Initiative, and if anyone knew what all of these numbers meant, then it was going to be her – or her team at least.

Vince decided to head back to the Captain's quarters and ask him about the communication protocol with Earth and Dr Mendez. As he walked, he went through the notes again, trying to see if he could make any sense of them. The numbers and equations were beyond him, but he did notice a diagram that looked like a power grid, with various nodes and lines connecting them. It seemed to be a plan for a new power system, but he couldn't quite figure out how it worked.

When he reached the Captain's quarters, he knocked on the door and waited for a response. After a few moments, the Captain opened the door and looked surprised to see Vince again so soon.

"Detective, is everything alright?" the Captain asked.

"Actually, I was wondering if you could tell me how to contact Earth," Vince said, holding up the notes. "I need to speak with Dr Mendez or someone on her team about these calculations. I think they might be relevant to the investigation."

The Captain frowned. "I'm not sure that's necessary, Detective. We have our own engineers here who can handle any power-related issues. Let me call Grace back and..."

"Please Captain, I understand why you want to keep this in house," Vince said quickly. "But I think it's worth looking into by people who aren't directly involved with the case. And besides, I'm sure Dr Mendez and her team would be interested to read up on whatever it was that Dr Whittaker had on his mind."

The Captain hesitated for a moment before finally nodding. "Very well. Here's the numbers to call," he said as he passed Vince a small booklet.

"Thank you, Captain," Vince said, taking the booklet. "I appreciate your help."

As Vince turned to leave, the Captain called out to him. "Detective, please keep in mind that we need to maintain a sense of unity and positivity among the crew. We don't want any unnecessary stress or concerns, especially with the limited resources and harsh conditions we face up here."

"I understand, Captain," Vince said. "But I also need to do my job, and that means exploring every possible lead."

Vince walked away and began to feel a small amount of frustration at the fact that he needed to constantly remind the Captain that he was simply trying to do his job. He understood that the Captain didn't want him to rock the boat too much, but if he needed to ruffle a few feathers in his pursuit of the truth, then he wouldn't hesitate in doing so.

Vince made his way back to his quarters again, booklet in hand, and sat down at his desk. He opened the booklet and found the number for contacting Dr Mendez on Earth. Taking a deep breath, he dialled the number and waited for someone to answer on the other end.

After a few rings, a voice finally answered. "Hello, Lunar Settlement Initiative Communications Centre, this is Alice speaking. How can I assist you?"

Vince cleared his throat. "Hello, Dr Mendez. My name is Detective Callahan, and I'm currently investigating the death of Dr Whittaker on the lunar settlement. I have some calculations and notes that were found in his quarters, and I believe they may be relevant to the case. I was wondering if I could speak with someone on your team who has knowledge of the power systems."

There was a pause on the other end before Dr Mendez replied. "I see. I know who you are Detective, and, well, as head of the initiative, I have knowledge of all aspects of the project, including the power systems. I would be happy to help you personally. What is it specifically that you are dealing with?"

Vince felt a sense of relief. "Thank you, Dr Mendez. If I start with what I can see in front of me, then you should get a feel for what I'm looking at."

"Of course, Detective."

"So I have been working through what looks like a power-sharing scenario, where the result of a requirement has been rolling blackouts throughout the entire settlement. Apparently it was Dr Whittaker who required additional power so that he could run some experiments," Vince said.

"OK," Dr Mendez replied.

Vince then described the diagram on the first page of the bundle he held in his hands.

"What you are looking at, Detective, is the current layout of the wiring between the solar arrays and the lithium-ion battery we sent up along with the habs. The solar array is currently covering an area of three-thousand square metres. Up there on the lunar surface, with the average solar irradiance of one thousand three hundred watts per square metre, and assuming an average efficiency of around twenty per-cent, the wattage per square meter would be around two hundred and seventy-two. All in all, this means that the numbers you should see on your piece of paper, should result in a power rating of eight hundred kilowatts, or thereabouts."

Vince took a moment to try to understand what Mendez had just told him, though when he looked down at the paper he did indeed see numbers similar to what he had just been given by Dr Mendez.

"That seems like a lot of power," Vince said eventually. "But you're right, that's what the numbers say."

"Yes, it's a significant amount of power, but keep in mind that we need to support the daily operations of the settlement, including life support systems, equipment, and lighting. And with a growing pop-ulation, our power needs will only increase. That's why we're always looking for ways to optimise our power usage and explore new sources of energy."

Vince nodded, taking in the information. "I see. And do you think there are any potential issues with the current power system?"

Dr Mendez paused for a moment, thinking. "Well, we're constantly monitoring the system and making adjustments as necessary. But I suppose there's always a risk of equipment failure or other unforeseen issues. That's why we have backup systems in place, and why we prioritise maintenance and repairs."

"And the battery system up here, it must be fairly big then too?" Vince asked.

"Yes, the lithium-ion battery we sent up with the habs is quite large. It has a total capacity of about fifteen hundred kilowatt-hours, which is enough to power the settlement for a short time in the event of an emergency or power outage," Dr Mendez explained. "I should say though, that the battery systems have not yet fallen below seventy percent within the settlement, not even once."

Vince furrowed his brow as he let the new information sink in. If the batteries hadn't been depleted yet, then why had there been rolling blackouts?

Vince couldn't help but feel puzzled. "That's interesting," he said slowly. "If the battery system has never fallen below seventy percent, then why were there rolling blackouts in the settlement?"

The phone clicked a few times before Dr Mendez replied. "I thought this was a hypothetical conversation, Detective?"

"I'm sorry, Dr Mendez, I didn't mean to mislead you. There was a situation a short time ago up here where power restrictions meant that Dr Whittaker's research meant that blackouts were necessary across the rest of the settlement. It was because of these blackouts that the surveillance cameras didn't catch what happened to Dr Whittaker, or could possibly corroborate the stories of the other suspects in my investigations."

Dr Mendez didn't reply.

"Dr Mendez?" Vince asked after a short pause.

"Yes... I'm still here, Detective. I'm sorry, I'm just having trouble processing what you're telling me right now. The power systems are so extensive in the lunar settlement... and when we are talking about the battery system and the solar arrays... we are talking about power in orders of magnitude greater than what would be required to simply keep the lights on... even if the systems were connected, which they aren't. Simply put, the low voltage lighting systems could function alone from the battery with no solar interaction for *thousands* of years. If you are being literal with your 'blackouts', then I simply don't see how this could be the case."

Vince felt a chill run down his spine as he realised the implications of what Dr Mendez was saying. "I assure you, Dr Mendez, I'm being quite literal. There were power restrictions in place that caused blackouts across the settlement, and they were severe enough to interfere with the surveillance cameras and other non-critical systems."

Dr Mendez was silent for a moment before she spoke again. "This is concerning, Detective. I'll have to look into this myself and speak with our engineers to see if there were any issues with the power systems that we weren't aware of. Thank you for bringing this to my attention."

Vince nodded again to himself, feeling a sense of relief that Dr Mendez was taking the matter seriously. "Of course, Dr Mendez. Perhaps then if you can tell me if there were any machines or diagnostic equipment that Dr Whittaker would possibly use that would even come close to something like this..."

"There aren't," Mendez replied flatly. "Unless you can tell me something else that I am yet to discover about what is actually going on up there?"

Vince looked down at his notes. "The only thing that I thought was strange, was a machine in Dr Whittaker's private quarters. About the size of a microwave oven, with the code "IODD2100" printed across the front."

Vince heard the tapping of keys on a keyboard, then Dr Mendez spoke again. "That's a Raman Spectrometer. At peak power consumption it would require no more than seven hundred watts. Certainly nowhere close to causing any issues at all."

"Is there anything up here that could require enough power to cause an issue?" Vince asked.

"Not on its own," Dr Mendez replied. "Possibly if every piece of diagnostic machinery was switched on and drawing all of its power at the same time, though I wouldn't ever see that happening."

"I'm sorry that I had to bring this to your attention, Dr Mendez." Vince said.

"It's OK Detective, I'd rather know about everything, as I should do about the settlement up there. It's a little shocking that you have uncovered so much in such a short period of time. I can't say that I'm not concerned, Detective."

"I'm just carrying out my investigation, Dr. I'm sure if it was you up here then you'd see these things too," Vince replied.

"...Is there anything that I can help you with, Detective?" Mendez asked.

"Just one thing," Vince said. "What is a Raman Spectrometer used for?"

"A Raman Spectrometer is a type of scientific instrument used to analyse the vibrational modes of molecules," Dr Mendez explained. "It's often used in chemistry, biology, and materials science to identify and study chemical compounds," Mendez replied.

"Right... can you give me the non-scientist version of that?" Vince asked.

"Sure," Dr Mendez replied. "Basically, a Raman Spectrometer helps scientists figure out what things are made of. It can be used to identify different chemicals or materials and understand their properties. It's a pretty useful tool in many different fields of science."

"Ah, that makes sense, and also why Dr Whittaker would have one," Vince said.

"Though not why he would have it in his private quarters," Dr Mendez replied.

Vince nodded in agreement. "Exactly, that's what's been bothering me. Do you have any idea why he would keep it there?"

Dr Mendez paused for a moment before responding. "I'm not sure, but I can look into it further. It's possible that he just wanted to have quick and easy access to the machine for his personal research. But it does seem odd that he wouldn't keep it in the lab with the other scientific equipment."

"Thanks, Dr Mendez. I appreciate your help with this."

"No problem, Detective. Please let me know if there's anything else I can do to assist with your investigation," Dr Mendez said. "But Detective. I want to know if you find anything unusual up there, anything at all. I feel as though there are many things happening that I should know but don't."

Vince took a deep breath and leaned back in his chair, feeling like he had again made some progress in his case. But there were still so many unanswered questions. He knew he had to keep digging to get to the truth.

Chapter 12: Prime Suspect

"So there was no need for blackouts," Vince said aloud to Eleanor as they both ate their meals of sausage, egg and beans. Dr Whitaker's wife had been absent as she'd prepared herself for her late husband's wake while Vince had been working, but she'd found him in the mess hall after he'd sat down with his metallic tray.

Eleanor looked up at him, her fork paused halfway to her mouth. "What do you mean?" she asked, confused.

Vince explained what he had learned from Dr Mendez about the power systems on the lunar settlement, and how it didn't seem to match up with the reported rolling blackouts. Eleanor listened intently, her expression thoughtful.

"That is strange," she said finally. "But what does it have to do with Adrian?"

"I'm not exactly sure yet," Vince admitted. "But it looks like someone was trying to cover something up by causing the blackouts on purpose – messing with the surveillance tapes. And if that's the case, then maybe they had something to do with Adrian's death too."

Eleanor looked at him sceptically. "But who would do something like that? And why?"

"Adrian did argue with someone about the power systems before he died, and in his room I found some calculations related to the power. He argued with Grace Thompson about it, but it all isn't adding up,"

"How do you mean?" Eleanor asked, having completely stopped eating now.

"Well the argument happened because your husband had asked for more power to run his experiments, and eventually a power sharing agreement was reached after some pushback from Grace Thompson. This ultimately resulted in rolling blackouts across the settlement and Ms Thompson is even now pretty upset about it."

"Right," Eleanor replied. "So what were the experiments that needed so much power?"

"That's just it," Vince replied. "According to Dr Mendez, there's nothing on the settlement that would require that much power on its own. And even if every piece of diagnostic machinery was turned on at the same time, it still wouldn't be enough to cause the blackouts we saw. So, it begs the question – why was this such an issue to begin with?"

"I think I may have missed something," Eleanor said slowly. "Why would Adrian go and ask for more power in the first place, if it wasn't going to be an issue?"

"That's a good question," Vince said, nodding. "And I don't have the answer to that yet. But it does seem like there's more going on here than meets the eye."

Eleanor looked down at her plate, her expression troubled. "I just can't believe that someone on this settlement would have something to do with Adrian's death. Everyone's up here for the same purpose – to further our understanding of the universe and improve life on Earth."

Vince nodded sympathetically. "I understand how you feel, Eleanor. But unfortunately, in any investigation, we have to consider all possibilities. And right now, it seems like there are some things that just don't add up, and when that happens, in my experience it's because someone nearby is guilty."

Eleanor sighed heavily, pushing her plate away. "I just hope that whoever did this is caught soon. Adrian deserves justice."

"I'll do everything I can to help make that happen," Vince replied with a half-smile.

"So what are you going to do next?" Eleanor asked.

"I think we need to get to the bottom of this power sharing issue," Vince replied. Either it was the cause of Adrian's death, or it wasn't. But someone knows more about it than I've been led to believe, and I can't help but feel like it's important."

Eleanor nodded in agreement. "It's worth investigating. Do you have any leads on who we should talk to about this?"

Vince thought for a moment before answering. "Grace Thompson was the one who opposed giving more power to Adrian. I think it's worth talking to her again and finding out why she was so against it. Maybe she has some information that could shed light on what's been going on. She wasn't in the best of moods with me the last time we spoke though."

Eleanor nodded, then looked thoughtful for a moment before she spoke again. "Adrian did tell me a couple of times that the chief engineer wasn't doing her job properly. It didn't happen too often, but over the last couple of weeks it seemed to get a little more frequent. I can't remember any of the specifics because it wasn't a focal point in our conversations, but if I do remember anything, I'll let you know."

"Thanks, that would be great," Vince said, noting the information. "In the meantime, I'll keep digging and see if there's anything else that might help us get to the truth."

Eleanor nodded again. "I appreciate everything you're doing, Detective. Honestly, I know I keep saying it, but with everything that's happening... well I just want you to know it really is appreciated."

Vince smiled at the genuine thanks he'd received. With the new revelations aired between the pair, Vince finished his food and stood up from the table, making his usual pleasantries as he left. He had a new destination in mind and until he followed this lead, he wouldn't be able to take his mind off it.

He called the Captain as soon as he was out of the mess hall and asked him to set up another meeting with Grace Thompson, though he made it clear that he wanted the Captain to be present at the same time. It wasn't an unreasonable request, seeing as how explosive their last confrontation had been.

As Vince waited for the meeting to be scheduled, he decided to do some research on Grace Thompson. He knew very little about her, except that she was the chief engineer on the lunar settlement and had opposed giving more power to Adrian. He searched through the settlement's database on his tablet and found some basic information about her – she had been working as an engineer for most of her life and had worked on several other space-bound missions before coming to the lunar settlement.

Vince also found some comments about her work that were less than positive. There were reports of missed deadlines, especially when she had been given clear instructions, which raised some red flags for him. He wondered if these issues with her work might be related to the power-sharing problem and the blackouts. But without context it was difficult to say.

A couple of hours after he had requested the meeting, Vince met with Grace and the Captain again in the small conference room. Grace looked tense and defensive from the start, but Vince did his best to keep the conversation civil.

"Ms Thompson, I'd like to talk to you about the power sharing agreement that you opposed," Vince began. "Can you tell me why you were against it?"

Grace leaned back in her chair, folding her arms across her chest. "I had concerns about the stability of the power grid," she said. "We're operating in a very fragile environment up here, and any disruption to the power supply could have serious consequences. I didn't want to risk it. We can see now that my concerns were well founded though, can't we?"

"But Dr Whittaker insisted that he needed more power for his experiments," Vince pointed out. "Why couldn't you accommodate that?"

"I did try to find a compromise," Grace said. "The Captain worked out a power-sharing agreement that would allow Dr Whittaker to get the power he needed without putting the rest of the settlement at risk."

"That's true," the Captain replied. "It was my idea to share the power."

"But there were still rolling blackouts," Vince said. "That doesn't sound like a successful compromise to me."

Grace sighed heavily. "Look, I did everything I could to make it work. But there were just too many variables at play. We're dealing with a complex system here and sometimes things don't go as planned."

Vince could see that Grace was already getting defensive. He exhaled loudly and opened his small notebook, apparently reading the information that he had noted down previously. "I read in your file that in your past, there have been accusations that you weren't doing your job properly. That you were missing deadlines and producing subpar work?"

Grace's expression turned cold. "I don't know what you're talking about," she said. "I've always done my job to the best of my ability."

"Is that entirely true?" Vince asked, his vision flicking almost imperceptibly towards the Captain.

Captain Armstrong, who evidently caught Vince's question, answered for Grace. "I have never had any issues with the quality of Grace's work," he said. "She has been exemplary in her dedication to her role here on the settlement, and other than a few tiny blips in her attitude, there is nothing that has concerned me, or concerns me for the future."

Vince smiled at the Captain. "Thank you, captain; you clearly run a tight ship up here. But tell me, how is Ms Thompson's work exemplary when there have been rolling blackouts that have resulted in the loss of surveillance data that could solve a possible murder case?"

Grace's face grew even colder at Vince's words and she interrupted the line of questioning before he could continue. "As I said before, Detective, sometimes things don't go as planned. We're dealing with a complex power system up here, and sometimes there are issues that arise that are beyond our control." Her voice had almost reduced to a growl.

Vince leaned forward, his tone serious. "But Adrian Whittaker seemed to think that you were doing something wrong. He was very insistent about getting more power for his experiments, and he argued with you about it. Why was that?"

Grace hesitated for a moment before speaking. "I didn't think his experiments were worth the risk to the rest of the settlement. We were already stretched thin when it came to our power supply and giving him more power could have put us all in danger."

Vince folded his arms. "But according to Dr Mendez, there wasn't anything on the settlement that would require that much power on its own, so why was Adrian asking for it in the first place? And why were there rolling blackouts if the power supply wasn't being stretched that thin?"

"I don't know," Grace snapped before she even seemed to hear what Vince had said, her voice filled with frustration. "All I know is that I do everything I can to keep the settlement running smoothly."

Vince nodded slowly. "I understand that, Ms Thompson. And I'm not suggesting that you had anything to do with Adrian's death. But I do think that there's more to this power-sharing agreement than I've been led to believe. Dr Mendez has assured me that the lithium-ion battery system that is in place here in the settlement has never, not once been reduced to less than seventy percent. Can you comment on that? Before you answer though Ms Thompson, please know that I already know more than you have been letting on so far."

Grace looked at him, her eyes narrowing. "If you're suggesting that I had something to do with Adrian's death, Detective, then you're barking up the wrong tree. I had nothing to do with it."

Vince held her gaze for a moment, though the Captain spoke before Vince could speak again.

"Answer the question, Grace," he said sternly.

Grace hesitated before responding. "It's true that the battery system has never been reduced to less than seventy percent. But that doesn't mean there weren't other factors at play that were causing the blackouts."

"Such as?" Vince prompted.

Grace sighed, looking tired. "There could have been equipment failures, or issues with the power grid that we weren't aware of. It's not always as simple as looking at the battery percentage."

Vince nodded slowly, considering her response. "I see... so you're saying that when Dr Whittaker came and asked for more power, you *knew* that there would be some failures somewhere, so you what? Decided to shut down much of the system as a preventative measure? I'm sorry Ms Thompson, but I am still struggling to understand why, if there was no issue in terms of raw power, that the lighting and CCTV systems were shut down in the habs and communal areas. You must see how this looks?"

Grace's expression turned even more defensive. "I didn't shut down anything intentionally. And as I said, there could have been other factors at play that caused the blackouts."

"But the surveillance cameras were surely switched off manually if there was no power issue," Vince pointed out. "Someone went to great lengths to make it seem as though there was a widespread power loss. Do you have any idea who that could have been? Or why?"

Grace shook her head. "I have no idea. I was focused on trying to get the power back up and running as quickly as possible. I didn't have time to worry about the how and the why."

Vince leaned back in his chair, studying Grace carefully. He could sense that there was something she wasn't telling him. "Ms Thompson, I understand you've been under much stress lately. But I need you to be completely honest with me. Do you know anything that could help us with this investigation?"

"Listen, Whittaker liked to take things into his own hands. I knew he was messing around with the power distribution systems – I can't prove it, but he was sticking his nose where it didn't belong. I knew that there were going to be some issues because of whatever it was that he was doing, so I was on hand and fixed the problem like I was supposed to, like a good engineer. I did my job, the problem was fixed and the place is running smoothly again. If people would just leave things be, then we wouldn't have all these issues in the first place."

Vince raised an eyebrow at Grace's response. "What do you mean by 'messing around with the power distribution systems'? Can you be more specific?"

Grace hesitated for a moment before answering. "I don't know exactly what he was doing, but I was told that he requested the power statistics and schematics for the settlement from Earth. That's all I know."

Vince made a note in his notebook. "And did you confront him about this?"

"No, I didn't. It wasn't really my place to interfere with his work. But I did express my concerns to the Captain, and he assured me that everything was under control."

Vince looked at the Captain, who nodded in agreement. "That's correct. Grace brought her concerns to my attention, and I spoke with Dr Whittaker about it. He assured me that everything he was doing was within the boundaries of safety protocols. And I even followed protocols and checked with Dr Mendez to make sure he couldn't actually do anything detrimental to the systems."

"And you believed him?" Vince asked.

The Captain shrugged. "I had no reason not to. Dr Whittaker was a respected member of this community, and I had no reason to doubt his word, or the assessment of Dr Mendez."

Vince nodded slowly. "I understand. But do you think it's possible that his experiments could have caused the blackouts?"

"It's possible," the Captain replied. "But I'm not an engineer. That's why we have Grace here."

"Captain," Vince said slowly. "I don't understand why this wasn't brought to my attention at the beginning of this investigation, or even why not when I began to ask questions about the power distributions issue."

"Well," the Captain said slowly. "Protocols were followed, the situation was resolved and it was an in-house matter..."

Vince interrupted, his tone firm. "Captain, I find myself reminding you of simple matters again, so forgive me for being blunt: The death of Dr Whittaker is no longer an in-house matter. It's a homicide investigation, and any information that could be relevant needs to be shared with me. You can't just pick and choose what to disclose. Now, do you have any other information that you think might be pertinent to this investigation?"

The Captain sighed, looking frustrated. "I'm afraid that's all I can offer, Detective. As I said, I'm not an engineer, and I don't have access to all of the details of Dr Whittaker's work. And as for potential motives, I can assure you that everyone on this settlement is dedicated to our mission and would never do anything to jeopardise it."

Vince nodded, but he didn't look convinced. "I understand. But I really would like to know what happened with this power situation," he turned back to Grace, who was looking down at the ground, her face red.

"Grace?" He asked, but she didn't reply.

Vince could see that he wasn't going to get much more out of Grace, so he thanked her for her time and left the conference room. As he walked back to his office, he couldn't help but feel like something wasn't right. The pieces again just weren't adding up, and he couldn't shake the feeling that there was still more to the story than he was being told.

Over the next few hours, Vince continued to pour over the power sharing agreement and the blackouts. He also went back over Adrian's notes and calculations, but nothing seemed to jump out at him.

Then a light knock came on the door, and when it opened, Grace Thompson slowly walked inside.

"Can I talk to you, Detective?" Grace asked in a very small voice.

Vince looked up from his notes and nodded, motioning for her to take a seat. He could see that Grace looked nervous and anxious, her hands fidgeting in her lap as soon as she sat down.

"What's on your mind, Ms Thompson?" Vince asked.

Grace took a deep breath before speaking. "Detective, I need to come clean about something. I know I wasn't completely truthful earlier when you asked me about the power situation. I got upset and angry, but I don't want you to get the wrong idea about me. I know how it all seems... but here," she took some folded paper from her pocket and held it out for Vince to take.

Vince leaned forward, his interest piqued. "What do you mean?" He asked as he took the paper from her.

Grace hesitated for a moment before speaking.

"It's the missing pieces of paper from Adrian's room. What you already have is just current information, but this was Whittaker's... Adrian's summary," she quickly corrected herself.

Vince unfolded the paper and looked down at it. There wasn't too much to go on past a few calculations and numbers, some of which he simply recognised from his conversation with Dr Mendez. The bottom line though, was a handwritten note by Dr Whittaker that stated in no uncertain terms, that the power consumption for the entire settlement, was less than thirty percent of the total available storage capacity within the batteries.

"I don't understand," Vince said honestly. "Why are you telling me this?"

"Because I wanted to explain," Grace said. "I'm not stupid, I know how this looks. The truth is, that I went to look for this once Adrian had been found missing. I knew how it would look, so I took his findings and shuffled his notes so it would be difficult to follow. It was a stupid thing to do... but I just didn't want anyone to know..."

"Know what Grace?" Vince asked.

As Vince watched, tears filled the engineer's eyes.

"I'm scared," Grace admitted, her voice barely above a whisper. "I've been an engineer my whole life, but technology is moving so fast, and I'm worried that I'm becoming obsolete. Even now, on the shuttle that you yourself arrived on, came younger engineers ready to join the settlement. I feel like I'm being left behind. So... I started manufacturing minor issues, just so I could fix them and prove my worth. Then I stupidly said that I would need to run some upgrades to facilitate Adrian's experiments... he didn't accept it and looked into it himself. Then it was too late. I needed to make it seem like I'd been right, then I could 'upgrade' the system afterwards and everyone would know just how vital I am to the mission... I'm... I'm sorry..." she began to sob quietly as her words trialled off.

Vince sat in silence for a moment, processing everything that Grace had just told him. He could see the fear and anxiety in her eyes, and he knew that she was finally being genuine with him. He didn't want to make her feel any worse than she already did.

"Grace," he said finally, "I appreciate your honesty. It takes a lot of courage to admit when you're wrong, and I can understand how you feel. But what you did *was* wrong, and it could have serious consequences for the settlement."

Grace nodded, tears still streaming down her face. "I know, and I'm sorry. I never meant for any harm to come from it."

Vince sighed, feeling a mix of frustration and sympathy for the engineer. "We'll have to figure out what to do from here. But just know that my concern is the investigation into what happened to Dr Whitaker, and nothing else." He wanted to tell her that what she did had no bearing on what he was there for, but he knew that what she had done would eventually come to light – perhaps even now the Captain was reporting her actions to Dr Mendez back on Earth.

"I understand," Grace said, her voice barely above a whisper. "I'll accept any consequences for what I've done, but please don't let it affect the mission."

Vince nodded, a sense of sadness settling over him. "I'll do my best to keep the investigation separate from the mission. But I can't make any promises, Grace. We'll have to see where the evidence leads us."

Grace nodded, wiping away her tears. "Thank you for listening, Detective. I'll cooperate with the investigation in any way I can."

Vince gave her a small smile. "That's all I can ask for. Now, do you think you could answer a few more questions about the case?"

Grace looked up at Vince, sniffing back her tears as she did so. "What did you want to know?" she asked in a small voice.

Vince stopped for a moment. He could see that the engineer still wasn't back to her old self, and when he thought about it, what he really needed to do right now, was reassure her.

"Actually, Grace, let's take a break from the case for a moment," Vince said gently. "I want to talk to you about your concerns. You're not alone in feeling worried about becoming obsolete in your field. Technology is always evolving and it can be hard to keep up. But I want to assure you that your experience and expertise are invaluable to this settlement. You have a wealth of knowledge that these new engineers don't have yet, and that makes you just as important to the mission as anyone else."

Grace looked up at him, her eyes still watery but with a glimmer of hope shining through. "Do you really think so?"

Vince nodded. "I do. And I'm sure the Captain and Dr Mendez feel the same way. You're a vital member of this team, Grace. Don't ever forget that."

A small smile formed on Grace's lips, and Vince could see some of the tension in her shoulders ease as they started to descend. "Thank you, Detective. I really needed to hear that."

"Anytime," Vince said with a nod. "Now, walk me through the search for Dr Whittaker again if you would."

Chapter 13: In the Know

"Captain, could you please tell me why you were so nonchalant when you found out that the blackouts had been so unnecessary at the time of Dr Whittaker's death?" Vince asked as he peered across the table at the Captain.

Captain Armstrong smiled back at Vince and for a moment it was as though the pair were locked in some unspoken, mental battle.

"Detective..." the Captain said slowly as though he was still making his mind up on what he was about to say. "I was nonchalant, because I already knew. It was not new information to me so therefore I lacked surprise."

"You knew?" Vice asked.

"Of course, Detective, you don't think I know everything that happens up here on this settlement? Well, I should say *almost* everything," he added as an afterthought.

Vince leaned forward in his seat, intrigued. "How did you know, Captain? And why didn't you share this information with me earlier?"

The Captain's expression grew serious. "I didn't share it earlier because it wasn't relevant to the investigation into Dr Whittaker's death. As for how I knew, let's just say that a dear friend told me about the problems that Grace has been having over the last few months or so. I chose to look the other way in all of this, because I believed that it was in the best interests of my crew."

"What do you mean, 'problems'?" Vince asked, knowing full well that he'd just told Grace that he'd do everything he could not to reveal the games she'd been playing.

The Captain hesitated for a moment, then sighed. "Grace has been struggling with feelings of inadequacy and obsolescence in the face of newer, younger engineers coming onto the settlement. She's been manufacturing minor issues to make herself look more vital to the mission than she actually is. I didn't think it was a big deal, just a coping mechanism for her. But clearly, it's escalated to something a little more serious."

Vince sat back in his seat, processing this new information. It made sense that Grace would feel threatened by the arrival of younger engineers, but he hadn't realised that the Captain had known all about it.

"Captain, I understand that you were trying to protect your crew, but hiding information from me isn't helping anyone. I need to know everything that's going on here if I'm going to get to the bottom of what happened to Dr Whittaker," Vince said firmly.

The Captain nodded. "You're right, Detective. I apologise for withholding information. From now on, I will be completely transparent with you and your investigation."

Vince nodded in acceptance, glad that they had cleared the air. He chose not to mention that this was in fact the second time the Captain had made him this promise. "Thank you, Captain. Now please tell me more about Grace, and why you allowed her to enact false blackouts that are right now, the only reason we don't have any evidence of what happened to Dr Whittaker through the CCTV systems."

The Captain's face grew solemn. "I allowed it because I believed it was in the best interests of the settlement. Grace is a vital member of the engineering team, and I didn't want to risk losing her or having her confidence in her own abilities further eroded. It was a mistake, and I accept responsibility for it. But I assure you, I had no idea that it would escalate the way it did."

Vince raised an eyebrow. "And what do you mean by 'escalate'?"

The Captain sighed heavily. "I mean the way Whittaker took it. It was like he was on some personal vendetta to get Grace removed from the mission once he'd figured out what she'd done. That was why he kept calling Dr Mendez, shouting and screaming to have Grace replaced. Eventually, Mendez just stopped answering the phone to him."

"I'm sorry Captain," Vince said as he flipped through his notes. "In your signed witness statement, it clearly stated that Dr Whittaker's conversations were 'hushed'. Were they hushed, or were they heated?"

The Captain frowned, as though remembering something unpleasant. "They were hushed at first, but as Whittaker became more convinced that Grace was responsible for the blackouts, his tone became more heated. He was very angry and upset about it, and he didn't hide it."

Vince nodded, taking notes. "And did you witness any of these conversations personally?"

The Captain shook his head. "No, I didn't. But I overheard parts of them from my office, and Dr Mendez told me about them later."

"So Dr Whittaker was calling Earth to complain about one of the crew up here, and he was so angry that it led him to scream and shout... and you thought that this information wouldn't be relevant to the ongoing murder investigation? Captain, you're a smart man and surely you can divulge motive from your own words?"

The Captain sighed again. "I know, Detective. In hindsight, I realise that it was a mistake to ignore those conversations. But at the time, I thought it was just a personality clash between Whittaker and Grace. In fact, I still do. I have no reason to suspect that Grace is capable of such an act, and in any case, she was the one who found Whittaker's body. These aren't the actions of a murderer and in my eyes, Grace is a deeply worried and anxious person. She needs support more than anything else, and a sense of belonging that this settlement can give her, if it hasn't already."

Vince raised an eyebrow sceptically. "I understand your loyalty to your crew, Captain, but as the lead investigator in this case, I have to consider all possibilities. And right now, Grace's actions and motives are suspicious. We can't rule her out as a suspect just because she found the body."

The Captain's expression grew stern. "I understand that, Detective. And I will cooperate fully with your investigation. But I won't stand by and let you accuse one of my crew members without solid evidence."

Vince nodded, understanding the Captain's position. "I appreciate your cooperation, Captain. And I assure you, I won't make any accusations without evidence to support them. Now, is there anything else you think I should know?"

The Captain shook his head. "No, that's all I have for now. But if anything else comes to mind, I'll be sure to let you know."

Vince nodded and stood up from his chair. He didn't believe that the Captain had nothing else to hide, but didn't want to press the issue. "Thank you, Captain. I'll be in touch if I have any further questions." With that, he left the Captain's office and headed back into the hallways outside of the room. He didn't have anywhere in particular in mind to go, but the last few days of uncovering the secrets of these people was just so tiring.

Deciding to simply take some time to observe the settlement as it worked, Vince began walking through the corridors and within the habs that these pioneers called home. He observed how the people worked together, how they laughed and joked, how they always seemed to know where they needed to be and what they were supposed to be doing. Vince had to admit that however the Captain had worked out these processes, they were certainly effective.

A few things were playing on Vince's mind now though. The metallic fragment of the mineral scoop that was found near Dr Whittaker's body, the fact that the Captain seemed to know an awful lot more than he had been letting on, the arguments that Whittaker had had with Grace Thompson... and then there were the falsified call logs. Vince still couldn't make his mind up about those – whether it was an honest mistake and someone else's calls had been passed over, whether they had been intentionally doctored, or a third possibility that Vince was yet to think about: that Dr Whittaker could have had a second phone. Was that really a possibility though?

Vince thought as he walked. He played each scenario out in his mind, examining it from every angle that he could, and the possible ramifications of each. If Dr Whittaker did indeed have a second phone, then perhaps it was in his room somewhere. But why would he? Maybe he simply used this phone to call people he didn't want anyone else to find out about – surely that's what the numbers would suggest. Though, no, the call logs were extensive and Vince had just called a handful of the most frequently dialled numbers – if this was a secret 'burner' phone, then there would surely have been far fewer calls made.

So that meant that the more likely possibilities were that the call logs were passed over in error, or intentionally doctored. Vince needed to find out which of these was the truth, and then he knew that it would either lead to more information that he could use in his case, or simply to a dead end. What he did know, was that he needed to keep these thoughts close to his chest.

Event: Funeral, Dr Adrian Whittaker

An account of Dr Adrian Whitaker's funeral, as told by Detective Vince Callahan.

Given that this is the first time that an event such as this has occurred on our celestial neighbour, I thought it prudent to produce a first-hand experience of the funeral as it happened. Death is something that we all may face, though it is how we deal with the aftermath that makes us human. I have only been within the celestial settlement for a short while, but what is most apparent to me up here, is just how close this community truly is. The people care for each other as though they are family, and that is no surprise given the fact that they have spent many years working together towards a shared goal and in close proximity.

I have been tasked with divining what has happened to Dr Adrian Whittaker, a geologist and head of his department up here. The passing of the Doctor has rocked the world, though I hope that in some small way, when this is all over I may be able to afford the settlement, and perhaps even the world, a sliver of comfort in the unravelling of the events that have caused this tragedy.

I want to preface this account with a few of my own observations during my short time here; I feel that it is important to do so due to the nature of my visit, and also so that the world may better understand what life on our celestial neighbour is truly like.

The pioneers that lead the settlement up here have carried out work that many have barely been able to dream about, though they have dedicated their lives to furthering the human race by way of exploration past our own orbital limits. Some of the members that I have met already have spent decades working tirelessly to generate this foothold that may well one day become vital in the expansion of our ambitious race.

But that is all to digress. My purpose within this account is to detail what I am seeing as a first hand perspective of the very first funeral to be carried out on the surface of the moon. I can only wish though, that the circumstances surrounding Dr Whitaker's death were different.

As I walk into the mess hall, there isn't much that has been done to decorate the place for the occasion. Not that I would have expected it to be so, but it screams to me of normalcy. The tables and chairs are of course bolted down to the ground in the wide open hab, and food and drink trays have been provided for people to serve themselves as they may. I note now that lead botanist Leo Martinez and his team have been very effective in creating not only a self-sustaining ecosystem, but also a stockpile of long-lasting foods that are available for the settlement. It is for these reasons that the settlement is about to undergo its largest ever expansion, with new habs being constructed for the scores of arriving engineers and scientists.

I also must commend the work of the lead scientists in the settlement. Dr Priya Nair, engineer Grace Thompson and Captain Jack Armstrong have created something here that I didn't ever think that I would see in my lifetime: a civilisation on the moon that is self-sufficient and although it receives technical assistance from the team back on Earth, it now requires no new supplies from Earth, though I am sure they would be available if it did.

People are standing all around in small groups, talking as though this world is entirely normal to them. They smile and joke like they are all the best of friends and I can detect no notes of anxiety or foreboding for the occasion ahead.

That is not to say that people are not upset with the passing of Dr Whittaker though. I have had the pleasure of speaking to his wife, Eleanor, on a number of occasions already. She had been sent up with the last addition of crew so that she may be a part of this historic moment and to say goodbye to the man she's called a beloved husband, and a devoted father.

Mrs Whittaker stands alone and I will make a point to speak with her again before the day is out, to offer my condolences and my assurance that I am doing everything that I can to bring her husband's killer to justice.

Dr Nair is also standing alone. She has her arms folded and a blank look upon her face. I know how dedicated she is to her work, and I wonder if she feels that this is a waste of time and resources.

Captain Armstrong, in the few moments that I've been in the mess hall has dropped in and out of no less than ten conversations, and I feel that he makes it a point to have some involvement in everything that happens within his charge. At this point I can only assess that he is a dedicated leader and will do whatever he can to make this mission a success.

I have not yet seen Grace Thompson nor Leo Martinez at this event and will assume that they are busy with their respective jobs in the settlement. After all, not everyone can leave their posts simultaneously to attend a funeral.

The funeral itself is not filled with ceremony or fanfare, and Mrs Whittaker will later explain to me that it is exactly how Adrian would've liked it; he was a man who did not enjoy the spotlight of attention, and that fact no doubt would have followed him into his own personal beyond.

I do not wish to minute the entire speech that Captain Armstrong gives as he stands next to the portrait of Dr Whittaker wearing the space suit that he had worn the day his shuttle had brought him up to the moon's surface. Rather I will paraphrase what I can and what I feel are the most appropriate parts.

'Dr Whittaker was a brilliant scientist, and during his career he managed to turn his hand to many fields of expertise. He would always see projects through to the end, and would do everything he could to abide by the rules of the settlement. He had few friends, though those he did have, he would do everything he could to make their lives better, or more comfortable. He was selfless, caring and respected everyone he could to the best of his abilities.'

Mrs Whittaker hadn't met any of the crew that her husband worked alongside, though she had been told about many of them in her conversations with her husband. In her own speech, she pointed out how nice it was to give names to faces, and that it was a testament to her husband's dedication that so many of the crew had come to say their final goodbyes to the Doctor.

All in all, the ceremony was short. I can note that there was a lack of the mention of deep friendships shared between the Doctor and any of the other crew members, though I know personally from the course of my investigation here, that Dr Whittaker was very much somebody who liked to keep himself to himself. I feel that the crew respected him and his work, though not many counted themselves among his group of friends.

Dr Whittaker is survived by his wife Eleanor, and his daughter Helen, back on Earth.

The event has now settled after the speeches given by the Captain and Mrs Whittaker, and I feel like a great weight has been lifted from the room. It had felt like all the while the funeral was in its progression, that we were all waiting for something to happen. I cannot say what it may have been, but the feeling finally lifted once Mrs Whittaker had said her final words and said goodbye to her husband.

As I work my way around the mess hall, I can't help but feel a sense of melancholy settle over me. It's the first funeral I've attended on the moon, and it's a sobering reminder of just how far humanity has come in terms of space exploration, but also just how far we have to go. I can't help but think about the impact that Dr Whittaker's death will have on the settlement, and the ripple effect that it will have back on Earth.

But I also can't help but feel a sense of admiration for the people up here. Despite the tragedy that has befallen them, they are still pressing on with their mission, still working tirelessly to expand and explore the moon. It's a testament to their resilience and dedication, and I feel privileged to be able to witness it first-hand.

The funeral has now concluded, and I will take some time to speak with some of the members of the expedition to see what their thoughts are surrounding both the funeral and Dr Whitaker's death. After this, I will speak with Mrs Whittaker to again offer my condolences and support for her loss.

As I speak with the crew members, I am struck by their resilience and determination to continue their mission. They are all mourning the loss of Dr Whittaker, but they are also focused on their work and the future of the settlement. They speak of Dr Whittaker with respect and admiration, but they also speak of the need to move forward and continue the work that he was so passionate about.

I also have the opportunity to speak with Mrs Whittaker, who is understandably still grieving the loss of her husband. She is grateful for the support of the crew members and for my own investigation, and she hopes that justice will be served for her husband's death. It's a sobering reminder of just how high the stakes are up here, and how important it is to ensure the safety and security of the people working and living on the moon.

I step outside, back into the habs that man has created up here in the harsh lunar environment and I'm reminded once again of the fragility of human life, and the importance of the work that's being done up here. It's not just about expanding our horizons or pushing the boundaries of science; it's about carving out a new home for humanity, a place where we can thrive and grow in ways that we never thought possible.

I take a deep breath and look up at the vast expanse of stars above me, feeling humbled and small in the face of it all. But I'm also filled with a sense of wonder and possibility, knowing that we are capable of so much more than we ever thought possible. And as I make my way back to my quarters, I know that I have a job to do, a mystery to solve, and a legacy to uphold.

This concludes my account of the first ever funeral held on the moon in human history. It is with certainty that I can say that it will not be the last, but it is my hope that the next will be through less distressing circumstances.

Chapter 14: Tireless

"Good morning Doctor," Vince said to Dr Nair as he walked into her workstation. She was a geologist at heart, but he knew that she held the title of 'Lead Scientist', so watching her pouring over pages and pages of notes that had nothing to do with rock formations or seismology didn't surprise the Detective at all.

"Good morning, Detective Callahan," Dr Nair replied, not looking up from her work. "What brings you to my little corner of the settlement?"

Vince leaned against the wall, watching her work. "I just wanted to check in on you, see how you're holding up. I know this has been a difficult time for everyone and sometimes it's easier to talk to people in an environment in which they feel comfortable, like at their work."

Dr Nair nodded, finally setting down her notes and turning to face him. "It's been tough, yes. But we're all trying to stay focused on the mission."

"I'd like to talk about the initial examination of Dr Whittaker's body again, if I may?" Vince asked, getting straight to the point.

Dr Nair's expression tightened slightly. "Yes, that's not a problem. I was the one who performed the examination, so any questions about it would be best asked of myself."

Vince took a step closer, studying her face. "Can you tell me again why you were the one to do it? I still don't understand why, given that you don't have any medical qualifications."

Dr Nair sighed heavily, rubbing her temples. "It's true that I don't have any medical qualifications, but I do have a background in biology and anatomy. And besides, there was no one else available at the time."

Vince raised an eyebrow. "No one else available? Surely there must have been someone else on the team who was more qualified to perform the examination? One of the medical doctors perhaps?"

Dr Nair shook her head. "No, there wasn't. We're a small team up here, and everyone has their own area of expertise. Dr Whittaker was a geologist, so I was the one who was most familiar with him and the potential injuries he may have sustained at the time. It was simply bad timing."

Vince frowned, not entirely convinced. "And how did you come to that conclusion? That Dr Whittaker had been injured?"

Dr Nair hesitated, then sighed. "It was just a hunch, really. There was an obvious sign of trauma to his spacesuit, and I felt that it was important to investigate further."

Vince leaned in closer. "Can you be more specific about this trauma?"

Dr Nair shook her head. "Everything that I saw I noted in my account of Dr Whittaker's disappearance and subsequent discovery. It looked as though a sharp object had punctured the suit and he died of a lack of oxygen."

Vince sighed, feeling frustrated. He could tell that Dr Nair was hiding something, but he didn't want to push her too hard. Instead, he decided to change the subject. "Can you tell me more about your work here on the settlement?"

Dr Nair's expression softened slightly as she turned back to her notes. "Of course. I'm primarily a geologist, but as Lead Scientist, I'm responsible for overseeing all of the scientific research that takes place here on the settlement. That includes everything from biology to physics to chemistry."

Vince nodded, watching her work. "And what are you working on right now?"

Dr Nair looked up, a small smile on her face. "I'm working on analysing some of the rock samples that we've collected from the surrounding area. It's fascinating work, really. Every rock tells a story, and it's up to us to decipher that story."

Vince chuckled. "I'll have to take your word for it. Rocks have never been my thing."

Dr Nair grinned. "It's not for everyone. But for me, it's a passion. I've been studying rocks and geology for as long as I can remember."

Vince watched her work for a few more moments, then spoke up again. "Can I ask you a personal question?"

Dr Nair looked up, curiosity in her eyes. "Of course."

Vince hesitated, then plunged ahead. "Do you think that Dr Whittaker's death has anything to do with the fact that he was also a geologist, and possibly even your main competition for the Lead Scientist position?"

Dr Nair's expression darkened, and she looked away from Vince. "Absolutely not."

Vince held up his hands defensively. "I'm not accusing you of anything, Dr Nair. I'm just trying to explore all possible angles in my investigation."

Dr Nair nodded, still looking unhappy. "I understand that, Detective. But I can assure you that I had nothing to do with Dr Whittaker's death."

Vince nodded, then paused for a moment before speaking again. "Can I ask you something else? I hope this doesn't come across as too forward, but I've noticed that you seem to be working twice as hard as anyone else up here. Is there a reason for that?"

Dr Nair's expression softened slightly, and she looked back at Vince. "Yes, there is. As a woman, I've always had to work twice as hard as my male counterparts to prove myself. And as the Lead Scientist up here, I feel a tremendous responsibility to make sure that everything runs smoothly and that the mission is a success. I know that my name will be on many educational papers in the future, and I want to make sure that I leave a positive lasting legacy."

Vince nodded, feeling a pang of sympathy for her. He knew the struggles of feeling like an outsider in a male-dominated field, and he could only imagine what it must be like for her up here on the moon. "I understand. And I have no doubt that you will leave a lasting legacy, Dr Nair."

Dr Nair smiled slightly, then turned back to her work. "Thank you, Detective. I appreciate that."

"No problem," he smiled. "Now, can you tell me about the last few interactions that you had with Dr Whittaker? Let's say the last interaction the pair of you had specifically, do you remember what you spoke about, or what happened?"

Vince couldn't help but notice that as soon as he had asked his question, Dr Nair began to sweat. She remained silent for a long moment, and then finally began to speak.

"There was nothing out of the ordinary really. We pretty much just spoke about work and small issues surrounding geology as it was his field of expertise," Nair said.

Vince furrowed his brow. He could tell that Dr Nair was holding something back. "I understand that, but can you be more specific? Did anything unusual happen during that conversation? Did he seem upset or agitated about anything?"

Dr Nair hesitated for a moment before responding. "No, not really. It was just a normal conversation between colleagues. Nothing stood out to me as unusual or noteworthy."

Vince leaned forward slightly, his voice lowering. "Dr Nair, I need you to be honest with me. I know there's something more to this and I need you to tell me what that is. I understand that you may be hiding something to protect yourself, or someone else, but all I care about is finding out what happened to Dr Whittaker. Now please, tell me what you aren't saying."

Dr Nair exhaled and her shoulders dropped visibly before she spoke. "OK Detective," she said. "A few days before Dr Whittaker went missing, he came to me with the results of a seismology report that he had conducted in the areas surrounding our habs. He argued that these reports showed that there were a series of underground caves not far from here and wanted to investigate. I looked at the reports, though I concluded that they were most likely false positives. I don't expect you to understand the intricacies of geological reports, but in essence these reports can be affected by a wide range of factors, such as rock density, faults and fractures. I didn't want to waste our time and resources investigating caves when we already have so much work to do here in the habs and nearby."

Vince leaned back, processing what Dr Nair had just told him. "So you're saying that Dr Whittaker wanted to investigate these supposed underground caves, but you believed that the seismology reports were inaccurate and advised against it?"

Dr Nair nodded. "Yes, that's correct. I didn't want us to waste our time and resources on a wild goose chase."

Vince tapped his fingers against the armrest of his chair. "And how did Dr Whittaker respond to your objections?"

"He was disappointed, but he ultimately agreed with my assessment," Dr Nair replied. "He didn't press the issue any further."

Vince leaned forward again. "Did anyone else know about these seismology reports?"

Dr Nair shook her head. "No, I don't believe so. Dr Whittaker shared them with me in confidence, and I didn't see any reason to involve anyone else."

Vince peered at the Doctor for a moment before he continued. There was still something there that he wasn't sure about. Something that she was hiding and he knew that it was something more personal than simple work discussions and disagreements.

"As a scientist, I would like you to divine a common denominator with the following facts, if you would indulge me, Dr Nair?" Vince asked, and the Doctor nodded silently in response.

"Dr Whittaker wanted to run some experiments or tests, to the point that he had some piece of equipment within his private quarters. You have told me that he wanted to go looking for some cave that you believed didn't exist. When he went, somehow in some unfortunate coincidence, the surveillance systems within the settlement were switched off, and by your own admission, Dr Whittaker had his eyes on your job. Dr Whittaker was found three kilometres away from the settlement and his private quarters had been ransacked. Furthermore, when the body was discovered, you ordered his body to be brought to you, who is not medically trained for assessment. Please, Dr Nair, tell me if I have missed anything?"

Dr Nair looked uneasy as Vince listed off the facts, but she didn't interrupt him. When he finished, she took a deep breath before responding.

"I understand how it might look, Detective. But I can assure you that I had nothing to do with Dr Whittaker's death. Yes, he wanted to investigate those supposed caves, but I didn't see any point in wasting our resources on something that I believed was a false positive. And as for his private quarters being ransacked, I have no idea who would do such a thing. I certainly didn't have anything to do with it."

"Dr Nair, I would like to see Adrian's body," Vince said shortly. It was not something that he was used to doing, having no training in the field himself, but something was telling him that perhaps the body held more secrets that he would be able to uncover.

Dr Nair looked hesitant, and Vince could tell that she was weighing her words carefully. "Detective, I'm afraid that won't be possible. Dr Whittaker's body has already been prepared to be sent back to Earth so that his wife can bury him as per his wishes. I would need to get permission from her and the rest of the team before allowing anyone to view the body."

Vince felt a pang of disappointment, but he knew that it was understandable. "I understand. Thank you for being honest with me, Dr Nair. Please arrange for the necessary permissions for me and we will continue this discussion at a later date."

Dr Nair nodded, her expression solemn. "Of course, Detective. I want to help in any way that I can. I just wish there was more that I could do."

~

It took the best part of a day, but eventually, Vince had been given the permission by everyone involved to examine Dr Whittaker's body.

Vince, accompanied by Captain Armstrong and Dr Nair, made their way to the room where Dr Whittaker's body was being held. The room was dimly lit, and the body was laid out on a metallic table in the centre. Vince donned a white lab coat, latex gloves, and a face mask before approaching the table.

Dr Whittaker was cold and still, and his skin was pale.

As he examined the body, Vince noticed nothing too out of the ordinary from what he assumed was a man of Dr Whittaker's age. General marks, skin tags and the like were present, he seemed thin but not to the point of malnourishment and Vince quickly began to think that he had made a mistake in asking to see the body.

Then Vince saw something, and picking up Dr Whittaker's arm by his left hand, he could now see a long, deep scratch along the man's forearm. Vince frowned, running his gloved fingers over the wound. "Dr Nair, can you tell me what caused this scratch?" he asked, looking up at her.

Dr Nair glanced at the wound and then looked away, seeming to feign ignorance. "I'm not sure, Detective. Dr Whittaker could have sustained that injury during his initial fall, or perhaps it was caused during the recovery process."

"I'm curious Doctor. I read your reports of your examination of the body, and they made no mention of this injury. Can you explain to me why that is?" Vince asked.

Dr Nair hesitated for a moment before answering. "I apologise, Detective. As I examined the body, I was looking for any other causes of death than asphyxiation. I didn't see it necessary to document a surface scratch."

Vince narrowed his eyes at Dr Nair. Her explanation didn't quite sit well with him, but he decided to let it go for the time being. Instead, he turned to Captain Armstrong.

"Captain, do you have any knowledge of how Dr Whittaker may have sustained this scratch?" he asked.

The Captain furrowed his brow, looking at the scratch closely. "I'm not sure, Detective. Could he have scratched himself on something during his fall?"

Vince turned back to Dr Nair. "Is there anything else you're not telling me, Doctor?" he asked, his voice hardening.

Dr Nair looked down, seeming to be deep in thought before she spoke. "There is something, Detective," she admitted, her voice barely above a whisper. "But it's not something I'm proud of."

Vince leaned in, intrigued. "Please, go on."

Dr Nair took a deep breath before continuing. "A few days before Dr Whittaker's disappearance, I became aware that he had taken one of the mass spectrometers from the research labs. It is a critical piece of equipment for our research. I confronted him about it, but he refused to return it. I tried to take it away from his room by force, and in the struggle, the machine caught him and scratched his arm."

Vince's eyes widened in surprise. "Why didn't you report this earlier?"

"I was ashamed of my behaviour," Dr Nair admitted. "I let my anger and frustration get the better of me, and I knew that I was in the wrong. I didn't want to cause any more trouble or tension within the team. I was worried that I could be removed from the mission as Lead Scientist if I was found to cause another crew member any physical harm."

Vince nodded slowly, processing the new information. "Thank you for being honest with me, Dr Nair. I appreciate it. But I have to ask, did you have anything to do with Dr Whittaker's death?"

Dr Nair shook her head vehemently. "No, Detective. I swear on my honour as a scientist that I had nothing to do with his death."

Vince nodded once and turned his attention back to Captain Armstrong. "Captain, can you have a closer look at the wound, please? I want to see if there are any other markings or signs of struggle that we might have missed."

"... are you just ignoring the fact that I hid this information from you?" Dr Nair asked incredulously.

Vince didn't even look away from Whittaker's body as he spoke. "I have come to the conclusion, Doctor, that if the crew are going to be unhelpful in this investigation, that I would be well suited to ask less questions and find more evidence on my own. That is if I am indeed correct in my assumption that the Captain already knew about this particular fact?"

The Captain smiled in response to this question.

"Yes, Detective. Dr Nair informed me of the incident shortly after it happened. I told her not to come forward with the information, but I understand your position. We are a team up here, and we rely on each other for survival. Any tension or conflict can have severe consequences. However, I agree with you that in a case like this, transparency is sometimes necessary for finding the truth."

Vince nodded in understanding, his eyes still fixed on the wound on Dr Whittaker's arm. "Thank you, Captain. Dr Nair, I appreciate your honesty, but I need to know if there's anything else you've been keeping from me."

Dr Nair shook her head. "No, Detective. That's all I know. I understand that it may seem suspicious, but I assure you again that I had nothing to do with Dr Whittaker's death."

Vince nodded slowly before turning back to the body. He carefully examined the wound, noting the length and depth of the scratch, as well as any other markings around the area. It was clear that it had been caused by a sharp object, but he couldn't tell for certain what it was.

After several minutes of examination, Vince stood up and removed his gloves and mask. "Thank you, Doctor, for your cooperation. I'll be in touch if I need any further information or assistance." Then he turned to look at the Captain and said: "Please, can we speak in private?"

Chapter 15: A Captain Who Goes Down with His Ship

"I'd like to tell you a few things before you begin your accusations," Captain Armstrong announced as the pair stepped into his office.

Vince nodded once. "Go on," he said.

"Firstly, I know how this all looks from the outside. I know that I hadn't told you about Grace and the way that she falsified problems to look as though she was doing a good job. I know that it looks bad that she argued with the Doctor. I also know that it looks bad that Priya didn't tell you about her little fight with the Doctor, but these things, I assure you are best kept out of the centre of your investigation. The eyes of the world are upon us, Detective, and I do not wish for us to be judged incapable of carrying out our tasks due to a few misdemeanours."

Vince raised an eyebrow at the Captain's words. "Captain, I understand the need for discretion, but withholding information from a murder investigation can have serious consequences. We need to find out what happened to Dr Whittaker, and that means considering all possible angles and information. We do not get to decide what is important and what is not."

The Captain leaned forward, his gaze intense. "I understand that Detective. But please understand that we are in a unique and precarious situation up here. We are a small team, isolated from the rest of the world, and we rely on each other for our very survival. Any conflict or tension between us could have serious consequences for our mission and for our lives. That's why I asked my crew to keep quiet about certain things."

Vince frowned. "I understand your concerns, Captain, but it's my duty to investigate this case thoroughly and fairly. If there's any information that you're withholding, I need to know about it."

The Captain leaned back in his chair, sighing. "Alright, Detective. What do you need to know?"

Vince took a deep breath before continuing. "First of all, I need to know if there's any reason to suspect anyone in particular for Dr Whittaker's death. Do you have any suspicions or leads that you haven't shared with me?"

The Captain shook his head. "No, Detective. We have no reason to suspect anyone in particular. Our investigations and interviews have not revealed any significant information."

Vince nodded slowly, taking note of the Captain's response. "Alright. And what about the incident with the mass spectrometer that Dr Nair told me about? You knew about that?"

The Captain nodded. "Yes, I did. Dr Nair came to me shortly after it happened and told me what had occurred. I advised her not to come forward with the information, but I understand that it might be relevant to your investigation. My thought was that the incident had been dealt with, and it was not worth putting Priya's job, and reputation on the line for."

Vince raised an eyebrow. "Why did you tell her not to come forward?"

The Captain hesitated before answering. "I was concerned about the potential consequences of Dr Nair's actions. For one I didn't want the incident to cause any more tension than necessary, but also I felt as the Captain, that Priya's work was more important than a little tension between colleagues."

Vince nodded slowly, taking in the Captain's words. "I understand your concerns, Captain. But I need to know about any relevant information, no matter how small or potentially damaging it may seem. Can I count on your cooperation from here on out?"

The Captain nodded. "Of course, Detective. I will do everything in my power to assist you in this investigation."

"Then please, tell me honestly what you think happened to Dr Whittaker," Vince said.

The Captain leaned back in his chair again, staring off into the distance as he gathered his thoughts. "I wish I knew, Detective. It's possible that he fell and injured himself, but the fact that his body was found so far away from the settlement raises some red flags. And then there's the issue of his private quarters being ransacked. It's all very concerning."

Vince nodded in agreement.

"But Detective, this is all for you to figure out isn't it?" the Captain asked. "If I knew what happened, then you wouldn't be here at all."

"That is true, and I can't help but reiterate the importance of your co-operation in all aspects of my investigation."

Captain Armstrong smiled. "Of course. Now what can I help you with?"

Vince sighed again before he spoke. "Well, there is one more person that I have yet to interview up here within the pool of evidence that I have been handed. Your Lead Botanist, a Mr Leo Martinez. What can you tell me about him?"

Captain Armstrong leaned forward, steeping his fingers in front of him. "Leo Martinez is a talented botanist and a valuable member of our team. He's been with us since the beginning of the mission and has made many contributions to our research on sustainable agriculture in space. He's also well-respected among his colleagues and has a good working relationship with everyone on board."

Vince nodded, taking note of the Captain's words. "Has there been anything unusual about his behaviour lately? Anything that might suggest he had a motive to harm Dr Whittaker?"

The Captain frowned, thinking for a moment. "Not that I'm aware of, Detective. Leo has been focused on his work as usual, and I haven't noticed anything out of the ordinary. But then again, I'm not always privy to everything that goes on among the crew."

Vince nodded again, considering his next move and thinking that in reality, regardless of what he just said, the Captain knew everything about everything. "Do you think it would be possible for me to speak with Mr Martinez next?"

The Captain nodded. "I'll arrange for you to meet with him, Detective. Just let me know when you're ready."

Vince could see something within the Captain's expression though, that told him once again, the man was not being entirely truthful. There was again something that he was keeping from Vince, and the Detective could only suspect that whatever it was, it was most likely something that the Captain had decided wouldn't be pertinent to the murder investigation.

Only a few hours passed before Vince caught up with the botanist. He hadn't yet told the Captain that he had planned to visit Leo Martinez at his place of work, given the way that the Captain had been protecting his friends and subordinates.

"You're Leo Martinez, right?" Vince asked as he approached the botanist. "The settlement's Lead Botanist?"

The man looked up at Vince from the ground that he had been tending to. He was on his hands and knees within a large dome that had been segmented to house a wide range of crops, all of which at a cursory glance looked to be thriving and healthy – a marvel given the fact that a few short years ago, the surface of the moon was a barren and unforgiving place.

Leo looked up at Vince and nodded, wiping his hands on a rag before standing up. "Yes, that's correct. Can I help you with something?" he asked, looking at Vince curiously.

Vince introduced himself and explained the reason for his visit. "I'm investigating the death of Dr Whittaker, and I was hoping to ask you a few questions about your interactions with him."

Leo's expression turned serious. "Of course, anything to help with the investigation. What do you need to know?"

Vince began by asking about Leo's relationship with Dr Whittaker and whether there had been any conflicts between them. Leo shook his head as everyone else had, explaining that they had a professional relationship, and that Dr Whittaker had often helped him with advice on mineral compositions of the lunar environment.

"I read your witness testimony," Vince said nonchalantly. "You're the only person to have stated that the best course of action was for you to stay within the habs."

Leo nodded. "Yes, that's correct. As the lead botanist, my role is critical to the success of our mission. If something were to happen to me, it would have severe consequences for the rest of the crew. That's why I felt it was best for me to stay in the habitat and continue my work while the others searched for Dr Whittaker."

"Something... happen to you?" Vince asked. "Like what? I understand that Dr Whittaker had been missing for days when he had been found, so what could have caused you to believe that you were in danger?"

Leo hesitated before answering, looking around at the plants in the dome before speaking. "I don't know, Detective. It's just a feeling I had. The moon can be a dangerous place, and we have to be cautious. I didn't want to take any unnecessary risks that could put the mission and the rest of the crew in danger. In fact, I try to remain safely indoors as often as possible."

Vince nodded, taking note of Leo's response. "I understand your concern for the mission and the crew's safety, but do you have any specific reasons to believe that you might be in danger?"

Leo shook his head. "No, not really. It's just a gut feeling, I guess."

Vince looked at Leo closely, studying his expression for any signs of deception. But the botanist seemed genuine in his answers, and there was nothing in his body language that suggested he was hiding something. What he did see, was a fair amount of anxiety within the man. He was clearly sweating and his eyes kept darting about as though he was talking to a fellow conspirator about things that should not have been mentioned aloud.

Vince decided to change tactics to try to put Leo at ease. "I understand that living and working on the moon can be stressful, and it's not uncommon for crew members to feel a bit anxious or uneasy at times. Is everything OK, Leo? Are you feeling alright?"

Leo seemed to relax a bit at Vince's words, and he nodded slowly. "Yes, everything's fine, Detective. I guess I've just been a bit on edge lately."

Vince nodded, still keeping his eye on Leo's behaviour. "Is there anything in particular that's been bothering you? Maybe something you've been keeping to yourself?"

Leo shook his head, but there was a hint of hesitation in his response. "No, nothing in particular. Just the usual stress and pressure of working up here, I guess."

"Mr Martinez," Vince said slowly, choosing his words carefully. "I have spoken with the other Leads in this settlement and all of them told me that there had been nothing out of the ordinary happen up here between them and Dr Whittaker. I want you to know that my capacity here is simply to investigate what happened to Dr Whittaker. I am not here to pass judgements or make reports on what the crew may or may not have done correctly. I have also spoken to the Captain, and he has assured me that all of the crew here will aid me to the best of their abilities and knowledge. Now I feel that although I cannot press you, I can ask my question again. Is there anything that happened between you and Dr Whittaker before his death that was out of the ordinary, or that caused conflict?"

Martinez froze for a moment as he looked down at his hands. Eventually, he spoke without looking up at Vince. "Listen, Detective..."

"You can call me Vince," Vince replied.

"Vince..." Martinez took a deep breath before continuing. "There was something that happened between me and Dr Whittaker a few weeks before his death. I was working on a project involving some rare plants that I had managed to grow successfully, and I was excited to show him my progress. But when I showed him the plants, he became very agitated and accused me of using resources that were meant for other experiments. I tried to explain that I had been very careful in my use of resources and that I was only trying to further our goals here, but he didn't want to hear it. He threatened to have my project shut down if I didn't stop using the resources."

Vince listened intently, taking notes on his tablet. "And how did you respond to this threat?"

"I was angry, of course. I felt like he didn't understand the importance of my work, and that he was trying to sabotage my efforts. But in the end, we simply decided to agree to disagree. Then... well you can see for yourself."

Martinez moved to a tiny corner of the habs that had been clearly set up to house a small amount of hydroponic pots, though they were half melted and charred, and whatever had been inside them previously had clearly been burnt beyond all recognition.

"He burnt the crops?" Vince asked with wide eyes.

"Yes," Martinez said with a grimace. "I woke up one morning to find my entire project destroyed, everything burnt to a crisp. There was no doubt in my mind that he had done it. I confronted him about it, but he denied everything, saying that it must have been a mistake. I didn't have any proof, so I couldn't do anything about it... and my project technically wasn't sanctioned by the settlement, so I couldn't really complain either."

Vince furrowed his brow. "That's a serious accusation, Mr Martinez. Are you sure that Dr Whittaker was responsible for the destruction of your project?"

Martinez nodded firmly. "Yes, I'm sure. I have no doubt that he did it, and it's been eating away at me ever since. But I didn't want to cause any trouble, especially with everything else that's been going on. I just wanted to keep my head down and focus on my work. The plants that I had though, were everything I had of their species, so I couldn't even restart the project if I wanted to."

"Does the Captain know about this?" Vince asked.

Martinez nodded. "The Captain knew about the project. He told me to keep it quiet but I thought that the other Leads would want to know, you know? We're supposed to all be in this together, but Whittaker... he just seemed to always know better than everyone else."

"And did the Captain confront Whittaker on your behalf after your crops were ruined?" Vince asked.

Martinez shook his head.

"No, he didn't. He said he would investigate the matter, but as far as I know, nothing came of it. I think he was trying to keep things calm and didn't want to cause any unnecessary tension among the crew."

Vince made a mental note to follow up on this and investigate further. "Thank you for telling me this, Mr Martinez. It could be a significant piece of information for the investigation."

Martinez nodded, still looking a bit uneasy. "Is there anything else you need to know?"

Vince paused for a moment before speaking. "Not right now thank you, but I will ask you some more questions later, I'm sure."

Vince gave Leo a smile as he left the botanist to his work. There was just so much more information to process now, and another possible motive for someone to want to cause Dr Whittaker harm.

It seemed to Vince that Dr Whittaker was not a liked and respected man after all; and if the Captain was hell-bent on keeping the status quo up here on the lunar settlement, then he had as much of a motive as anyone else to keep the late Doctor quiet.

Chapter 16: A Shot in the Dark

Vince had only taken a couple of steps away from the botany lab when his phone began to ring. Answering the unknown number, he was greeted by the familiar female voice of Dr Mendez, head of the Earth-side science team working in tandem with the lunar settlement.

"Detective?" Mendez asked.

"Speaking, Doctor," Vince replied. "How may I help you?"

Mendez was quiet for a short moment before she finally spoke. "Its just... I'm calling to see if you have made any progress in your investigation. I must admit that I am... we are all waiting with bated breath down here to learn what you've discovered.

Vince took a deep breath, feeling the weight of the pressure on his shoulders. "I'm still working on it, Doctor. It's a complex case, but I'm doing my best to find the answers we need. I'll be sure to update you when I find anything of note."

Mendez sighed audibly. "I understand, Detective. But time is of the essence. We need to know what happened up there so that we can adjust our mission parameters accordingly. Every day that passes without answers is a day lost in the pursuit of our goals."

"I'm aware of that, Doctor," Vince replied. "I'm doing everything in my power to solve this case as quickly and thoroughly as possible. But I can't rush the investigation. I need to be certain that I have all the facts before I make any conclusions."

Mendez seemed to consider this for a moment before speaking again. "I trust in your abilities, Detective. But please, do keep me updated on any developments. We're all counting on you up there."

Vince nodded from habit as the Doctor couldn't see him. "I will, Doctor. Thank you for your support."

"I wonder if you could tell me what you have learned so far? I may be of use as somewhat of an outsider down here," Mendez replied.

Vince furrowed his brow. It was a pretty normal request from someone that was close to the settlement, though he couldn't help feeling that something was slightly off about this phone call.

"I'm not sure that you can be of much assistance..." Vince began, though Mendez quickly interrupted him.

"Perhaps I can assist with what Dr Whittaker had been working on around the time of his death?" She asked.

"Dr Mendez..." Vince began to speak though again was interrupted.

"Or have you uncovered some motives that are as yet unknown to the rest of us?" She asked.

"Dr Mendez... I do not want to speak out of turn, and the last thing I want to do is to implicate innocent parties. There is something that you can help me with, however. Could you tell me why each of the Head of Departments were chosen to lead this mission and their teams respectively? I would like to know more about Grace Thompson, Leo Martinez, Priya Nair and Captain Armstrong."

Mendez was quiet for a moment before she eventually clicked her tongue into the phone. "Do you think one of them actually killed Doctor Whittaker?" She asked with a very high-pitched inflection to her voice.

"I would not like to say at this very moment, though I am interested in hearing about the selection process that led to each of them being sent up here – possibly for the rest of their natural lives. I think it would help me with my investigation."

Mendez let out a sigh before answering. "Very well, Detective. I suppose it's only fair that you have a complete understanding of the people you're investigating. Grace Thompson was chosen for her expertise in engineering. Leo Martinez was selected for his knowledge of botany and agriculture. Priya Nair was chosen for her experience in both geology and leadership. And Captain Armstrong was selected for his leadership skills and experience in management."

Vince took note of the information, though it didn't seem particularly enlightening. "Thank you, Dr Mendez. I appreciate your assistance. Is there anything else you'd like to add? I mean it would stand to reason that these people were chosen for their skill sets and abilities."

Mendez hesitated for a moment before speaking. "Just that we're all hoping for a swift resolution to this investigation. It's been a difficult time for all of us, and we're eager for justice to be served."

"Listen," Vince said slowly, trying to steer Mendez back in the right direction. "I know that these people are all very capable, they wouldn't have been chosen otherwise. But I want to know more about them personally, their personality types, their resiliencies and their weaknesses. For example, you must have known that Grace Thompson is an anxious person at heart? Dr Whittaker was arrogant and abrasive. Dr Nair is dedicated to achieving the most that she possibly can and the Captain is stalwart in his determination to keep a tight ship. Please, Dr Mendez, tell me something that I may be able to use."

Mendez was quiet for a moment before responding. "Well, I can tell you that Grace Thompson is very driven and passionate about her work, sometimes to the point of obsession. She's also quite private and doesn't share much about her personal life. Leo Martinez is a bit of a perfectionist and can be overly cautious at times. Priya Nair is a natural leader, but she can be stubborn and headstrong in her decision-making. And as for Captain Armstrong, he can be a bit rigid in his thinking and can sometimes struggle to adapt to unexpected situations."

Vince listened carefully, taking note of the information. "Thank you, Dr Mendez. That's what I wanted to hear."

The information wasn't particularly useful, but it gave Vince the knowledge that the team back on Earth had carried out a range of personality tests, and these people had all passed. He couldn't have been certain that his own tests would've been similar or yielded the same results, though what Dr Mendez had said did seem to match up with what he was thinking.

Then Dr Mendez spoke again as Vince was lost in his thoughts. "I'd really like to know if there is anything that I can do to help, Mr Callahan," Mendez said. "Do you have any leads, anything at all to go on?"

"Dr Mendez..." Vince said slowly.

"Please, call me Alice," the Doctor replied quickly.

"Uh... Alice," Vince replied. "There's nothing that I can honestly tell you that you don't already know. I am yet to discern what truly happened and am currently working my way through personnel and motives."

"But you have found some motives?" Dr Mendez almost interrupted.

"Dr Mendez, there are always motives. And in a place like this, there are generally lots of them. I will keep you updated as and when I discover more. Until then, I am afraid you are going to have to be a little patient." Then Vince cancelled the call and put his phone back in his pocket. He always hated it when people tried to help a little too much.

Vince continued down the hallway mulling over the information he had just received from Dr Mendez. It was true that it didn't provide any concrete leads in the case, but it did give him a better understanding of the people he was investigating. And he couldn't shake the feeling that there was something off about Mendez's eagerness to help. He made a mental note to look into her as well.

As Vince walked, he noticed the sound of footsteps echoing down the hallway from behind him, and he turned to see Captain Armstrong quickly approaching.

"Detective," the Captain greeted him with a nod. "How are things going with the investigation?"

Vince returned the nod. "It's slow going, but I'm making progress. I spoke with Leo Martinez earlier, and he gave me some information about a conflict he had with Dr Whittaker before his death."

The Captain's expression shifted slightly, but it was hard to tell if it was surprise or concern. "I see. And what did he tell you?"

"He said that Whittaker destroyed a project he was working on, and that they had a heated argument about it. Martinez is convinced that Whittaker was responsible for destroying his plants, though he didn't have any concrete proof."

The Captain furrowed his brow. "That's concerning. Did Martinez mention anything else?"

"Not really," Vince replied. "Just that he's been feeling stressed and on edge lately. But that's not exactly surprising given the circumstances."

The Captain seemed to look past Vince as he answered the question, and Vince couldn't help but think that there was more to this.

"Is there anything more that you'd like to add?" Vince asked, pulling on the thread that he had seen dangling.

The Captain shook his head. "No Detective, I think you're doing great work. Let me know when you have any updates."

The Captain seemed eager to leave the conversation and in a moment the pair parted and turned away from each other, Vince then heard the Captain speak again.

"Hello Mrs Whittaker," he said. "Is there anything I can do for you today?"

Vince turned just in time to hear Eleanor say: "No thanks, I actually wanted to catch up with the Detective," and she looked past the Captain and met Vince's eyes. She smiled, and he returned the gesture. The Captain then disappeared around a corner and it left the pair to walk and talk.

"Hello Mrs Whittaker," Vince greeted her as they walked together. "How are you holding up?"

Eleanor let out a small sigh. "I'm... I'm doing my best. It's just been so difficult to process everything that's happened."

"I can only imagine," Vince replied sympathetically. "But I want you to know that I'm doing everything in my power to get to the bottom of this. And if there's anything you can think of that might help me in my investigation, please don't hesitate to let me know." Sometimes Vince felt like a bit of a broken record, but he was always amazed at what people seemed to 'remember' later.

Eleanor nodded gratefully. "Thank you, Detective. I appreciate all of your efforts."

Vince studied her for a moment, noticing the bags under her eyes and the tension in her shoulders. "How about we sit down and talk for a bit?" he suggested.

Eleanor hesitated for a moment before nodding. "Alright. I suppose it couldn't hurt to talk."

Vince led her to a nearby seating area, and they both took a seat. "Now, can you tell me a bit more about your husband?" Vince asked gently.

Eleanor looked down at her hands, which were clasped tightly in her lap. "Adrian was... he was brilliant. He had a sharp mind and a strong will, and he was always pushing himself to be better. I miss him."

Vince nodded. "That's what I've been hearing. But he could also be a bit abrasive right? Some would say that he would stick his nose in where it didn't belong."

Eleanor's expression grew pained. "Yes, that's true. Adrian had a tendency to be very opinionated, and he didn't always consider other people's feelings. He was so focused on his work that he sometimes forgot about the people around him. Sometimes I would joke that he would either see other people as obstacles, or furniture."

"I see," Vince said, jotting down a mental note. "And how about his relationships with the other members of the settlement? Did he have any conflicts with anyone in particular?"

Eleanor sighed. "He had his disagreements, of course. But nothing that I would consider a major conflict. He was always focused on his work, and I think he believed that everyone else should be too."

Vince nodded again. "And what about you, Mrs Whittaker? Did you notice anything different about your husband in the days leading up to his death?"

Eleanor's expression grew even more pained, and she looked away from Vince. "He was... distant, I suppose. More preoccupied than usual. But he was always like that when he was working on something important. Like he would get ultra-focussed on something and nothing else could make it through to him."

Vince studied her for a moment before speaking again. "Do you think there's anyone on the settlement who might have wanted to harm your husband?"

"I... I don't know. I wouldn't have said so if I hadn't come up here myself... but, well people didn't seem to get along with Adrian very much."

"Why do you think that was?" Vince asked.

Eleanor paused for a moment and eventually her shoulders dropped. "Adrian was under so much stress. It was partly my fault, but you don't know what it's like..." Vince could see her eyes filling with tears and moved to comfort her.

"What what's like?" Vince asked.

Eleanor covered her face with her hands as she spoke. "Our daughter... Helen... she has to live in a care facility... they say that she can never leave..."

Vince's heart sank at those words. He had known that the Whittakers had a sick daughter, but he had no idea that things were as serious as that.

"I'm so sorry," Vince replied. "It must have been so hard for Adrian to have been away for so long."

"It's just... so hard," Eleanor said through sniffs and tears. "I have to be the one to sit by her bedside in any free time I have. The one to talk to her and tell her about all the great work her father is doing... to explain why he can't be there with her, to cuddle or kiss her..."

Vince listened with empathy as Eleanor poured out her heart, her grief and her frustrations. He could feel the depth of her pain, the weight of her responsibilities and the helplessness that she must be feeling. He had seen it before, the way that the stress of living apart could amplify every problem, every challenge, and every setback.

"I can't imagine how difficult that must be for you, Mrs Whittaker," Vince said, offering her a tissue from his pocket. "It sounds like you're carrying a heavy burden on your shoulders."

Eleanor took the tissue gratefully and wiped her eyes. "It's been tough," she admitted. "And then to lose Adrian... it feels like everything is falling apart."

"I can only imagine," Vince said again. "But I want you to know that you're not alone in this. We're all here to support you, and we're going to find out what happened to your husband. I promise you that. Beyond that I'm sure there's a wealth of help available to you."

Eleanor gave him a small smile, her eyes still red-rimmed from tears. "Thank you, Detective. I think I just need to know what happened so that I can put all this behind me..."

Vince nodded. "I think we all need a little closure. It helps us to move on and fully understand the reasons behind why such things happen."

Eleanor nodded silently again.

Vince sat with Eleanor for a few more minutes, letting her compose herself. As she took a few deep breaths, he realised that he had been so focused on the investigation that he hadn't fully considered the impact that Adrian's death had on his family.

"Detective..." Eleanor said slowly. "Do you have any idea what happened? Any suspects, or leads to follow yet?"

Vince thought about what he could say to the woman. He knew that she needed hope, but he didn't want to give her any false hope or the idea that he could be close to figuring all this out. Instead, he said: "I have a few leads that I'm following up on but at this stage, I can't say for certain what happened. However, I can assure you that I'm doing everything I can to get to the bottom of this. And if I do find anything out, you'll be the first to know."

Eleanor nodded, seemingly grateful for his honesty. "Thank you, Detective. I appreciate everything you're doing."

Vince stood up from his seat, signalling the end of their conversation. "If there's anything else you can think of that might help me with my investigation, please don't hesitate to let me know."

"I will," Eleanor said as she stood up as well. "And thank you again, Detective."

As Vince watched her walk away, he couldn't help but feel a sense of sadness and frustration. He knew that he had a job to do, but he also knew that there was a family grieving for their loved one. He made a silent promise to himself that he would do everything in his power to bring the killer to justice, for the sake of not just the settlement, but for Eleanor and her daughter too.

Evidence: Video Tapes 2

It took a while for Vince to sift through some of the rubbish that the CCTV systems in the habs had caught, but eventually, he found what he was looking for: The interaction between Dr Whittaker and Leo Martinez that he knew he wouldn't be able to get any more information about from the crew.

The video tape started with a view of a large greenhouse that Vince already knew was where Martinez worked and tended to his crops. It was filled with rows of various plants and within the frame, Vince could see Leo Martinez tending to some plants and the lab seemed empty apart from the botanist. The plants in question though, mysteriously seem to be purposely out of view of the camera. Martinez was wearing gloves and a face mask as he worked, and the camera captured the sound of the plants rustling as he moved around them. Martinez also seemed to be merrily humming to himself as he worked.

After a few minutes, the sound of footsteps was evident, entering the greenhouse. Dr Whittaker entered the frame, looking agitated and angry.

Whittaker: What the hell is this, Martinez?

Martinez: What do you mean, Whittaker?

Whittaker: These plants. They're not supposed to be here. They're taking up valuable space that could be used for more important projects.

Martinez: This is just a personal project that I'm working on. I thought you might understand...

Whittaker: You really think this is what I wanted? This is exactly the kind of thing that's been holding us back!

Martinez: I don't think that's fair. These plants could have significant medical applications. And they're not wasting any resources - I'm using my own time and materials.

Whittaker: Oh, well that makes it all better, doesn't it? Look, Martinez, I don't have time for this. Get rid of these plants and focus on the projects that actually matter. I don't want to have to remind you again.

Martinez: With all due respect, Whittaker, I think you're being short-sighted. We need to be exploring all avenues of research, not just the ones that fit into your narrow view of what's important. You aren't the boss around here no matter what you might think.

Whittaker: Excuse me? Are you questioning my judgment, Martinez? After what you've been doing here?

Martinez: I'm questioning your ability to see the bigger picture. If we only focus on the projects that are easy or convenient, we're never going to make any real progress.

Whittaker: You're out of line, Martinez. I won't tolerate this attitude from anyone, least of all from someone like you.

Martinez: I'm not trying to be insubordinate. I'm just trying to do what's best for the settlement. And I think that means exploring all possibilities, not just the ones that fit into your preconceived notions.

Whittaker: You have no idea what's best for the settlement, Martinez. And if you can't do what you're told, then maybe it's time for you to leave.

Martinez: Is that a threat?

Whittaker: Consider it whatever you want, Martinez.

Whittaker then turned, and Vince could see that within his hand, he held a portable camera. Raising it up to his eye level, Whittaker began to take pictures of the crops, which were immediately printed by an attachment at the bottom of the antiquated machine.

Martinez: What are you going to do with that, Doctor?

Whittaker: I'm going to use it as evidence, Martinez. Evidence of your insubordination and your refusal to follow orders. Don't think for a second that your personal project is more important than the work that we're doing here. If you can't understand that, then maybe you're not cut out for this kind of work.

Martinez: I understand perfectly well, Whittaker. I just don't agree with you. And I'm not going to give up on something that I believe in just because you don't like it.

Whittaker: Then you leave me no choice, Martinez. I'll have to report this to the rest of the crew. I'm sure they'll be interested to hear about your little project.

Martinez: Go ahead, report it to whoever you want. I stand by my work.

Whittaker: We'll see about that, Martinez. We'll see about that.

With that, Dr Whittaker stormed out of the greenhouse, leaving Leo Martinez standing there with a determined look on his face.

Vince peered closely at the screen and as he did so, he watched as Martinez pulled a shoot from one of his plants and brought it up to his nose. Vince's eyes grew wide as he immediately recognised the plant for what it was. The leaves were immediately recognisable as that of the cannabis plant.

Chapter 17: Paranoia

Vince was absolutely certain that cannabis plants wouldn't have made it into the settlement's library of plants, but he needed to be sure. Somehow though he knew that if he was to ask the Captain about this, that the response was going to be a 'yes I knew, but I covered it up'. So, Vince did the only other thing that he could think of: he would confront Leo Martinez himself, and ask about the plants.

Vince found Martinez in the greenhouse, tending to his plants once again. He watched as the botanist carefully sprayed the leaves of a small plant with a water bottle, humming to himself as he worked. Vince cleared his throat to get Martinez's attention, and the man turned around, clearly surprised to see the Detective there.

"Detective, what brings you here?" Martinez asked, his tone friendly but guarded.

"I wanted to ask you about the plants you were tending to in this greenhouse," Vince said, trying to keep his voice neutral.

"What about them?" Martinez asked, still spraying the leaves of the plant.

"I saw on the video tapes that you were growing cannabis plants," Vince said bluntly.

Martinez paused in his work and looked up at Vince with a mixture of surprise and concern.

"I'm not sure what you mean, Detective," Martinez said slowly. "I don't know anything about any cannabis plants."

"Don't play dumb with me, Martinez," Vince said, his voice starting to rise. "I know what I saw on the video tapes."

Martinez sighed and set down the water bottle. "Look, Detective, I'll be honest with you. Yes, I was growing cannabis plants. But I swear, it's not what you think."

"And what do I think, Martinez?" Vince asked, folding his arms.

"You think I'm growing marijuana to get high, right?" Martinez said, his voice tinged with frustration. "But that's not it at all. I'm growing it for medicinal purposes. There are so many medical applications that it boggles the mind." Then Martinez took a deep breath before continuing. "Did you know that one of the most significant factors in the illegalisation of cannabis was the competition it posed to other industries, particularly the paper and textile industries. Hemp, a strain of the plant, was used extensively in paper production, and its fibres were used to make durable textiles. However, the paper and textile industries lobbied against the plant because they saw it as a threat to their businesses. In the nineteen thirties, powerful industrialists like William Randolph Hearst and DuPont family member Andrew Mellon also campaigned against cannabis, fearing that the rise of hemp-based products would affect their businesses. They played a significant role in the criminalisation of marijuana through lobbying and propaganda campaigns, which helped to create a negative image of the plant in the public eye."

Vince didn't quite know what to say in response, and just stared at Martinez with his mouth slightly open for a short while. Eventually he managed to respond to the only part of Martinez's statement that he could comment on.

"Medicinal purposes?" Vince managed.

"Yes, medicinal purposes," Martinez said firmly. "Cannabis has been used for thousands of years to treat a variety of ailments. It can help with pain, nausea, anxiety, depression, and a host of other conditions. I had the idea that we could grow the perfect strain here so that we can maximise the medicinal benefits from the plant."

Vince was silent for a moment, considering what Martinez had said. He knew that cannabis had been used medicinally on Earth, but he had never considered the possibility of it being grown on the moon. Still, he couldn't help feeling uneasy about the whole situation.

"But growing illegal drugs is still a serious offence," Vince said finally. "You could get in a lot of trouble for this."

"I know that," Martinez said, nodding. "And I'm willing to take that risk. But in a lot of places, it isn't illegal, and I'm not going to let some arbitrary law on a planet a quarter of a million miles away stop me from helping the people who need it."

Vince shook his head. "I don't know what to say, Martinez. I understand that you believe in this, but..."

"But it's still breaking the law in a technicality, right?" Martinez finished for him. "I know. And I'm sorry for putting you in this position, Detective. But I truly believe that this is important work. And I'm not the only one who thinks so. There are many scientists and medical professionals who are advocating for the use of cannabis for medicinal purposes."

Vince sighed. He could see that Martinez was passionate about what he was doing, and he couldn't deny that there might be some merit to his arguments. But at the same time, he couldn't ignore the fact that what Martinez was doing was most probably illegal.

"I'll have to report this to the Captain," Vince said finally. "I'm sorry, Martinez. But I have to do my job."

"I understand," Martinez said, nodding. "But the Captain already knows."

"He knows?" Vince asked, and he had to try very hard to inject some surprise into his voice.

Martinez' shoulders dropped. "It was the Captain's idea to burn the crops. I told him about the argument that Whittaker and I had about the plants. He said that because Whittaker had taken those photos and was kicking up such a fuss... it would just be better to burn the plants. I guess it doesn't really even matter anymore now does it, not now that Whittaker's gone..."

Vince wasn't taken aback by this revelation. The Captain had known about the cannabis plants all along and had even ordered them to be destroyed. It made sense, though, given the possible illegal status of the plant and the potential consequences of being caught growing it.

But Vince couldn't help feeling frustrated by the secrecy surrounding the issue.

"Why didn't the Captain tell me about this? And why did you give yourself motive by saying the Whittaker burnt them?" he asked.

"I don't know," Martinez said with a shrug. "Maybe he thought you didn't need to know. Or maybe he was afraid that you would try to shut us down. Either way, it's not like we were trying to hide anything. We just didn't want to cause any trouble. I told you Whittaker did it because he may as well have done. After all, if he didn't stick his nose in to my business, I'd still be growing the plants, right?"

Vince thought for a long moment. "You know what this means, don't you?"

Leo Martinez nodded thoughtfully. "It means I've just given you a great motive for why I would want Whittaker out of the picture."

Vince nodded in return. "That's exactly what it means."

"Only there are two issues with that, Detective, one: the plants were burnt before Whittaker even went missing and two, I don't have any more seeds to cultivate new plants. So Whittaker being out of the picture would make no difference, so to speak."

"Except for the fact that he could've cost you your job with the photos he took. Did you ever find them, by the way?" Vince asked.

"Find them? I never even saw them," Martinez replied with a bemused expression on his face.

"You know Whittaker's room was ransacked after he went missing... it seems that you would have a good reason to go looking through his things, no?"

Martinez shook his head. "I didn't go through Whittaker's things. Why would I? I didn't have anything to do with his disappearance."

Vince nodded slowly, considering Martinez's words. It was possible that Martinez was telling the truth, but he couldn't be sure. He decided to change the subject.

"Well, regardless of whether or not you had anything to do with Whittaker's disappearance, we still need to figure out what happened to him," Vince said firmly. "And I have a feeling that the answer lies somewhere in this settlement."

"I agree," Martinez said, nodding. "But I don't envy you in your task. Seems like it's a needle in a haystack to me."

Vince sighed. "Yes, it's not going to be easy. But we have to try. We owe it to Whittaker and to the rest of the crew to find out what happened."

Martinez nodded in agreement. "I'll do whatever I can to help."

Vince gave him a small smile. "Thanks, Martinez. I appreciate it."

The two men stood in silence for a moment, each lost in thought. Vince couldn't help but feel like they were missing something, some clue that would help them unravel the mystery of Whittaker's disappearance. He just hoped they would find it before it was too late. One thing that he certainly couldn't do though, was remove Martinez from his list of suspects. It just seemed like as more time went by, more and more people had reason to want Doctor Whittaker out of the picture.

It was again clear to Vince though, that all roads were, as they say, beginning to lead to Rome. Or more specifically, the Captain was hiding way too much from Vince, and he didn't like it.

Vince spent the next few hours going over the evidence he had gathered so far. He still couldn't shake the feeling that he was missing something important, so he went back over the video tapes, the statements from the crew, and the notes he had taken during his interviews. He hoped that something would jump out at him, some clue that he had missed before. But no matter how hard he looked, nothing did.

He decided to take a break from the investigation and head back to his quarters. As he walked down the empty corridors of the settlement, he couldn't shake the feeling that he was being watched. Something had changed and the more he dug into this case, the worse he was feeling.

He had felt this way since he had arrived on the moon, but he had always dismissed it as paranoia, or the fact that the cameras up here were always rolling. Now, he wasn't so sure.

Vince entered his quarters and locked the door behind him. He sat down on his bed and tried to relax, but his mind was racing. He couldn't shake the feeling that someone was watching his every move. Even now when he was alone, he felt eyes upon him and it made his stomach churn. Eventually, he managed to tell himself that this was simply a side-effect of such a high-profile case and as long as he kept moving in the right direction, he was going to be fine.

Deciding to call the Captain and confront him about the secrecy surrounding the cannabis plants, Vince dialled the Captain's number and waited for him to answer.

"Detective," the Captain said, his tone formal. "Is there something I can help you with?"

"I want to know why you didn't tell me about the cannabis plants," Vince said flatly, his voice firm.

There was a pause on the other end of the line. "I didn't think it was relevant to the investigation," the Captain said finally.

"It's illegal to grow cannabis," Vince said. "And it could be a motive for Whittaker's disappearance."

"I understand your concerns, Detective," the Captain said. "But I assure you, there is no connection between the cannabis plants and Whittaker's death."

"Then why did you order them to be destroyed?" Vince asked.

"Because I didn't want to risk any trouble for Martinez or for the settlement," the Captain said. "As I'm sure you're aware, there could have been consequences for everyone involved, even if we could argue away the legal technicalities. Leo brought those seeds with him of his own accord, and that wouldn't pass muster with the team back on Earth."

"I still don't fully understand why you insist on hiding information like this from me Captain," Vince said. "But I will get to the bottom of this case, with or without your help and eventually, the truth, and everything that comes along with it will be revealed.

"Uh-huh," the Captain replied almost rudely. "So what do you think you're going to uncover next then Detective?" Armstrong asked. "What small piece of evidence is going to blow this whole thing wide open? Perhaps you'd like to know what brand of toothpaste each of my crew members use? Or what they typically have for breakfast?"

"You know what Captain," Vince replied through gritted teeth. "I want all of the heads of departments in for a meeting as soon as it can be arranged. We're going to get to the bottom of this and I've had enough of being given half-truths. I think we all need to sit down together and talk like adults. The sooner I can leave this place the better."

The Captain was now clearly smirking. "Of course, Detective, anything you wish for. Give me a couple hours and I'll make the arrangements. Don't worry, there'll be coffee and biscuits too."

Chapter 18: J'accuse

"Mrs Whittaker, I didn't expect you to be here for this, I…" Vince started as soon as he walked into the room and saw that not only were Grace Thompson, Priya Nair, Leo Martinez and Captain Armstrong present, but also Dr Whittaker's widow, Eleanor.

"I know…" Eleanor said quietly. "But if this is your pool of suspects, and you're about to make your ingenious reveal, then I want to be here. I want to look into the eyes of the person who killed my husband and I want to know why they did it. They can explain to me why I no longer have a husband and why Helen no longer has a father."

Vince looked at the Captain, who gave a slight nod as though to say that it would be Ok. Vince wanted to object, though he didn't feel like Eleanor's presence would cause any great issue.

"Please, sit down Detective and tell us what you've found," the Captain said.

"I would rather prefer to stand for this," Vince said, straightening out his clothes. "I would like to play a little game with you all. It's something that helps me organise my thoughts, but also, I feel that you will all find what I have to say about each of you illuminating."

As Vince looked around the room at the faces staring back at him, he couldn't help but take note of each of their expressions. The Captain was smirking, his arms folded across his chest as though this was all some big game that was somehow beneath him. Dr Nair was standing, her posture perfect and unwavering. Leo Martinez was sat in a chair looking down at the table in front of him as though he wanted to be anywhere else, and Grace Thompson was fidgeting, picking her nails and making an effort not to make any eye contact with Vince at all.

"The game is called j'accuse. I assume you know what the word means?" A few nods came in response. "I will reveal what I have learnt about each of you in turn, and then we will all share in the knowledge of this case. Understood?"

Again, the room returned with nods, but no words.

"Now you are all here together, because each of you is a suspect in this investigation."

Dr Nair opened her mouth to speak, but Vince quickly interrupted her. "Please don't interrupt me. What I mean by the word 'suspect' is that you each had motive and opportunity to commit this crime. Nothing more and nothing less. Yet. Now if I may move on?" he paused for a moment and received no reply.

"Dr Nair," he looked at the Doctor, who made no move to answer. "You are the lead scientist up here. It's a very stressful position and one that you worked tirelessly to achieve, correct?"

Priya nodded silently.

"But it was clear that Dr Whittaker wanted your position, and he wasn't above doing what he needed to do to step into your shoes so to speak. You fought, and you caused an injury to the Doctor's body. You were worried that this small misdeed could cost you your position here, so when you carried out the initial assessment of Dr Whittaker's body, you conveniently ignored the wound that you yourself had caused. But the question begs, why were you the one to examine the body when you have no formal medical training? I put it to you, that you requested the body be brought directly to you so that you could carry out this cover-up and save your career."

Dr Nair didn't move an inch, but everyone in the room seemed to be staring at her with surprise in their eyes.

"Dr Nair," Vince continued. What you did screams of guilt, and it is not something that I would easily overlook. This is where your motives lie, and you have already proven the lengths that you will go to in order to keep your position here safe."

"So you're saying it was the Doctor?" the Captain asked with a raised eyebrow.

"Please Captain, let me continue," Vince said. "The game is still afoot."

"Leo Martinez," Vince announced loudly, causing the botanist to look up from the table. "An amazing botanist. In fact, so amazing that he was able to cultivate cannabis plants right here on the moon. Something that even I hadn't seen coming. Forgetting the legalities of such cultivation, these plants – or more accurately the seeds that they grew from – were not a part of the mission pack and therefore had technically been smuggled here, right?"

Martinez nodded slowly but didn't speak.

"And the cannabis plants grew well, but Whittaker found you with them, even taking photos of the plants as he warned you that he was going to turn you in. You would lose your position at the very least here in the settlement, but if it was deemed that what you had done was illegal, then you would have been facing a far worse punishment. Furthermore, when everyone went out to look for Dr Whittaker, you stayed within the habs. This would have been the perfect opportunity to search through Whittaker's quarters to look for those photos, would it not? Especially if you knew that the Doctor would not have been back any time soon."

"What!?" Martinez exclaimed. "That is not..." but Vince held a hand up to silence him.

"So they both did it?" Captain Armstrong asked sarcastically. "Sounds like you have this all figured out, Detective."

"Ah now you bring me swiftly on to you, Captain. When I arrived here, you were cordial, helpful even. But as time has progressed, you have proven yourself to be controlling to the point of obsession. You have hidden fact after fact from me in the pretence that you are saving your crew and this mission from ridicule and quite frankly, I have come to the realisation that your obtrusiveness has pushed me to the point of avoiding asking you questions wherever possible. So let's talk about your motive, shall we, captain?" Vince continued, ignoring the Captain's eye roll. "You are so hell-bent on keeping this mission within your grasp and to keep out any outside agencies sticking their noses in where they don't belong, that you would do anything to keep any and all issues in-house. Whittaker was a threat to that status quo, was he not?"

The Captain leaned back and folded his arms, his face betraying no emotion. "You're making some pretty serious accusations, Detective," he said calmly. "But you haven't provided any concrete evidence to support them."

"I have motive, Captain," Vince said firmly. "You had everything to lose if any of Whittaker's messing led to an investigation from outside agencies. You could have lost your position, and this mission could have been compromised. And let's not forget, you were the one who ordered the destruction of the cannabis plants, and you have been withholding information from me from the very beginning."

The Captain raised an eyebrow. "And what information, exactly, have I been withholding?"

"Well for starters, the arguments between the crew members and Dr Whittaker. The issues that each of your crew members have brought to you but you have chosen to cover up. Quite frankly, I am surprised that you didn't simply cover up Dr Whittaker's death and pretend that he was still working here like some sort of morbid puppet!"

The Captain's expression remained unchanged. "You're making assumptions, Detective," he said. "I've kept some things from you, yes. But it was for the good of the mission. As for the arguments, those are normal disagreements that happen on any mission, especially one as long as this. And as for covering up Dr Whittaker's death, I would never do such a thing. That would be a breach of trust with our sponsors and with the public."

"Then why did you order the destruction of the cannabis plants?" Vince pressed.

"Because it was the responsible thing to do," the Captain replied. "Martinez brought them here without authorisation, and it was a liability for the mission. We can't afford to have any unauthorised activities going on up here, especially when we're representing the future of space exploration."

Vince shook his head. "I'm sorry, Captain, but I can't ignore the facts that I've uncovered. There's too much evidence pointing to each of you as suspects."

The Captain sighed. "Fine, Detective. Investigate all you want. But remember that we're all on the same team here. We're working towards a common goal. Don't let your suspicions blind you to that fact."

"Oh I am well aware of how you feel about your team, Captain," Vince said. "But please, so that I can put more of this together, I would ask at this juncture that you provide me with each of your phone records so that I can peruse them and see if there is anything else you have been hiding from me."

Vince watched then as the Captain's expression softened slightly, apparently happy to be somewhat out of the spotlight. Then the Captain nodded slightly at Grace, who announced that she would have the call records sent over to Vince's quarters.

"That leaves us with one last suspect, our engineer, Grace Thompson." The engineer shuffled her hands, and it was clear that she forced her gaze up to meet Vince's.

"Ms Thompson. By your own admission, you have been generating faults within the settlement so that you could 'fix' them, and in doing so ensuring that you are seen as a vital part of this team, correct?"

Grace nodded once and Vince continued.

"You were aware that Dr Whittaker had discovered one of your games, in the way of the power consumption issue that you had posed, and if he brought this up, then you could lose your job and every shred of credibility that you ever had as an engineer. Furthermore, it was during one of these manufactured blackouts that Dr Whittaker went missing and was subsequently killed without any trace of recording from the many, many security cameras around the settlement."

Grace opened her mouth to speak, though apparently thought better of it.

"And finally, you were the one who happened to find Dr Whittaker's body, though it was far from the settlement and when nobody else was around. I put it to you, Ms Thompson and everyone else in this room, that you are to be placed within a holding cell until such a time arrives that you can be transported back to Earth and held to account for what you have done."

The room fell silent as Vince finished his accusations. Each member of the crew looked at one another, unsure of what to say or do. Finally, the Captain spoke up.

"Detective, you have made some serious allegations against each of us," he said, his tone grave. "But I would caution you against rushing to judgement before all the evidence is in. We need to continue working together to solve this case, not tear each other apart."

Vince nodded. "I understand, Captain. But I have to follow the evidence where it leads me. And right now, Ms Thompson is the only one of you who I believe is responsible for this crime."

The Captain sighed heavily. "Very well, Detective. We will cooperate with your investigation, but I will remind you that Ms Thompson is still innocent until proven guilty. We will all have to deal with the consequences of this investigation, whatever they may be."

Vince nodded once more. "I understand, Captain. But I have the authority to request confinement, and that is what I am doing, for the safety of everyone within this settlement."

The Captain looked as though he was going to object, but eventually just exhaled and let his shoulders drop.

"Can I say something?" Grace Thompson asked in a very small voice.

Vince turned to look at her. "Yes, Ms Thompson. What is it?"

"I didn't do it," she said quietly. "I mean, I did tamper with the systems, but I didn't kill Dr Whittaker. I didn't even know he was dead until I found his body. I was scared," Grace said, tears welling up in her eyes. "I didn't know what had happened or who had done it. And I didn't want to be the one to find him, but I was the only one in the area at the time."

"Don't worry Grace," the Captain said. "The truth will always win out. If you say you didn't do this, then I believe you."

"Then who did?" Dr Nair spoke up, unfolding her arms. "It was one of us in this room, and if you're saying that it wasn't Grace, then you're saying that it was either Martinez or me, right?"

"Hey I didn't kill anybody!" Martinez objected loudly, but before the room could descend into declarations of innocence, Mrs Whittaker's voice cut through the rest and the room fell instantly silent except for her words.

"All I want, is for my husband's killer to be caught," she said slowly but loudly. "The Detective has been sent here to make a determination, and he has made one. Mr Callahan is not the judge, jury and executioner and what he says is not binding... but I know how hard it is to lose somebody you love, believe me." She paused for a long moment to let her words settle in. "The way I see it, is that this settlement can't effectively run without the majority of you four. And there are two options that I can see before you: either you accept the Detective's view that Ms Thompson is the most likely suspect and allow her to stand trial and defend herself, or you all stand trial and let a jury decide on the best course of action."

"What Mrs Whittaker has said is correct," Vince cut in. "Ms Thompson here must be confined, as the only alternative is to place you all in confinement and risk the future of this mission. I assume that you don't want that to happen, captain?"

The room fell totally silent for a long time. Each of the crew seemed to be looking at the rest with suspicion in their eyes, but eventually they all turned to Grace, who had begun quietly sobbing.

"I didn't do it," Grace was managing to breathe out between her quiet cries. "I didn't do it."

"Priya, Leo," the Captain said finally. "Will you take Grace to her quarters and arrange for a watch on her door." Then he turned his attention to the engineer. "Grace... you won't be treated like a criminal in this settlement. To me you are innocent until proven guilty, and you will be waited on hand and foot until all of this is sorted out, on this you have my word. But you must promise me that you will not leave your quarters. Do you understand?"

Grace managed to nod slowly before standing up and was escorted from the room by Leo Martinez and Dr Priya Nair. That left just the Captain, Vince and Mrs Whitaker in the room alone.

"I must ask you, Detective," the Captain said levelly, all humour now absent his tone. "What makes you so sure that it was Grace? Surely the circumstantial evidence is not enough to sway your opinion so strongly?"

Vince glanced sideways to Mrs Whittaker before he replied. "Actually, this meeting was a bit of a ruse, something that I wouldn't have been able to do without Mrs Whittaker here."

"Me?" Eleanor asked, shocked. "I didn't do anything."

"Oh but you did, Mrs Whittaker. You showed me that the call logs from your husband's phone had been falsified. I couldn't ask outright who could have done such a thing, or even let on that I knew, because that would have raised suspicions and potentially put the perpetrator on alert. I asked for all of your call logs to be provided rather than say that I knew that they had been doctored, and by doing so I discovered that Ms Thompson was the person responsible for providing those logs. I can assume, Captain, that Ms Thompson provided the first set of logs?"

Captain Armstrong nodded silently, clearly trying to let all of this information settle in.

"Then my assumption is well founded. Not only does Grace Thompson have both motive and opportunity, but she has also purposely falsified information on the course of this investigation. I'm sorry Captain, but I feel that there is no alternative here."

"I can't believe it," Mrs Whittaker said slowly. I never thought that Grace..." it was clear that she was having a hard time believing that the engineer had done such a thing, but she offered no alternatives and simply buried her face in her hands.

"I thought it would feel good, you know..." she managed to say through the cracks in her fingers. "To find out who is responsible for Adrian's death. But it doesn't feel good at all. It feels terrible."

"I'm afraid that the truth is not the great healer that many think it to be," Vince said soothingly. "Time is the only healer that I know of, and I truly hope that in time, your pain will dissipate."

Chapter 19: Life, Insured

Vince was in his quarters, collecting his notes and evidence so that when he would come to pass over the insights he'd made to the team on Earth, he would be able to do so in a logical and collected manner, when a quiet knock on his door stole his attention. He sighed, somewhat feeling that something else was about to unveil itself in this mystery, but knew that whatever it was, he couldn't ignore it.

"Come in," he answered and to his surprise, Mrs Whittaker stepped in.

"What can I do for you, Mrs Whittaker?" Vince asked.

"Please, I asked you to call me Eleanor," she replied in a small voice. "I wanted to thank you for all of your effort in cracking this case, and to bringing justice for my husband. You have no idea how much it means to me. I still can't believe..." she trailed off, her voice growing smaller and smaller.

"Mrs... Eleanor," Vince corrected himself. "I only did what I was supposed to do. I feel that your husband would've enjoyed that. Plus, the case is far from over; I have merely provided a possibility – who I think is the most likely suspect in all of this. I have provided no insights to what actually occurred, nor am I the judge, jury and executioner here."

Eleanor nodded, tears welling up in her eyes. "I know, but still, I am grateful for what you've done. And there's something else I wanted to ask you about."

Vince raised an eyebrow. "What is it?"

"I know it's not really the done thing... but..." she struggled with whatever it was she was about to ask, then visibly composed herself. "I wanted to go out and see the place where my husband's body was found, I know it may seem a little morbid... but I think it might give me a little bit more of an insight into what happened, and the fact that I'll never see Adrian again."

Vince felt a weight on his chest and a lump form in his throat. After a moment to think on the request, he said: "I think we can make that happen. Besides, I think it would be best for me to go back to where Dr Whittaker was found again anyway, just in case there's anything I missed the first time around."

Eleanor nodded gratefully. "Thank you, Detective. I appreciate it. You really have done so much for me and I don't know how I'll ever thank you."

Vince stood up from his desk and gestured for Eleanor to follow him. Together, they made their way to the Captain's office where they would ask for permission to leave the settlement to make their way to where Dr Whittaker had ultimately met his maker. Of course something like this happening on Earth wouldn't ever have happened, but up here the rules were different.

Upon arriving at the Captain's office, Vince and Eleanor found him sitting at his desk, poring over some paperwork. He looked up as they entered, and his expression softened when he saw Eleanor.

"Mrs Whittaker," he said, rising from his seat. "Is there something I can help you with?" He seemed to soundly ignore Vince in his welcome.

"Yes, Captain," Vince spoke up. "Mrs Whittaker here would like to visit the site where her husband's body was found, and I believe that it would be beneficial for me to revisit the site as well, in case there is anything that I missed the first time around."

The Captain nodded thoughtfully. "I understand. And I think it's important for both of you to get some closure on this matter. I'll authorise a rover for you to take, and I'll arrange for a chaperone to accompany you."

Eleanor looked grateful, and Vince nodded his thanks to the Captain. "Thank you, sir. We'll be sure to take all necessary precautions," Vince said.

The pair left the office and made their way to the rover garage to await their chaperone. Vince couldn't help but feel a sense of unease. He had a feeling that there was still something missing, something that he hadn't quite uncovered yet that could change everything that had happened so far. But he pushed those thoughts aside and focused on the task at hand. He was sure that Eleanor would become emotional visiting the place her husband had been found, and before anything he needed to be able to offer her some emotional support.

The pair that eventually joined them were less 'security' and more scientists that were just finishing their rotations. It made sense, as the settlement didn't have security per se, but Vince couldn't help but feel that the pair of one botanist and one geologist weren't really necessary for their little expedition. Especially given that none of the suspects in the murder of Dr Whittaker were going to accompany them so the threat level was low, though a little experience wasn't going to be unwelcome.

The group of four, once they had all suited up, then entered one of the longer rovers in the garage that were designed for four people and began their journey to the place three kilometres away from the settlement where Adrian Whitaker's body had been found.

"It's a pleasure to meet you, Detective," one of the two scientists finally said through the headpiece embedded into the inside of Vince's helmet. "I've read up on some of your cases and I have to say, you really know what you're doing."

"Thank you," Vince replied. "It's not been on too many occasions that my reputation has preceded me, but I do appreciate it. How long have you been up here, may I ask, uh... I apologise but I haven't yet taken your name."

"Bill. Bill Palmer. And I've only been up here a short time, actually I arrived on the same shuttle as you did Detective, only we didn't have the chance to speak then."

"Nice to meet you, Bill," Vince said with a small smile evident in his tone. "And what about you?" he asked the other scientist, who had been quiet until now.

"I'm Jane," she said, her voice slightly muffled by the helmet. "I'm a botanist, and I've been up here for a little longer than Bill – from the beginning actually. It's a pleasure to meet you, Detective."

Vince nodded in acknowledgement. "Likewise, Jane."

As they approached the site where Dr Whittaker had been found, Vince couldn't help but feel a sense of unease. This was the place where a man had lost his life, most likely where someone had taken it from him. It was a heavy burden to bear, and he wondered how Eleanor was going to take it.

Eleanor was similarly subdued, but Vince could sense a certain determination in her as well. She wanted to be here, to face the reality of what had happened to her husband.

When they finally came to a halt as they arrived at the site, Vince and Eleanor stepped out of the rover and began to survey the area, though again it just seemed like such a vast array of nothingness. The two scientists stayed in the rover, offering any assistance they could from a distance but it was clear that they were giving Vince the chance to carry out his work, and Eleanor the space to grieve.

As the pair walked around the area, Vince couldn't help but notice that Eleanor was unusually quiet. She seemed lost in thought, and he wondered if there was something on her mind that she wanted to talk about. After a moment passed, he decided to break the silence.

"Mrs Whittaker," he began, breaking the silence. "Can I ask you something?"

"Of course, Detective," she said, turning to face him.

Vince hesitated for a moment before speaking. "I couldn't help but notice that you seemed hesitant to believe that Grace Thompson could have been responsible for your husband's death. Is there a reason for that?"

Eleanor sighed heavily. "It's not so much the fact that it's Grace. I suppose I just find it hard to believe that anyone could do something like that. But I know that you have evidence that points to her, and I trust your judgement. It's just hard to accept, you know?"

"I understand," Vince said sympathetically.

"I know I'm being a bit quiet, Vince," Eleanor offered. "It's just that... well we aren't... weren't wealthy people. The life insurance policy that was offered to my husband wasn't as substantial as you may think. We bought our house at the height of the market and as we stand right now, I find myself in the position of negative equity, so what I stand to inherit doesn't even pay off what we owe. Sure, things will be a little easier, but for what it's worth and as morbid as it may sound... it's not a life changing amount of money and truly I don't yet know what I'm going to do."

Vince nodded, understanding the financial burden that Eleanor was facing. "I see," he said. "It must be tough to go through all of this and not even have the financial relief you were hoping for."

Eleanor shrugged, her eyes focused on the barren landscape. "It is what it is," she said. "Money can't bring my husband back, and it can't change the past. But at least justice is being served, and that's something."

Vince nodded again. "You're right," he said. "Justice is important. And I'm glad that we were able to bring some closure to this case."

They stood there in silence for a few moments longer, each lost in their own thoughts. Vince couldn't help but feel a sense of admiration for Eleanor. Despite everything she had been through, she still had the strength to come out here and face the truth. It was a testament to her resilience and determination.

"What do you think happened to him?" Eleanor eventually asked as Vince was looking around the lunar landscape. It was just all so alien to him. Barren lands littered with rocks, hills and craters as far as the eye could see. Mrs Whittaker's question brought something to the forefront of his mind though: What *was* Whittaker doing out here?

Vince turned to face Eleanor, his thoughts still lingering on the question she had just asked. "Honestly, I'm not sure," he said. "There are still some missing pieces to this puzzle, and I can't help but wonder why your husband was out here in the first place. It's not exactly a place that someone would come to without a good reason."

Eleanor nodded, her gaze turning back to the spot where her husband's body had been found.

Then something clicked in Vince's mind. Someone *did* know what he was doing out here, because he actually asked to come here once before, didn't he?

Vince immediately moved to pull his phone from his pocket, though he had forgotten one small fact: he was wearing a space suit. Even if he could've managed to pull the thing from his pocket and somehow use it through his gloved hand, there would be no way he could actually talk with it. Instead, he spoke through his helmet's communicator.

"Eleanor, we need to speak with Dr Nair! Your husband was working with some seismology reports and wanted to investigate, but she told him no. Tell me, what would your husband do if he asked for permission to do something, and the boss said no."

Eleanor was silent for a moment before she cottoned on to what Vince was saying. "He would go and do it anyway..." she said slowly.

"Can we contact Dr Nair directly through these communicators?" Vince asked, but the reply came from Jane who was still in the river with Bill the geologist.

"We're on a closed circuit here Detective, but we can call home base and ask Dr Nair to patch into the comms. Otherwise, anyone could just call whoever they wanted at any point!" She explained.

"Please," Vince replied. "I know this is going to shed some light onto what happened here, I can feel it."

It took all of three minutes for Dr Nair's voice to come through the communicator in Vince's helmet and he excitedly greeted her.

"Dr Nair, thanks for answering," he said.

"No problem Detective, what can I help you with?" she asked.

"The project that Dr Whittaker brought you... the seismology reports that you turned down... do you still have them? I think that Vince was following up on this project when he came out here and I think knowing what he was doing would be a huge leap in figuring out what actually happened to him."

Dr Nair was silent for a moment, but it sounded as though drawers were opening and papers rustling and then she announced: "I have them, Detective. I did take a moment to read through his reports on the subject, but I concluded that his assumptions were unfounded and I didn't want to waste our resources following inconclusive data."

"But was the project related to the place where he was found?" Vince asked.

Nair was silent for a moment again and Vince assumed that she was comparing the reports that she had been given by Dr Whittaker, and the co-ordinates of where his body was found.

"It is not the same location, Detective, but in truth it is not too far away. About another kilometre and change from your current location on a heading due east. But Detective, I do not see why anyone would..."

"What were the reports of, Dr Nair?" Vince interrupted the Doctor.

"They were simply seismology reports of the lunar surface and what potentially lies beneath to a depth of about fifty metres or so. Dr Whittaker brought me these reports because he thought that he had found what he was calling a cave system nearby. Seismology reports are famously inconclusive for determining such features though, and even if there was a cave system, I would not risk sending in team members only to find a large empty cavern. We have enough rocks to analyse up here as it is, without risking collapses, or people getting trapped."

"Do you know if he found a cave system?" Eleanor interrupted the conversation and in doing so Vince was now aware that all four of his expedition party had been included in his discussion.

"I am sorry, Mrs Whittaker. I told your husband not to follow up on this project and as far as I am aware, he followed my orders," Dr Nair replied.

Vince could feel the tension in the air as Eleanor processed Dr Nair's response. It was clear that she was hoping for some kind of revelation, but it sounded like Dr Nair had no more information to give."

Vince turned to Eleanor and said: "Well it looks like we're on our own then. Due east, was it?"

The first response, however came from the geologist still sat in the rover. "Don't worry Detective, the suits have hours of oxygen, and the communication system uses the rover as a relay so we can realistically travel up to around ten kilometres from the settlement without fear of losing contact."

Vince nodded to himself, grateful for the reminder. "Good to know, Bill," he said. "But let's not push our luck. We'll head due east and see what we can find."

With that, the group set off towards the coordinates that Dr Nair had given them, trekking across the rugged lunar landscape. It was slow going, with the bulky suits and the low gravity making each step feel like a chore, but both Vince and Mrs Whittaker had decided that if they walked the distance whilst the rover went on ahead, then they would be sure not to miss anything, if there was indeed anything to see.

As they walked, Vince couldn't help but think about what they might find. A cave system, perhaps, or some kind of physical evidence that could shed light on what had happened to Dr Whittaker.

Eleanor was quiet again, clearly lost in her own thoughts, but Vince could sense the anticipation building in her as well. This was a chance for her to get some answers and he knew how important that was to her.

After what felt like hours of walking, they finally came to a halt. They had reached the coordinates that Dr Nair had given them, and they could see nothing but more barren moonscape, hills and divots all around. Granted, the hills and craters seemed a little more numerous than before, but still, it was a lot more of the same-same.

As they walked, Vince and Eleanor scanned the area, searching for any sign of the cave system or anything that could be of interest. They carefully navigated the rocky terrain, checking their surroundings every few steps.

After a short while, Eleanor spoke up. "Where's the rover?" she asked, her voice tinged with concern.

Vince looked around, scanning the area for the rover. It was nowhere in sight. "It must have gone on ahead," he said, trying to reassure her. "I'm sure it'll be back in a moment."

But as they walked further, there was still no sign of the rover. Vince's concern grew as he tried to radio through to Bill and Jane, but there was no response.

"Something's not right," Vince finally announced, his voice tense. "They should be here."

Eleanor nodded, her own worry now apparent. They continued to call out for the missing scientists and rover, but there was no response.

Vince took a deep breath and made a decision. "We need to head back to the settlement and report this," he said, turning to Eleanor. "It's not safe out here without the rover, and we don't know what's happened to Bill and Jane."

"Don't you think we should look for them?" Eleanor asked. "They could just be behind a rock formation or a small hill... couldn't their communicators just be blocked by the terrain? Plus what if it is the worst, and they need our help. Surely we should stay and look, even if it's just for a few minutes?"

"Eleanor... protocol states that we have to do what we can to save ourselves... but perhaps if it was just me here then I would look the other way... but I won't risk your life."

"But Detective," Eleanor said slowly. "We can't just leave them here if they need help, can we?"

Vince hesitated, his mind racing with conflicting thoughts. He knew that Eleanor was right, they couldn't just abandon Bill and Jane if they were in trouble. But at the same time, he didn't want to put Eleanor in any danger.

"You're right," Vince finally said, his voice resolute. "We can't just leave them here. Let's split up and search the area. But stay nearby, OK? If this starts taking too long then I want you to start heading back."

Eleanor nodded, her expression serious. "I'll head towards that larger hill over there," she said, pointing in the direction of a nearby formation. "You search the other side."

Vince nodded in agreement and they set off in opposite directions, calling out for Bill and Jane as they went. Vince searched the area with increasing desperation, but there was still no sign of the missing rover or scientists. His communication with Eleanor didn't break for even a moment either, which made it more unlikely that some terrain was simply blocking the radio waves.

After what felt like an eternity, Vince's communicator crackled to life with Eleanor's voice. "Detective," she said urgently. "I found the rover. It's been abandoned, and there's no sign of Bill or Jane."

Vince's heart sank. "I'm on my way," he said, turning to run towards the direction that Eleanor had searched.

When he reached the rover, he saw it was indeed abandoned, and there was no sign of Bill or Jane anywhere in sight. They had to assume the worst. Vince's mind raced as he tried to think of what to do next. They needed to report this back to the settlement and get a search and rescue team out here as soon as possible. But they also needed to secure the area and make sure that no one else was in danger. The first thing that Vince noticed though, was that the rover was in complete darkness, as though its battery had been entirely depleted.

"Settlement, this is Detective Callahan, do you read me?" Vince said into his communicator, but after a short pause, no response came.

Vince tried again, his voice growing more urgent. "This is Detective Callahan, do you copy? We have an emergency situation out here, the rover is down, and we've lost contact with two of our team members. We need immediate assistance."

Still, there was no response. Vince's frustration and concern grew with each passing second. He tried calling again, but the communicator remained silent.

"Looks like the long range communicator's down too," he muttered to himself, feeling a sense of helplessness wash over him. "We're on our own out here."

He turned to Eleanor, who had been standing by the rover, looking out at the desolate landscape. "We need to find them," he said.

Eleanor nodded, her expression grim. "I'll start searching the area again," she said. "We need to find some clues as to what happened to them. Surely they would have left footprints that we can follow?"

Vince nodded in agreement, and the two of them set off, searching the area around the abandoned rover. They carefully examined the rocky terrain, looking for any sign of footprints or disturbances in the ground.

It was slow going, and after several minutes of searching, they still had no answers and there were no signs of disturbances on the ground. Vince's frustration was mounting, and he could sense Eleanor's own sense of despair. They were running out of time, and they had no way to call for help.

As they walked, Vince noticed something in the distance. A small glint of light, reflecting off some object on the ground. He quickened his pace, hoping that it might be a clue as to what had happened to Bill and Jane.

As he approached the object, Vince saw that it was a small piece of metal, glinting in the sunlight. He picked it up, examining it closely. It was clearly the same as the other metallic fragment that he had found near Dr Whittaker's body, and if anything, it looked like it was the other half of the broken mineral scoop that still sat atop his desk back at the settlement.

"That's not good," Eleanor said, appearing over his shoulder. "What do you think happened to it?"

"It looks like the other half of the scoop. The fragment that could've been a part of the Doctor's death..." Vince said cautiously. "I can't be sure without having the two together, but it's sure what it looks like to me."

Eleanor took a large step back from the object as though it was radioactive, and Vince could see the pained worry etched on her face. It was clear that she was afraid of whatever was happening, and he couldn't blame her. They had no idea what they were up against and were slowly running out of options.

They continued to search the area, but there was still no sign of Bill and Jane. Vince's concern grew with each passing moment, and he couldn't shake the feeling that they should turn around and leave. It was a difficult pill to swallow, though, to leave two other people out here to potentially die alone.

Just as they were about to give up hope, Vince's communicator beeped to life once again. It was Bill's voice, but it was weak and distorted.

"Detective... help... injured... can't move... north..." the message cut off abruptly, leaving Vince and Eleanor in a state of panic.

"We need to find him," Vince said, determination in his voice. "Let's move north and see what we can find. He can't be too far if our communicators are working. Then once we find them we can make our way back to the habs."

Chapter 20: Stranded

Within a few minutes of moving north, Vince finally found two pairs of footprints in the ground. It was strange though; why hadn't there been any prints at all, and then all of a sudden it was like the feet that made them had appeared as though from nowhere.

Vince followed the footprints as they led him and Eleanor further north. They walked for what felt like an eternity, the terrain becoming increasingly rough and rocky. But they didn't give up hope, knowing that they were getting closer to finding Bill.

As they crested a small hill, Vince immediately saw something that he hadn't been expecting to see: a formation of rocks surrounding a crater that very clearly led into a tunnel, and then underground.

"Eleanor, look at this," Vince said, pointing towards the formation. "That could be the entrance to the cave system we've been searching for. Maybe they're inside?"

Eleanor nodded, her eyes widening with anticipation. "Let's go check it out," she said, and they both hurried towards the opening, bounding through the reduced gravity.

The tunnel was dark, and the only light came from the beams on their space suits. Once they were inside, they slowed down and carefully made their way down the tunnel, the ground becoming steeper as they descended further inside.

Suddenly, they heard a loud rumbling sound behind them, and as they turned to see what was happening, the entrance to the tunnel quickly filled with stones, rocks and rubble, and then total darkness. The entrance had been blocked by a cave-in.

"No!," Eleanor said, panic rising in her voice. "How are we going to get out of here?"

Vince ran back up the tunnel and tried to push the rocks out of the way, but they were too heavy and too firmly wedged in place. Whenever he did manage to move anything, more rocks and gravel simply slid down and filled the gaps.

"We're going to have to find another way out," he said, turning back towards the tunnel. "But we're going to have to be quick. We've already been out for a long time, so we only have a few hours of air left in the tanks at most."

Eleanor nodded, trying to steady her breathing as they regrouped and pressed on into the darkness. The tunnel seemed to go on and on, twisting and turning with no end in sight. The only sounds were the soft hum of their oxygen tanks and the occasional scrape of their boots against the rocky ground. Neither felt like talking was the best course of action right now.

They continued to make their way deeper into the cave system, the narrow passageways becoming increasingly treacherous with jagged rocks jutting out from all around them. They had to squeeze through tight spaces and climb over pointed rocks, and their progress was slow and arduous.

As they pressed on, they became acutely aware of their dwindling oxygen supply. They had only hours of air left, and they knew that they had to find a way out soon.

"We have to keep moving," Vince said, his voice strained. "We can't give up now. There must be another way out of here."

Eleanor nodded, but her movements were sluggish, and he could see the fear in her eyes. They were both exhausted, and then slowly and quietly reducing oxygen was starting to take its toll.

But they couldn't stop. They had to keep going, no matter what.

"Do you think we should've stayed and tried to dig our way out at the entrance? And I've not seen any signs of the others... do you think they're alright?" Eleanor asked, her speech slightly pressured.

Vince took a deep breath, trying to steady his nerves. "I don't know, Eleanor. It's hard to say. But right now, we need to focus on finding a way out of here before we run out of air. We'll worry about the others when we get out."

Eleanor nodded, but he could see the worry etched on her face. They both knew that the situation was dire. Their only chance was to keep moving forward and hope that they would find another way out.

Reluctantly, the pair moved deeper into the tunnel and walked for at least a hundred metres before anything seemed like it was going to change. The tunnel itself had been descending steadily and Vince didn't want to voice his concern that if the tunnel didn't level out soon, then their hopes were descending as quickly as the ground beneath them.

Vince looked down at the floor as his attention was drawn that way, and then he saw something. He looked towards the ground at his feet and followed what he saw all the way back behind him and then said quietly into his communicator: "Eleanor. I think you need to see this."

"What is it?" she began to ask, but then her gaze followed the light of Vince's headlamps and she too saw what had caught his attention: a single line of footprints led up from the tunnel before them and back away to the entrance from which they'd arrived.

"It has to be..." Eleanor started.

"I have no doubt in my mind, that these footprints belonged to your husband," Vince said, feeling a cold chill run down his spine as he spoke the words. It was strange. Dr Adrian Whittaker had gone, but this reminder of his presence seemed so real, and so present. As though he was with them right there, right now and for a moment, Vince couldn't comprehend that these were the footprints of a dead man.

"Adrian was here?" Eleanor said with wide eyes. "We need to follow them, right?"

Vince furrowed his brow. It was only moments ago that the pair were battling with the realities of their own mortality, and now the Doctor's widow wanted to go searching for her late husband's last project? Who was he really to question how people processed grief, though. In truth, they had no other choice anyway, so what difference would it really make?

Vince nodded, his determination returning. "Yes, let's follow the footprints. Maybe they'll lead us to another way out or even some kind of clue as to what happened to Bill and Jane."

They carefully followed the footprints, the path leading them further down the tunnel. The footprints were clear and defined, as if someone had just walked through the tunnel moments before them.

Then the tunnel came to an abrupt halt, and before Vince and Eleanor now stood something that Vince could have never imagined in his wildest dreams. They could only have been a few hundred metres beneath the surface of the moon, but they had found themselves within a cave the size of a large barn, filled top to bottom with what could only be described as bright, shimmering diamonds, reflecting the lights from their spacesuits like they were twinkling stars.

Vince and Eleanor were both taken aback by the sheer beauty of the sight before them. The diamonds, of various shapes and sizes, were everywhere, covering the walls, the ceiling, and the floor. The space was alive with the sparkling light they cast and it danced around the cavern as though in some beautiful silent melody. Vince had never seen anything like it before, and he couldn't help but stare in awe.

Eleanor gasped, her eyes wide with wonder. "It's like we're standing inside a giant diamond," she breathed, her voice barely above a whisper.

Vince nodded, his eyes still fixed on the magnificent display of natural wonder. "It's breath-taking," he said, his voice filled with wonder.

They both began to move cautiously into and through the space, their suits reflecting the light and creating a kaleidoscope of colours around them. Vince could feel his heart pounding in his chest, the sheer grandeur of the place overwhelming him.

"I guess your husband was right," Vince said. "This place was certainly worth checking out. I can only assume that this was the last place he ever saw, and I feel quite glad that he was vindicated in his request to search for this place."

Eleanor clicked her tongue as she looked around the diamond-filled cave, though she offered no additional sentiment to Vince's words.

"This is it, Eleanor said under her breath as though she had completely forgotten that Vince could hear her through her communicator. "You were right..."

"Uh, Mrs Whittaker?" Vince said. "What do you mean by 'you were right'?" he asked.

"What?" Eleanor said as she somewhat returned to herself. "Oh, it's nothing... I mean..." she stopped for a moment before continuing. "Adrian always said he thought there was more to see below the surface of the moon... so I guess he's been vindicated, right?"

Vince wasn't convinced by the reply. Eleanor had seemed like she had been expecting this place to be here, and that didn't sit well with him.

"Listen, Detective," Eleanor said in a newly assured tone. "You know about Helen, right? You know what this place could mean for me back on Earth... and am I right to assume that this place is probably the most valuable thing you've ever seen in your entire life as well?"

Vince looked around the cave again. At all of the pinpricks of light dancing, reflecting his light back at him as though they were whispering to him of their vast value.

He replied slowly. "I once read an article that said one ton of diamonds had a value of around half a billion pounds sterling. With the cave the size that it is... we could be looking at tens of billions of pounds here..."

"No Detective... that's not right," Eleanor replied cautiously. "If we take the size of this cave multiplied up into cubic centimetres... and diamonds with a density just shy of two grams per cubic centimetre..." Vince tried to do some quick calculations as Eleanor spoke, but the numbers grew so quickly that he could only assume he was wrong.

Eleanor continued when Vince didn't reply. "We could be looking at thirty *thousand* tons here... that means..."

"Forty-five trillion pounds..." Vince finished Eleanor's sentence, catching up with what she was trying to explain.

His mouth hung open.

Forty. Five. Trillion.

"Detective I..." Eleanor started but didn't continue.

"Detective, Mrs Whittaker," a clear voice came through their helmets, and it snapped the pair back to reality.

"Bill?" Vince asked incredulously.

"That's my name," Bill replied without a semblance of the past communications issues that he'd experienced.

"Where are you? Are you OK?" Eleanor asked worriedly. She hadn't yet picked up on something that Vince had: that Bill no longer sounded as though he was in trouble, rather he sounded happy. No, not happy, cocky.

"Where are you, Bill?" Vince asked in a far more serious tone than Eleanor had. "What's going on here?"

Bill chuckled on the other end of the line. "You really think you're the only ones who can explore the moon, Vince? You really think you're the only ones who can find something valuable down here? Oh, and by the way, we estimated it to be a little over fifty trillion, but I'll forgive you that oversight."

Vince and Eleanor exchanged confused looks. "What are you talking about, Bill?" Vince demanded.

"I'm talking about the biggest diamond heist in history," Bill said, his voice now cold and calculating. "You see, I knew about this place long before you did, and I've been planning this for a while now. Now that you've led me straight to it, well... let's just say you're going to have to stay here for a little while... at least until those oxygen tanks of yours finally deplete, right?"

"You did this?" Vince asked. "But how? And why?"

"Look around you, Detective. Are you telling me that the famous Vince Callahan, Detective extraordinaire can't see a motive when it's staring him right in the face?"

"But you arrived here on the shuttle?" Vince said. "There's just no way you could be involved in all of this."

"Ah Detective. So short-sighted," Bill replied. Well, I'm a resourceful guy. I made sure I was on this mission, and I made sure I had the necessary equipment to carry out this plan. It's just a shame that I couldn't convince the Captain to let me chaperone you two out here alone, what with me being new to the settlement. Never mind, though, what's another loss to the barren lands of the moon in the great scheme of things?"

Vince clenched his fists, anger boiling inside him. "So you trapped us in here, just to get your hands on these diamonds?"

Bill laughed. "It's not personal, Detective. It's just business. I've been one step ahead of you from the moment we arrived here. And now, well, I'm afraid you're just loose ends that need tying up."

Eleanor's voice trembled with anger. "You're a monster. You're condemning us to die down here, all for your own selfish gain."

"Oh come, Eleanor," Bill goaded into the communicator. "You know, I had nothing to do with your husband's death. In fact, when he died, I had no knowledge of this place whatsoever! You have nothing to be angry at me for... well I suppose other than trapping you in here and eventually cashing in on trillions of pounds worth of profit. Surely you can understand how important that is, right?"

Vince's mind raced, trying to think of a way out of their predicament. Their oxygen was running low, and the cave was a death trap. But there had to be a way to turn the tables on Bill and find a way out.

"Bill," Vince said, forcing himself to remain calm. "You may have the upper hand right now, but don't forget that we're still alive. And as long as we're alive, we're a threat to you." It was a simple deception, but Vince had no other options.

Bill scoffed. "You're in no position to make threats, Vince. You're trapped in a cave with no way out, and your oxygen is running out. I think I'll take my chances."

Vince turned to face Eleanor as he spoke. He needed to do something that would rebalance the scales of war, but he knew what he planned on saying could put them both in danger, and he didn't like the idea of doing that to Eleanor.

"Bill," he said. "We're going to shout as loudly as we can about this. And I don't mean that we're going to literally shout. We're going to get communications up and running somehow, and when we do, we'll be telling the Captain and the rest of the settlement exactly what's happened here. Besides, people know where we went, so sooner or later they're going to come to find us and when they do, if we are no longer living, they'll find the notes we leave behind, pointing them all in your direction."

Bill's voice wavered for a moment, betraying a hint of uncertainty. "You're bluffing. You can't get communications working down here, and even if you could, nobody would believe you. I'm a respected member of this mission, and you two are just desperate, oxygen-starved lunatics."

Vince didn't let Bill's words deter him. "You underestimate us, Bill. We have more than enough evidence to convince the others. And even if they don't believe us right away, they'll investigate. They'll find this place, and they'll figure out the truth eventually."

Eleanor chimed in, her voice cold and determined. "That's right, Bill. You can't keep this secret forever. And when the truth comes out, you'll pay for what you've done."

There was a brief silence on the other end of the communicator, and then Bill's voice came through, sounding slightly more subdued. "Fine. But you'll never make it out of here alive, so it won't matter."

Vince and Eleanor exchanged glances, knowing they had to act quickly. The only thing they could do was to search the cave for any possible exits, their determination renewed by the confrontation with Bill. The walls of the cave were rough and uneven though, and even after a thorough search, they could see no other openings or passageways.

"Are you still there, Bill?" Eleanor eventually called through her helmet. The man didn't reply, but Vince suspected that Bill had decided to stay behind to listen in to what they had planned.

"Just to let you know, if you can still hear us up there... that we've found another way out. We'll beat you back to the settlement and we're going to tell everyone what you did."

Silence.

Eleanor looked at Vince and he simply shrugged.

"What I don't get though, is how you're involved in all of this when you only arrived in the settlement so recently," Eleanor continued as she walked the perimeter of the cave, still searching for any signs of exits. "I mean, surely you wouldn't think that you could just come up here and run the show all by yourself?"

"No," Vince inserted himself into the one-way conversation. "Someone is using him. Using him to get what they want, we just don't know who it is yet," then he paused theatrically. "It's just a shame that Bill's going to have to take all the heat, do all the hard work up here while his puppet master sits comfortably in his ivory tower. Tell me Bill, how does it feel to be used?"

Silence.

"I bet whoever it is, they're sitting in their comfortable chair and laughing happily to themselves about what you're doing, just to benefit them," Eleanor added.

Bill's voice finally crackled through the communicator, filled with frustration and anger. "You think you're so clever, don't you? I'm not being used by anyone. This is my plan, my operation. And I'll make sure you never make it out of that cave to tell anyone about it."

Vince and Eleanor exchanged knowing looks. They had managed to rattle Bill, make him doubt himself and his position, and that would certainly play to their advantage.

"Come and show us just how in charge you are then, Bill," Eleanor said. "See if you can do the job right, or if your boss is going to tell you off."

Both Vince and Eleanor knew that they couldn't speak with each other without Bill listening in, so that made making any detailed plans impossible. What they both understood though, was that if they could get Bill to unblock the cave for them somehow – presumably he could do so if he wanted to eventually come back to take the diamonds for himself – then they would need to either overpower him or make their escape. Either way, they would need to make their way back up to the tunnel that led from the entrance to the cave so they could ambush their captor.

It was their only chance.

Chapter 21: Help Me

Vince communicated as best he could with Eleanor that he wanted the pair to move up to where the tunnel entrance had been so they could begin to make somewhat of a hiding place there. It was his plan that as soon as Bill would unblock the tunnel, they would be able to ambush him. The pair of them combined with the difficulty of moving quickly within the reduced gravity of the lunar surface would make it difficult for him to fight back.

It didn't take long for their silent chat to make sense, though and within a minute or so, the pair were making their way up towards the blocked tunnel entrance to see what they could do.

They needn't have made the effort.

Before they were even half-way up the tunnel, there was a loud crash from the blocked entrance ahead, and the rover smashed through the entrance, sending dirt, debris and rocks cascading through the tunnel.

"Down!" Vince cried as he flattened himself to the ground. The last thing he needed was for some small rock to pierce his spacesuit.

Eleanor quickly followed Vince's lead, throwing herself to the ground as well. They watched as the rover came to a halt just a few feet away from them, its sturdy bull bars glinting in the dim light. It was clear that the tunnel was too narrow for the vehicle to come any closer – a fact that had surely saved their lives. What was more, the blocked exit to the outside lunar landscape, was now open and free.

They could see Bill inside the rover as the dust settled, his face contorted with anger.

"You thought you could hide from me?" he shouted, his voice echoing through the tunnel. "You thought you could outsmart me?"

Vince and Eleanor exchanged a quick glance, both of them realising that their plan had been foiled. They were completely exposed now, with no cover and no escape route. Bill had them trapped.

Something odd had happened though, the rover was completely stuck inside the tunnel, and not only could Vince and Eleanor not pass it to escape if they so wanted, but Bill couldn't open any of the doors on the thing either. He was just as stuck as they were.

"What do you want, Bill?" Vince called out, trying to keep his voice steady. "Why are you doing this? What's so important about this cave? It can't just all be about money now, can it?"

Bill laughed bitterly. "You still don't get it, do you? This cave is the key to everything. With these diamonds, I can buy my way into any position I want. I can be the most powerful man in the world. And you two are just in the way."

Vince and Eleanor shared a look, both of them realising that they were dealing with not just a greedy, crazy man, but a desperate man as well. They knew they had to be careful; that one wrong move could mean the end for both of them.

"Bill, listen to me," Eleanor said, her voice calm and steady. "We don't want to fight you. We just want to get out of here alive. We can work something out. We can share the diamonds, come up with a plan that benefits all of us."

Bill snorted. "You expect me to believe that? You think I'm stupid?"

"No, we don't," Vince said, his voice firm. "But you have to realise that you're not going to get away with this. Eventually, someone is going to find out. And when they do, you're going to be in a lot of trouble."

Bill's eyes narrowed. "I don't think so," he said, his voice low and dangerous. "You see, I have a plan. And part of that plan involves making sure that you two never make it back to the settlement alive. Just like Jane."

The scene that was playing out before Vince though, made him smile. As he was threatening, Bill was clearly attempting to open the door of the rover so that he could make his way out into the tunnel, but no matter how hard he struggled, the door wouldn't budge against the solid stone wall.

Vince and Eleanor exchanged another look, both of them realising that they had a momentary advantage.

"Hey Bill?" Vince asked in a somewhat conversational tone. "Now I can see that you're stuck in there and all... but I have to ask. Did you damage the communications repeater, or simply switch it off?"

"I..." Bill said absently, but then his eyes widened as he realised what Vince was asking. He redoubled his efforts to open the door, and when that didn't bring about any results, he began to hit the windows and windscreen with his elbows and feet, to no avail.

Bill had just one option before him if he wanted to get the rover away from Vince, who was slowly walking towards it: he would have to see if he could reverse the rover from the tunnel, but in doing so he knew that he would free his two captives, and the game would be up.

Vince crossed his arms as he watched Bill struggle with his entrap-ment.

"Come now Bill, you know the communications array is situated on the outside of that thing... so why don't you just sit tight and let me see if I can get the thing up and running?" Vince asked.

Of course, Vince was bluffing. He knew the antenna, or antennae, were situated on the outside of the rover, but he had no idea how they worked, or even if the circuitry that managed them was inside the vehicle or not. What he was banking on though, was the fact that Bill didn't know this information either.

Vince walked casually up to the rover and began to feel around one of the antennae as though he knew exactly what he was doing.

"Eleanor, please could you come and give me some assistance? I need to reroute this power cable from the antennae into the battery pack on my suit, then we should be able to call for help. You just hold tight up there Bill."

Eleanor hesitated for just a moment, and then she noticed the expression on Vince's face and finally understood the ruse. She quickly moved to stand beside him and made it look as though she knew what she was supposed to be doing.

Vince continued to tinker with the antenna, hoping that his bluff would work. He couldn't believe his luck – somehow, Bill had managed to trap himself inside the rover, and now all of a sudden, Vince and Eleanor had the upper hand.

As he worked, Vince cast a glance at Bill, who was still struggling to free himself. Sweat was beading on the man's forehead, and his face was red with exertion. Vince knew that he needed to keep Bill as off-balance as possible.

"Come on, Bill," Vince said, his voice taking on a coaxing tone. "Just sit tight for a few more minutes. We'll have this fixed in no time, and then we can all go home."

Bill didn't reply, but Vince could see the anger and frustration in his eyes.

Finally, Bill stopped struggling to escape and Vince watched as the man hatched his new plan. He could see the realisation in his eyes that he had just one option left to take.

Vince watched as Bill's expression switched to a grin, he re-seated himself in the rover, and switched it to reverse gear.

They watched in silence as Bill slowly backed the rover out of the tunnel, its wheels crunching on the loose gravel and rock and the sides of the vehicle screeching as they scraped along the tunnel walls.

As soon as the rover cleared the entrance, Vince and Eleanor would make a break for it. It was a risky move, but it was their best chance to escape and they prepared themselves.

Vince quickly signalled to Eleanor, and the two of them were ready, waiting for the right moment to make their move. They watched in silence as Bill slowly backed the rover out of the tunnel.

The rover finally cleared the entrance and Vince and Eleanor sprang into action. They sprinted towards the opening and the rover, the reduced gravity of the lunar surface making their movements appear slow and graceful.

But Bill had taken the opportunity to really think about what was happening, and as his rage subsided, reason returned to him.

He realised that if he didn't act fast, he would lose everything. He knew that he needed to stop Vince and Eleanor from escaping, or his entire plan would be ruined.

Bill waited for the pair to make their escape from the tunnel and then switched back to forward gear the moment they thought they were home free. Realisation dawned on Vince that now they had nowhere to escape to. The plan had been basic, but they'd had no alternative.

The rover quickly built up speed and careened towards the pair who didn't know what to do, but they did the only thing they could do: they leapt to the sides of the entrance and Bill, unable to decide which way to turn in the heat of the moment, pulled hard to the left to where Vince had dived and hit the back of Vince's legs, sending him flying across the moonscape, far away from where he had been impacted.

Vince felt the pain in his legs as he was sent flying, though the lack of gravity somehow reduced the impact and where he would've assumed he might've been seriously injured by such a hit on Earth, rather here he was more pushed than hit. He couldn't help himself from spinning through the air though, watching the ground beneath him hurtle by all the way until he eventually crashed back down with a loud scraping sound and an 'oof'.

The first thought that Vince had, was to check his helmet and space-suit for damage, and after a quick cursory examination, he determined that he had been somehow miraculously unharmed.

Vince quickly got to his feet and turned his attention back towards Eleanor and the entrance of the tunnel. He saw Eleanor, who had managed to avoid the impact that had sent Vince flying, and the rover which had overturned and smoke was rising from its undercarriage.

He ran towards Eleanor, who was now standing at the entrance of the tunnel, and together they slowly made their way towards the overturned rover.

As they approached, they could see that the damage to the vehicle was extensive. Smoke was pouring from the engine compartment, and the wheels were twisted and broken. It was clear that the rover was not going anywhere any time soon.

Then when they cautiously rounded the vehicle, they saw what had happened to Bill.

There was no blood in the rover, but it was clear that Bill's helmet had taken the brunt of the impact when he'd flipped the vehicle; the glass in front of his face had a long crack across it and a hole the size of a tennis ball right where Bill's mouth was. Bill would've had just seconds to live after such a breach, and it was clear that even having those seconds, there was nothing that he could do to prevent his demise.

Vince and Eleanor looked at each other in shock, neither wanting to break the silence.

"Do... do you think the communicator is still working?" Eleanor asked eventually.

Vince looked back at the vehicle, but it was clear that the rover was completely beyond salvation. It wasn't igniting as one would expect of a smoking vehicle back on Earth, but the antennae had been snapped clean off when it had rolled over, and even if Vince knew how to repair them, he wouldn't risk getting any closer than was comfortable.

"Not a chance," Vince replied. "We need to get back to the settlement now, we have enough air in the suits, so I think we're in the clear. Are you OK?"

Eleanor visibly checked herself and nodded, still in shock from what had just happened. "I'm fine," she said, her voice barely above a whisper. "Let's just get out of here."

Vince took one last look at the wreckage of the rover and then turned towards Eleanor. "Come on," he said, gesturing for her to follow him. "We need to start making our way back to the settlement."

"Wait," Eleanor announced as Vince turned away to begin their trek. "Do you think we could go and get a sample of the diamonds so that we know what this place is?" she asked.

Vince hesitated for a moment, considering the risk involved in straying from their planned route. But then he thought about the discovery they had made, and the potential scientific value of the diamonds.

"Okay," he said finally, nodding towards the direction of the tunnel. "Let's go get that sample. After all, it's what Dr Whittaker would have wanted, right?"

Eleanor nodded and quickly led the way. Together, they made their way carefully through the tunnel and back into the diamond-encrusted cavern below. When they reached the cavern, Vince again looked at the glittering diamonds all around, mesmerised by their beauty.

Eleanor then retrieved a metallic device that Vince instantly recognised to be a mineral scoop from the small bag attached to her spacesuit and carefully placed it between the hard cavern wall and one of the larger-looking diamonds.

She struggled for a few minutes, trying to wiggle the tool back and forth to tease the gem free, though it was clear from her face and annoyed grunts that the diamond did not want to break free from its position within the wall.

Then she placed a foot against the wall and pulled on the lever that the mineral scoop created with all her might. The scoop started to bend, but before Vince could say anything, the tool abruptly snapped and Eleanor fell back onto the ground with a thud.

Vince couldn't help but snort at the sight of Eleanor on the ground, but after a moment of silence that was cut by the faint sound of hissing, the realisation of what had happened struck him, and his face dropped in shock horror.

He rushed over to Eleanor and helped her up, checking her suit for any signs of damage. "Are you OK? Is your suit breached?" he asked urgently.

Eleanor slowly nodded, her face pale. "I think so," she said, her voice trembling. "How bad is it?"

Vince quickly checked her suit and found a small tear near her shoulder. "It's a small breach, but we need to get you back to the settlement as soon as possible," he said, his voice urgent.

"I... do you think we can make it?" Eleanor asked, still in shock. "The rover..."

There was no way that Vince could answer that question. He knew that they were already on limited supplies, but with a leak... he feared the worst, and without transport, this was going to be a very long walk.

Chapter 22: Please, I Don't Want to Die

"We have to try," Vince said firmly. "Come on, let's move quickly and get back to the settlement. We'll monitor your suit and do everything we can to keep you safe along the way. Just speak up if you feel lightheaded or anything like that."

Truthfully, Vince had no idea and no experience of what Eleanor might encounter if her suit began to run too low on oxygen. All he did know, was that the little time they already had, was running out.

Eleanor nodded and they set off, moving as quickly as possible through the tunnel towards the outside of the cave. They had at least four kilometres to go and at a normal walking pace, Vince knew that would be over an hour's worth of walking. After a few moments though, it became apparent that the pair would be able to move much faster than normal due to the less restrictive nature of the lunar gravity.

Vince held back behind Eleanor and kept a close eye on her suit, monitoring her movements and looking for any signs of further damage. He knew that time was of the essence and that they had to get back to the settlement as soon as possible, but he also knew that if there was any more damage then it could spell disaster.

"Just keep your hand pressed over the leak as tight as you can," Vince said through slightly laboured breaths. "The less you leak out the easier this is all going to be."

For a while, they moved in silence, the only sound the soft hiss of the suit as they walked. Vince kept a close eye on Eleanor, watching for any signs of distress. He could see that she was struggling, but he also knew that she was strong and determined.

"Are you doing OK?" he asked after a while, his voice low and soothing.

"Vince... Detective," Eleanor corrected herself. "Do you think Bill killed Jane, or do you think she's back out there and in need of our help?"

"I don't know," Vince replied quickly. "But there's nothing that we can do right now; we can't turn back on the off chance that she's still alive while we absolutely know that you are alive, and in danger. I know how morbid it may sound, but if she isn't already dead then there's nothing we can do. When we reach the settlement or at least to within communication range, then we'll tell them to send out a rover and they'll find her."

"And the diamonds..." Eleanor added quietly.

"The diamonds?" Vince asked. "Who the hell cares Eleanor? You're in huge trouble here, we just survived a run in with a mad man and all you're thinking about is those damned diamonds?"

Eleanor stopped jogging and Vince managed to catch himself before he ran into the back of her. She turned and faced him, and he could see the pained expression in her face.

"Detective I... I don't think I can keep going. I'm getting a bit out of breath and I... I just need to sit down for a moment."

"No Eleanor we need to keep moving!" Vince raised his voice to almost a shout. He looked over her shoulder to see if the settlement had made it into view yet, but they were still too far away.

"Just a minute..." Eleanor repeated, and Vince watched as her eyes began to slowly close.

He tapped her on the shoulder and she opened her eyes to look at him again, though now her expression was filled with something other than fear; now Vince could see regret in her eyes.

"We need to keep going, and you need to keep your hand over that hole," Vince ordered.

"It's too late..." Eleanor said. "I can already feel it coming... but before I die, I need to tell you something."

"You aren't going to die," Vince said reassuringly, but Eleanor simply rolled her eyes in response.

"Detective, I knew about the diamonds," Eleanor replied. "I knew all along."

"What!?" Vince replied incredulously. "What are you saying?" he couldn't believe what he was hearing, though nothing seemed to fit into place for him anymore. Eleanor wasn't even on the moon when her husband had been killed, there was no way that she could have had anything to do with it.

"I know what you're thinking..." Eleanor continued. "I had nothing to do with Adrian's death. But I know what happened. And I need to tell you so that you can tell the world."

Vince looked up and away from Eleanor, not knowing exactly what to do next. In the end he decided to try to calm her down.

"We can talk about this when we are back in the settlement, Eleanor. Just please, you can do this."

"No Detective, please don't let me take this to my grave... I need you to know. I need the world to know what happened to my husband. He was a good man, and he didn't deserve to die out here alone... it was my fault."

"How could any of this have possibly been your fault?" Vince asked, his voice again raising. He had now quickly come to the conclusion that she had started to become delusional in her oxygen-starved state.

"Adrian called me when he was told by Dr Nair not to go looking for this cave system. I told him to just follow the rules and forget about it; the mission was too important to worry about such stupid little things... then the next time he called me, he told me he had gone to investigate. He described to me the wonders that he saw in that cave – the diamonds upon diamonds and how he wanted to tell the world how amazing his discovery was. Only... he wasn't supposed to have gone. I saw an opportunity... our Helen..."

"Your daughter," Vince said quietly.

"Yes... she needs constant care, but also experimental treatments do exist... but we could never afford them. I told Adrian to see if there was any way he could get just a few of those diamonds so that we could pay to make our daughter's life just a little better. I would do anything for Helen, and I know that Adrian would too..."

"But how would you have got them back to Earth?" Vince asked.

"I know it seems mundane... but packages do get sent up and down fairly regularly. Nobody would have even realised what they were, and everything would've been brighter for us and for Helen. But if Adrian told the world, or even just another person about the diamonds, then they could be seized by the governments of Earth to prevent widespread economical chaos in the diamond industry and markets. Adrian needed to keep them a secret, and that's what I told him to do."

"You are right of course," Vince replied homing in on the facts rather than the emotion behind Eleanor's words. "If that quantity of diamonds became common knowledge, then the price of diamonds would fall significantly and industries around the world would feel the repercussions..."

Eleanor nodded slowly and Vince could see that she was fading.

"Yes... and Adrian told me about the blackouts too, his arguments with Grace Thompson. Eventually I managed to convince him to go and get some of the diamonds to test. He said he had commandeered a mass spec to do the testing in private. When the next blackout came and the CCTV systems were offline, he would make his move."

Vince simply couldn't believe what he was hearing. This woman who he'd actually started to trust was now telling him that she knew what had happened all along?

"I know it's awful..." Eleanor choked out with tears in her eyes. "I know it was wrong... but you don't understand how difficult it is to sit there and watch your child as she's in pain... I'd do anything to give her that little bit of hope, to be better, to get out of that place and live a normal life..."

"I understand," Vince replied softly. "And what's happened has happened." He swallowed hard. "It wasn't your fault."

"But it was," Eleanor replied practically sobbing. "Adrian snuck out when one of the blackouts started. He agreed to go to the cave to bring back some samples and he said that he wouldn't risk taking a rover because then people would know he had gone. He said that he would go out on foot because the suits had plenty of oxygen in them and he could easily make his way from the hab to the cave and back... now I can see what happened so clearly..."

Vince's eyes widened as Eleanor said those last words because now he also understood.

"He tried to pry one of the diamonds from the wall with his mineral scoop and just like when you did the very same thing, it proved difficult," Vince said.

Eleanor nodded. "I can see it all... his mineral scoop snapped just like mine and it pierced his spacesuit. He had no rover and no way to call for help. He must've run as fast as he could back towards the habs until he could run no further, and that's where he fell and died. He was alone and must've been so scared..." And that was where Eleanor would break down into floods of tears, unable to say another word or listen to Vince as he attempted to soothe her.

Vince could see that Eleanor was in a state of emotional distress, but he also knew that they had to keep moving if they were going to make it back to the settlement in time. He gently placed a hand on her shoulder and pulled her to her feet, encouraging her to keep moving.

"Eleanor... there's an innocent woman being held back in the habs. You know she didn't kill Adrian and no matter what's already happened, we can't let her stand trial for something that she hasn't done," Vince said sternly. He knew they would need to talk about Bill and Jane too, and how Bill somehow knew what was happening up here, but for now he decided that the better course of action was to try to appeal to Eleanor's more caring side.

Eleanor nodded weakly, ignoring her tears as best she could. "You're right," she said softly. "Grace is innocent and she doesn't deserve to be punished for something she didn't do."

Vince gave her a reassuring smile before they continued their journey towards the settlement. He could tell that Eleanor was struggling to keep up, her movements still slow and uncoordinated and becoming more so with every passing moment. But Vince knew that they were so close to safety, and he encouraged Eleanor to keep going with every part of his being.

However, as they made slow progress, Eleanor's movements began to slow even further until she was barely shuffling her feet along the surface of the moon. Vince could see the desperation in her eyes as she tried to push through the pain and exhaustion.

"Just a little further, Eleanor," he said, his voice filled with urgency. "We're almost there."

But it was no use. Eleanor's legs finally gave out beneath her and she crumpled to the ground, her hand slipping from the tear in her suit and the breach hissing loudly. Vince rushed to her aid, trying to hold her upright, but it was too late. Eleanor's eyes had rolled back into her head and she had slipped into unconsciousness.

Vince's heart raced as he frantically searched for a way to help her. He had no idea how much time they had before it was too late. But no matter what he tried, Eleanor remained unresponsive.

Then the hissing from the suit slowed and an eerie silence replaced the sound that no astronaut would ever want to hear. The silence was somehow worse though; it meant that Eleanor was finally out of the oxygen stored in her tanks.

Vince fumbled around almost in shock for the place where Eleanor's oxygen tanks fed into her spacesuit from the outside and unclipped the hose. His hands weren't working properly through the anxiety though and it took him precious seconds longer than he'd anticipated to un-couple the system. Then he took a deep breath in and repeated the procedure with his own hose. Then, he placed his air line into Eleanor's suit and clipped it shut. He wouldn't have long, but he knew that this was the only chance for them both to survive.

Vince knew that he had to get her back to the settlement as quickly as possible or they would both be lost. He carefully lifted Eleanor up in his arms, trying to distribute her weight evenly so that he could move as quickly as possible and placed a hand tightly over the now hissing breach in her suit. The sound comforted him, as though it was a reminder that Eleanor at least had some small lifeline to cling onto.

With Eleanor cradled in his arms, Vince began to run towards the settlement. He could feel his own suit beginning to strain under the effort, but he knew that he had to keep going and he pounded his feet into the ground as fast as he could will them.

The next minute or so felt like an eternity to Vince. His muscles burned and his lungs cried out for him to take a breath, but he refused to stop. He could again feel Eleanor's shallow breathing with every passing moment, but he knew that he had to keep going.

Then finally, Vince caught sight of the settlement. He pushed himself even harder, running as fast as he could towards the array of habs. But just as he felt like they had almost made it, he couldn't help but allow the breath that he had been holding to release and as he tried to take in another breath, it was evident immediately that there was no oxygen present in his suit. This was it. He had come so close to salvation but there was nothing more that he could do.

Idly as he failed to take his last breath, Vince wondered if he should have clipped and unclipped the air line to take turns getting oxygen, but there was no more time for thinking and beneath him, his legs gave way and he felt himself crashing down to the ground with Eleanor still held in his arms.

Almost immediately, his vision began to blur and fade, and all that he saw at the end of his life, were the elongating lights of the lunar habitats: a stark reminder of how uninhabitable this rock really was.

Chapter 23: The Truth Will Out

When he came to, Vince was lying in a hospital bed, surrounded by medical equipment and blurred, worried faces. He groaned as he tried to sit up, but a hand gently pushed him back down.

"Lie still, Detective," a woman's voice said soothingly. "You've been through a lot, haven't you?"

Vince frowned in confusion. "Eleanor..." he croaked. "What happened to Eleanor?"

There was hesitation for a moment before a soft reply came. "I'm sorry, Detective. We did everything we could, but... well Mrs Whittaker hasn't woken up yet. There is the chance that her lack of oxygen could've caused permanent damage and we don't really know if she'll ever wake up."

Vince felt his heart sink at the news. "No... I gave her my oxygen... just a few minutes... she'll be OK..." he croaked out and opening his eyes fully, he realised that the person speaking to him was Dr Priya Nair.

"Completed medical school since I went out?" Vince managed to ask alongside a forced smile. "I don't know how much I like having a geologist looking after my wellbeing..."

Dr Nair chuckled softly. "Don't worry, Detective. I'm just filling in while the regular medical team takes a break."

Vince let out a sigh, feeling a wave of exhaustion wash over him. "Can I see her?" he asked, referring to Eleanor.

"I'm afraid not," Dr Nair replied gently. "She's still in critical condition and we need to monitor her closely. But you need to rest now, Detective. Your body has been through a lot and you need time to recover."

Vince nodded slowly, but his mind was already racing with questions and concerns. What would happen to Eleanor? And what about the case? They still needed to prove Grace's innocence and reveal the truth behind Adrian's death.

"I need to speak to the Captain," Vince forced out. "There's something he needs to know."

Dr Nair then placed a gentle hand on Vince's shoulder. It was both reassuring and a reminder that he wasn't going anywhere until the medical team had seen to him properly.

"We know about Jane and Bill," she said softly with a sad frown. "You don't need to explain right now."

"But Jane... she might still be out there..." Vince replied.

"Detective... Bill and Jane... they didn't make it I am afraid to say. But none of that matters right now, what you need to do is focus on getting a little rest, OK? That is unless you have anything else to say that could mean life or death for anyone here?"

Vince managed to shake his head, before adding: "Only I was wrong about Ms Thompson. You can tell the Captain to release her from her quarters, and tell him to come and see me as soon as you allow it."

Dr Nair nodded and made a note of Vince's request before stepping away to check on some of the equipment in the room. Vince let out a deep sigh and closed his eyes, trying to process everything that had happened over the past few days. He couldn't believe that Bill and Jane were gone, and that Eleanor was in critical condition. But he knew that he couldn't let those thoughts consume him, not if he wanted to continue the investigation and get to the whole and complete truth.

As he drifted off into a much-needed sleep, Vince made a silent promise to himself that he would do everything in his power to ensure that justice was served for Adrian and Grace, and that Eleanor would have a chance to make things right.

Vince didn't know how much time had passed when he eventually awoke again, though again it was not of his own accord; it was the voice of Captain Armstrong that roused him from his slumber.

"Detective?" the Captain asked sternly. "Priya told me that you wanted to speak to me, well, here I am. I would like to know why my settlement and our mission has turned to shit ever since you seem to have got yourself involved. I want to know why I have two injured people in my medical bay, and I want to know why two of my team members are dead." Then he added quickly: "In addition to Dr Whittaker, of course."

Vince took a deep breath before responding. "Captain, I'm sorry for the loss of your team members, but I can assure you that I'm doing everything I can to reveal what happened and who is responsible. As for what happened to them, I'll get to that in a minute. Grace Thompson is innocent. I was wrong about her and I need you to release her from her quarters."

The Captain's expression remained unchanged as he listened to Vince's words. "And what evidence do you have to support this claim? After all, you were sure enough to have me remove her from the mission before," he asked.

Vince hesitated for a moment before speaking. "I have evidence that points to Adrian being responsible for his own death. I know it may be difficult to hear, but it is my belief that Adrian Whittaker's death was an accident, and that's the conclusion that I will be reporting back down to Earth."

"An... accident?" the Captain's eyebrows raised, and Vince couldn't help but feel like the Captain seemed relieved at this development.

"Yes... I guess you're going to find out about this anyway but," Vince looked around the room conspiratorially to make sure he wasn't overheard before he brought the Captain up to speed on what happened at the cave, to Bill and Jane, and Eleanor's confession.

"I... don't understand..." the Captain finally said after Vince had stopped speaking. Then he let out a sigh, running a hand through his hair. "This is a mess, Detective," he said, shaking his head. "But if what you're saying is true, then I have a few more questions to ask. Why were you so sure that Grace was involved, and how the hell did Bill get onto this mission in the first place, knowing what he knew about the diamonds?!" his voice raised as he spoke, but he made an effort not to outright shout his question.

"This is where I have arrived as well, Captain," Vince replied. "And I can come to just one conclusion. It's not something that I want to voice without evidence, but if you could hand me one last piece of this puzzle, I believe that we can have this all solved."

"And what is that?" the Captain asked.

"The reason that I was so sure that Grace was the culprit, was because of one of the first pieces of evidence that I surveyed after arriving here. Dr Whittaker's phone records had been purposely doctored to throw off my investigation, but whoever had doctored them clearly didn't think that Mrs Whittaker would see their error: that they had removed all of his conversations with his own wife. Then when we played our game of j'accuse - and I must admit that the game was somewhat of a ruse – I asked for all of your records, at which time you told Ms Thompson to arrange that. I falsely assumed that Ms Thompson would get the records for herself as a part of her duty, ergo she was the one who doctored the first set."

"Ah," the Captain said simply, catching on to what Vince was saying. "But why didn't you simply ask, rather than play that stupid little game with us?"

"Because if I started asking questions about the phone records, then whoever tampered with them would know that I knew they had been falsified. I couldn't let that happen as you may well imagine," Vince said.

"Well I can tell you now that there's just one person who has access to the phone records as per our data protection policies. One person who can view and sign off on all calls that we make and receive up here, and that person is Dr Mendez, back on Earth."

"Captain I..." Vince began to ask his next question but before he could finish, the Captain shook his head.

"This is one of the very few tasks that Dr Mendez can't delegate," he said. "She has full access to the communications both ways, so nobody else has that clearance."

"So that means that we have just one last possibility, meaning we have arrived at the truth," Vince said. "Dr Mendez doctored those call logs so that, well presumably I would assume Vince was a bad person and therefore dilute the seriousness with which I would approach my investigation."

The Captain nodded slowly. "So Mendez wanted you not to discover the truth about Whittaker?" the Captain asked. "But that doesn't make any sense."

"There is one way to look at this that does lead to all of this making perfect sense, Captain. When you say that Mendez had access to the communications to and from your settlement, does that include call recordings too?"

The Captain nodded thoughtfully.

"In that case, when Dr Whittaker spoke on the phone with his wife and he told her about the diamonds... Dr Mendez would have known about it," Vince said. "Dr Mendez knew that there were diamonds up here to be had, and she knew that Dr Whittaker was the only person who knew about them."

Vince remained silent for a long moment before he knew what he needed to say next. He needed to be absolutely sure of himself before he made any accusations, but he could see no alternative.

"Then Dr Mendez sent Bill up here to find the diamonds and send them back down to Earth," he said calmly.

The Captain stroked his chin but didn't respond. It was clear that this revelation pained him, but there were still some things that he simply couldn't place.

"But what did Dr Mendez have planned? How could she do any-thing while she was back down on Earth and the Whittakers were going to run this diamond smuggling operation?" Armstrong asked.

"Well Captain, just going with a hunch here, but how long has Bill been on the rotation roster for?"

"A couple of weeks actually," the Captain replied immediately. "Nothing happens instantly but usually the rosters are prepared further in advance than Bill was. I didn't question it though as Mendez has full oversight into the settlement's members."

"So he was chosen presumably after the diamonds had been found, but before Dr Whittaker had passed?" Vince asked. "I know it may sound like a mighty coincidence, but I think that Bill was sent up here by Dr Mendez to run the lunar half of the operation. It was just pure dumb luck that Whittaker died before he could begin the operation, but I would not have put it past Bill to have planned to kill Dr Whittaker. Then of course Eleanor's arrival was another spanner in the works so to speak."

"So your assessment is that Dr Mendez send Bill up here to kill Whittaker, but the Doctor unfortunately and coincidentally died before Bill had the chance. Then you're saying that Bill was so hell-bent on murder that he simply killed someone else?"

Vince nodded.

"Well then the last thing for me to ask, I guess, is for you to show me these diamonds."

"No problem Captain," Vince said. "But before all of this becomes public knowledge, I believe that we should consider the ramifications of such a discovery to markets and economies back on Earth. Now I'm not saying that I have the answers to this, but such a quantity of the precious stones could swing the supply and demand of diamonds to a degree that we are yet to understand."

"I don't believe that's something we can decide by ourselves, Detective," the Captain said. "But in the meantime, I'll have Ms Thompson released. It seems to me like she's been held for long enough."

Vince nodded in gratitude. "Thank you, Captain." In truth, he was pleased with the Captain's response. He had said that the diamond decision wasn't up to him rather than trying to cover it up and Vince knew that he had been right to trust the man.

The Captain then turned to leave but paused at the doorway. "And Detective?" he said, looking back at Vince. "I hope you know what you're doing."

Vince watched as the Captain left the room before settling back into the bed, feeling a sense of relief wash over him. All of this was still far from over, but at least he had the Captain's support, and he could start to piece together what needed to happen to close this chapter.

Call Recording: Adrian & Eleanor Whittaker

"Adrian?" Eleanor asked eagerly.

"Eleanor, it's me," Adrian's voice crackled through the line.

"Adrian, it's so good to hear your voice," Eleanor said, her voice filled with relief.

"Yeah, it's good to hear yours too," Adrian said, his voice sounding tired and strained. "Listen, I have something to tell you."

"What is it?" Eleanor asked, feeling a knot forming in her stomach.

"I've found something," Adrian said, his voice filled with excitement. "Something amazing."

"What is it?" Eleanor asked, feeling a sense of dread creeping up on her.

"A cave," Adrian said, his voice barely containing his excitement. "A cave filled with diamonds. Wall to wall. And they're huge. I'm talking *millions* at least."

"Adrian, we can't tell anyone," she said, her voice serious.

"What?" Adrian said, his voice filled with confusion. "Why not?"

"Think about it, Adrian," Eleanor said, her voice soft. "If people find out about this, everyone will want a piece of the pie. It'll be chaos. We have to keep this a secret, just between us. Think of what we can do with them, the difference we can make."

"I don't know, Eleanor," Adrian said hesitantly. "I feel like this is something we should share with the world."

"Think about Helen," Eleanor said firmly. "Think about how much we need the money for Helen's treatments. We can't afford to have the government or some corporation come in and take everything."

There was silence on the other end of the line. "You're right," Adrian finally said, his voice resigned. "But how are we going to get the diamonds back to Earth without anyone noticing?"

"We'll have to do it slowly, a few diamonds at a time," Eleanor said, her mind racing with possibilities. "We can't just send them all down at once."

Adrian sighed. "I suppose you're right," he said, his voice still deflated. "But I'll need to do some tests on the diamonds first. Make sure they're real and see what they're worth."

"Of course," Eleanor said, her mind already working on a plan. "Just be careful, Adrian. I don't want anything to happen to you."

"I will be," Adrian said, his voice serious. "I promise."

Chapter 24: A Ghost in the Machine

"Detective?" Grace Thompson's voice filled Vince's mind as he stirred from his sleep. His entire body ached but he knew from the fuzziness in his head that it was finally time for him to get out of the bed; he'd been asleep for far too long.

When he opened his eyes, he was greeted by the familiar faces of Eleanor Whittaker, Captain Jack Armstrong and Grace Thompson.

Vince groaned as he sat up slowly, his mind still foggy from the long rest. He looked around the room, trying to gather his bearings again before focusing on the group in front of him.

"Detective, how are you feeling?" Captain Armstrong asked, his tone laced with concern.

Vince rubbed his eyes and took a deep breath. "I'm... I'm OK, I think," he said, his voice hoarse. "What happened? How long was I out?"

Eleanor stepped forward, her expression grave. "You've been asleep for hours, Vince," she said softly. "We were all worried about you."

Vince nodded slowly, trying to process the information. He couldn't believe he had been out for so long. "What about you? How are you doing? I thought I might've lost you out there," he asked. Vince couldn't help but feel a little hard done by that Eleanor actually seemed fine, where he seemed to have paid a far harsher toll for the whole ordeal.

"I'm OK, thanks to you," Eleanor smiled. "I really thought I was done for. I don't know where you found the strength to... well, you know. But in any case, we're all here and I've brought everyone up to speed on what I told you, what we found and everything else. They had me in the critical care unit as a precaution, but in the end, you were without oxygen for longer than I was... so again, thankyou, Vince."

Vince managed to nod. His throat was sore and he wanted a drink more than anything else in the world.

"So we all know?" Vince asked finally and he was answered by nods from both the Captain and Grace.

"We four in this room are here right now, because categorically we have nothing to hide between us," the Captain said. "We know that Dr Mendez planned something behind our backs, and we know that we can all trust each other. What we need to do next, is figure out what we're going to do about it."

"No secrets?" Vince managed to croak out. "In that case... can you tell me why you felt the need to ransack Dr Whittaker's room, captain?"

The Captain grinned sheepishly. "I wondered if you had managed to figure that part out. Of course I was the only one with the opportunity to do so, and when I found Adrian after he was reported missing, I took it upon myself to see if there was any evidence of his meddling. I am afraid that I may have taken it a little too far, though I believe that I acted in the best interests of the settlement as a whole."

Vince nodded, blinking a few times. In truth, he wasn't surprised.

Grace stepped forward and did her best to turn the conversation back to Mendez and what they had to do next, with a determined look on her face. "I've been going over the call logs and I think I've found something."

Vince sat up straighter, his interest piqued. "What did you find?" he asked eagerly.

Grace pulled up a tablet and showed it to Vince. "There's a ghost in the machine, so to speak" she said, pointing to a section of the data, though Vince didn't really know what he was looking at. "I've found proof that Mendez has been tampering with the logs, deleting records and altering the timestamps. I think it'll come in handy as evidence when it's needed."

Vince leaned forward, squinting at the tablet. "How did you manage to find this?" he asked, impressed by Grace's sleuthing skills.

"I started going through the logs again, looking for any irregularities or patterns. And then I noticed that some calls were missing altogether, but I could see them in the metadata. That's when I knew I had proof that someone had been tampering with the logs," Grace explained, her eyes shining with satisfaction.

"That's fantastic work, Grace," Eleanor said, placing a hand on Grace's shoulder. "But what do we do with this information?"

"That's the question," the Captain said. "Any communications from the base will go directly through Mendez's office and I don't think that it would be a good idea to alert her to the fact that we know. This isn't just a case of theft or fraud, she sent Bill up here with the intent to kill Whittaker. She has too much power and we honestly don't know who we can and can't trust either."

The group all looked at each other silently for a moment, wondering what their next steps would be.

"Well," Vince said slowly. "My investigation here is complete. I have made my determinations and I will be passing that information on to the authorities as I have been charged to do so. In that case... I suppose that I am free to return to Earth, and I believe the same to be true for Eleanor too?"

The Captain nodded. "So that's two of us with reason to get back down there. But I don't like throwing the rest of you to the wolves like that."

"I don't see another choice, Captain. If any more decide that their time here is up and want to leave, it could raise suspicions. We do have another problem though."

"What's that?" Armstrong asked.

"I assume that Bill would need to check in with Mendez at some point. Please tell me that you haven't made a report of his death yet?"

"I haven't," the Captain said. "I didn't know what was going to happen, so nobody else knows about what happened to Bill and Jane."

"In that case, I have an idea," Eleanor said before Vince could say another word. "Why don't the Detective and I return to Earth as scheduled, but take a parcel to Dr Mendez supposedly from Bill with a sample of the diamonds inside. She'll think that the plan is still on-going, and we'll know for sure that she's the culprit for all of this, and we'll have the evidence!"

Vince raised an eyebrow at Eleanor's suggestion, but couldn't deny the cleverness of the plan. "It's risky," he said. "But it might just work."

The group fell into silence, each considering the risks and potential outcomes of the plan. Finally, the Captain spoke up. "Alright, I'll support this plan. But we need to be careful. Mendez is a powerful woman with connections, and we don't know what she's capable of."

Vince nodded in agreement. "We'll need to make sure we have everything in place before we make any moves. And we need to make sure that the evidence we have is rock solid. I don't want any doubt in any of this."

Then the group turned to leave Vince after agreeing to their roles in the plan. The Captain and Grace would continue on as normal, and Vince and Eleanor would return to Earth as scheduled. It was the only way that they wouldn't raise any suspicions.

"Grace, can we talk for a moment," Vince said as the engineer was leaving the room with the Captain and Eleanor.

"Of course, Detective," she said.

"I... I uh wanted to apologise to you," he said. "I made an accusation that was false and it resulted in you being placed under guard. I'm sorry for causing you that stress and anxiety. You're a great engineer and I wanted you to know that my apology is sincere."

Grace looked at Vince for a moment, her expression unreadable. "Thank you for apologising, Detective," she said finally. "I appreci-ate it."

Vince could tell that Grace really did appreciate his words. Her expression had softened and there was a new kindness in her eyes that he knew meant mutual trust and respect. He knew that he'd caused her a great deal of hardship, but it was a mistake that he wasn't going to make again.

Grace turned and left the room, but called out over her shoulder. "Better get packing Detective, the next transport off this rock leaves in just two days."

Vince's mind immediately turned to the fact that he now had just two days to form a plan to catch Dr Mendez in the act.

In truth, Vince had recovered as much as he thought it was necessary for him to be able to leave the medical bay. Of course, he hadn't been discharged as yet *per se*, but he knew how he felt, and other than a little lethargy and dizziness, he was pretty much ready to go. What he needed to do, was to start thinking properly, rather than lying around in a bed.

With that in mind, Vince got up, assessed his balance as he stood and checked to make sure he was still wearing all of his clothes – which he was – and then he walked towards the door and made his way out into the hallway and back to his room.

When he arrived back at his room, everything was just as he had left it. He had no reason to believe that it wasn't going to be, but he had seen so many unexpected twists in the last few days that at this point, frankly nothing would surprise him.

Picking up his suitcase from under the small bed, Vince began to pack his things, making sure he had everything he needed for the journey back to Earth. As he packed, his mind drifted to the Whittaker family, and specifically to Helen. He couldn't imagine what they were going through, with Adrian having passed away and Helen still in need of expensive and experimental treatments. Vince resolved to do everything in his power to help them, but right now, he just wanted to make sure that Mendez was made to pay for what she had done. He only hoped that he and Eleanor could pull off their plan and get the evidence they needed to bring her down.

After finishing his packing, Vince made his way to the Captain's office. When he arrived, he found that the Captain, Grace and Eleanor were already there, discussing what they should do about Mendez.

"Vince, you made it," the Captain said, looking up from the tablet in his hands. "How are you feeling?"

"I'm feeling much better, thank you," Vince replied, taking a seat at the table.

"Good. So, we've been discussing what we should do next, but we seem to just hit a dead end at every turn," the Captain said. "We can't speak about any of this over the comms network, or even call down to Earth, because Mendez will see it and cover her tracks. The problem that we have, is that we have no evidence of, well anything."

Vince scratched his chin. He knew what the Captain was saying was right. Even if Mendez had fast-tracked Bill into the settlement so that she could use him to smuggle the diamonds back down to Earth, surely she wouldn't have left a paper trail that incriminated her in any of this. It was a tough situation, and it was made even more difficult by the fact that they were essentially cut off from the entire world.

Eleanor spoke up, "What if we use an independent satellite to send a message down to Earth, explaining the situation and asking for backup? We could encrypt the message and use a code that only trusted authorities would understand."

"No," Grace said. "We don't have any independent satellites just laying around in orbit you know? This mission was designed to run on a secure link only between Earth and the moon."

Vince nodded in agreement with Grace. It was a good idea in theory, but the reality was that they simply didn't have the resources to make it happen. They needed to think of another way to communicate safely.

The Captain leaned forward, resting his elbows on the table. "We need to think outside the box here. Mendez is smart, but so are we. There has to be a way to catch her in the act."

Vince rubbed his temples, trying to think of a way forward. Then he said slowly: "We have just one thing that can work to our advantage up here, and that's the fact that Mendez doesn't know Bill is no longer with us." It wasn't so much a lead in to a detailed plan, but Vince knew that this could be the cornerstone to at least *something*.

"But how can we use that?" Eleanor asked.

Vince thought for a moment before answering. "Well, if we can make her think that Bill is still alive and working with her, maybe she will slip up and reveal something incriminating. But I just don't know how we can keep up this ruse for long enough for it to be effective."

"I have an idea!" Grace announced loudly. It was so loud in fact, that her exclamation made Vince start. "I can create an issue in the communications repeater..." she paused for a moment when the rest of the group looked at her as though she had grown three heads.

"I know... it sounds bad that I even know how to do it, but honestly we need something big here, right?"

Vince was the first to agree, nodding slowly after thinking through the engineer's words. "I believe that in this case, the end may justify the means," he said.

"I agree," Captain Armstrong quickly followed up. "We all know what Grace has done, but I think that we can all agree that what has happened is going to stay within this room?" He pointedly looked to Vince and Eleanor, who each nodded once in confirmation.

"I don't need to report anything that isn't an intrinsic part of my investigation and I think that Ms Thompson has been through enough already," Vince agreed. "Please, Ms Thompson, do continue."

Grace looked at the Captain rather sheepishly and continued once he had nodded to her.

"If I made an issue – not something too critical – then we could blame that on the fact that Mendez wouldn't be able to contact Bill," Grace explained.

"No, that wont work," the Captain said. "If the communications system is down, they won't let us send a shuttle down to Earth."

Vince scratched his chin again. Then it hit him. "We don't need to turn off the comms array," he said with a smile. "Grace, do you think that you could cause an issue that would disable voice communications, leaving just text?"

Grace thought for a moment, then replied with wide eyes: "Yes!"

Eleanor leaned forward, intrigued. "How would that help us?"

Vince then explained his idea. "If we can make it seem like Bill is still alive and working with Mendez, but just unable to communicate via voice, we can pretend to be him and tell Mendez that everything's still going ahead as planned. And even better, we can tell Mendez that 'Bill' is going to send a parcel back down to Earth with us so that she can finally get her hands on the diamonds!"

The Captain nodded in agreement. "That's a great idea. And if Mendez takes the bait, there'll be no backing out of any of this; she'll be caught red handed. All we need to do is make sure nobody finds out about what's happened to Bill because if anyone at all talks about it, then Mendez is going to hear about it."

"But how do we ensure that nobody talks?" Eleanor asked. "Plus, won't people start asking more questions now that Bill and Jane haven't returned?"

"I don't think that Bill we be a huge problem, but people will notice Jane missing," the Captain replied. "We're going to have to let people think that the pair of them are alive and well, but uncontactable..."

Vince nodded in agreement. "Why can't we say that they've gone out to explore something?"

"Nope," the Captain replied. "There's nowhere up here that they could go for more than a day, and why would they both need to go? We need something that won't raise any suspicions or alarms. If Mendez gets wind of any of this, the whole game's up."

The group sat in silence for a long while. They knew that they were so close to a solution, but with the limitations in place due to their location, coming up with something was proving difficult.

"OK so what we have here," Vince began to summarise, "is a situation where we can Doctor the communications array with the help of Ms Thompson here, but we need to ensure that nobody asks any questions regarding the whereabouts of Bill or Jane, especially of Earth." He waited for a moment to see if anyone would cut in, but eventually he decided to continue when nobody in the room offered anything. "OK so why don't we switch the internal communications systems over to text based too, and then we act like its business as usual, but we can also speak with the rest of the settlement as though it's Bill and Jane doing some of the talking. Nobody will ever see them of course, but they'll at least be a part of the conversations..."

The Captain nodded slowly in agreement. "I think it could work... Grace, do you think you can do that, and make it seem believable?" he asked.

Grace nodded enthusiastically, clearly happy to have an important role in their plan. "I can even write a program that'll send a few messages as though they're from those two too! We already have a text-based intranet set up as it is!"

It sounded to Vince as though they had a plan, but he couldn't help but worry about the look on Eleanor's face.

"What's wrong, Eleanor?" Vince asked.

"It's just..." she said slowly. "I know we're glad we're figuring things out and all... but I think we're starting to forget that three people up here are dead... I just don't want to forget that."

Vince nodded in understanding. "You're right, Eleanor. It's important to remember that this is a serious situation and lives have been lost. But we're also working to make sure that justice is served and that nobody else gets hurt. It's a delicate balance, but we need to keep that in mind as we move forward."

The Captain also nodded in agreement. "We can't lose sight of that. And we'll make sure that the memory of those who have passed is honoured."

Chapter 25: Mission Failed

It only took Grace a few hours to get the communication system broken enough so that only text-based messages could be sent back and forth to Earth, and between everyone currently in the lunar settlements. Vince had been surprised at just how effective she had been, but he knew that she had been chosen as a lead engineer in the first place for a reason. He was also surprised by the fact that she had managed to write a program that sent out a few sporadic messages from each of their small group, as well as Bill and Jane so as to give the impression that everything was business as usual.

It was an odd sensation for Vince, sitting at the communications terminal and pretending to be someone who was no longer alive. But he had to keep reminding himself that it was all for the greater good, and that they needed to catch Mendez before she could cover her tracks.

The days passed quickly, with the team going about their business as usual. They made sure to keep up appearances, talking to each other as though nothing had changed, while secretly playing the game that nobody else knew was afoot.

On the morning of the shuttle launch, the team gathered in the small docking bay. The shuttle was still there from their arrival, its engines humming softly as it prepared for lift-off. Thankfully, the communications problem that was due to be 'fixed' within the next few days hadn't been serious enough to cause Mendez to halt the shuttle launch. Vince also wondered if it had anything to do with the message that he'd sent to Mendez from 'Bill' that said he was sending down some rock samples for her to analyse down on Earth.

"Here are those samples for you to give to Mendez," the Captain said loudly for everyone to hear as he approached Vince and Eleanor. "Please, if you wouldn't mind passing them along when you see her next?" It was a bit showy for Vince's tastes, but he knew that if anyone was watching or listening, this would at least go some way to help in the long run if they would eventually speak with Mendez.

"Thankyou Captain," Vince said, taking the package. It was marked as 'private and confidential' and it fit into Vince's hand comfortably. He quickly put it into his pocket and held a hand out for the Captain to grasp.

"It's been a pleasure having you up here with us, Detective. I only hope that your conclusions will bring some peace to the Whittaker family, and close this dark chapter in the history of our mission," the Captain said.

Vince shook the Captain's hand firmly. "Thank you, Captain. I hope so too," he replied.

Eleanor stepped forward and hugged the Captain. "Thank you for everything," she said softly. "You've been wonderful to us."

The Captain patted her on the back. "It's been my pleasure, Mrs Whittaker. Safe travels."

With that, Vince and Eleanor checked their bags once more, making sure that they had everything they needed for the journey back to Earth and turned their backs on the Captain.

As they waited for the final checks to be completed, Vince found himself thinking about the Whittaker family once again. He knew that he had to make sure that Mendez was brought to justice, not just for the sake of his own career, but also for the sake of Adrian and Helen. He hoped that they would find some solace in the fact that justice had been done.

The final checks were completed, and Vince, Eleanor and ten scientists and engineers boarded the shuttle, their time on the lunar settlement finally reaching its end. Vince took his seat, feeling a sense of relief wash over him, and Eleanor sat next to him, though she looked straight ahead clearly feeling uneasy about what had passed, and what was still yet to come.

Vince was going home, and he was going to make sure that justice was done.

The same shuttle that had been used to bring Vince and the rest up to the settlement had been waiting to take them home, and again Vince was surprised at how luxurious the Luna's Promise truly was. The soft lighting, plush seating, and array of amenities designed to make the journey as pleasant as possible almost made him feel guilty for leaving the inhabitants of the settlement having to deal with the realities and struggles of lunar habitation.

The ascent from the lunar surface was different to what Vince had experienced when he had left Earth. Presumably the Earth's hold on the shuttle combined with the additional gravity and atmosphere were the cause for the need to accelerate away from Earth at such high speeds, but lifting up from the moon seemed even smoother, or perhaps even calm. The ion thrusters seemed to have to make no effort for the shuttle to glide effortlessly up from the ground and within a few minutes, the settlement on the surface of the moon was nothing but a fading beacon on the viewscreens.

As the shuttle took off, Vince watched as the lunar settlement receded into the distance. It was a strange feeling, leaving behind the place that had held so many secrets. But he knew that he had to move on, and that there were more important things to focus on.

Eventually, the excitement of leaving the surface of the moon dissipated, and Eleanor turned to speak to Vince.

"Do you think it's going to work?" she asked in a very small, hushed voice.

"I think that this is the best chance we have to catch the person responsible for all of this. But I want you to know, no matter what happens, we did the right thing here," Vince reassured her. "It's the only way to bring about justice for Adrian and... well you know..."

Eleanor nodded. "I guess I just never thought that I would be so close to this..." she said, still careful with her words.

"I know, Eleanor."

"Thanks, Vince."

Vince smiled at her, "Anytime, Eleanor." He leaned back into his seat, the weight of the mission still heavy on his shoulders. He couldn't help but wonder what would happen once they reached Earth. Would Mendez take the bait and reveal herself? Or would she be too smart for their plan to work?

The journey back to Earth proved uneventful, with the shuttle coasting smoothly through space. Vince spent most of his time in his seat, lost in thought as he tried to make sense of everything that had happened. It was a strange feeling, knowing that he had played a part in something so big, but also feeling like he had been swept up in events beyond his control. There was still so much to do as well.

Eventually, nearing the end of their voyage, the shuttle began its descent into Earth's atmosphere. Vince watched as the ground grew closer, feeling a sense of relief wash over him as he realised that he was finally home and as the shuttle touched down, he couldn't help but smile to himself. It was good to be back on solid ground. He could already feel the familiar weight of Earth's natural gravity bearing down on him.

The scientists and engineers disembarked from the shuttle before Vince and Eleanor, though it seemed like all the attention was on the pair that weren't really a part of the lunar mission. The shuttle had landed on a pad next to a series of large buildings and Vince could see television cameras and reporters watching the shuttle from where he stood. What Vince had to tell the world was going to be momentous and they knew it.

"Please, follow me," a man in a white coat ordered before Vince could even make his introductions and the pair dutifully followed him into a small room, where there were hot drinks and mugs already waiting on the table for them. Vince didn't take any of them.

"How are you feeling?" the man asked.

"We're fine," Vince said. "But would it be rude for me to ask who you are?"

"Oh, I'm sorry, my name's John, John Telford. I'm just here to make sure you're OK before I let you move onto debriefing."

"So you're a Doctor?" Eleanor asked.

"That's right," Telford said with a warm smile. "How are you feeling, Mrs Whittaker?"

"I... I'm fine," she replied slowly, almost caught off guard by the question.

"I must apologise, Doctor," Vince said. "But Mrs Whittaker lost her husband, and we have had a very long few days... I'm sure that you can understand..."

"Of course I understand, Detective," Telford said, still smiling. "I'm just here to ensure that you're both physically and mentally stable before you move on to debriefing. Now can you tell me if you encountered anything unusual during your time up there in the settlement?"

The question was certainly one that Vince hadn't been expecting and it caught him off guard. Speaking slowly, he managed to force out a response. "We... were on the surface of the moon... with people who had been living together for many years. I was sent to investigate a murder and Ms Whittaker was only there because her husband was suspected to have been killed. I wonder what you could mean by 'unusual' beyond these circumstances, Doctor?"

Telford chuckled softly. "Fair point, Detective. I suppose what I meant to ask is if you experienced any physical or psychological stress while on the lunar settlement? It's not uncommon for people to feel a sense of isolation or anxiety when they're away from Earth for an extended period of time."

Vince considered the question for a moment before responding. "I wouldn't say that we experienced anything out of the ordinary for a mission of this nature. It was certainly challenging at times, but we were able to handle it." He was being short in his answers, and it was primarily because Vince had no idea who this man was, why he was asking questions, and he had no idea if this man had been sent to find anything out about any diamonds, or even the arrival of Bill.

Eleanor nodded in agreement, though she didn't seem as uncomfortable with Telford as Vince was. "Yes, it was difficult being away from home and dealing with the loss of my husband, but the team up there was very supportive, and we were able to work together to get through it."

Telford nodded in understanding. "I see. Well, I'm glad to hear that you had a supportive team up there. It can be tough being away from home for so long, but it sounds like you were able to cope with the situation."

He paused for a moment before continuing, "If you don't mind me asking, how did you find the living conditions on the lunar settlement? Was everything up to standard?"

Vince and Eleanor exchanged a quick look before Vince replied, "Yes, the living conditions were adequate. We had everything we needed to survive and complete our mission."

Telford nodded again. "That's good to hear. And were there any issues with the equipment or technology up there? Anything that needed to be repaired or replaced?"

Vince hesitated before answering, "There were a few minor issues that needed to be addressed, but nothing that significantly impacted our mission."

Telford raised an eyebrow. "Can you elaborate on that, Detective?"

Vince shook his head. "I'm sorry, I can't give specifics. We were up there to investigate a murder, not to assess the condition of the equipment."

Telford nodded slowly, but Vince could tell that he wasn't satisfied with the answer. "Alright, fair enough. And what about the other members of the team up there? Did you have any issues working with them?"

Eleanor spoke up this time, "No, everyone up there was professional and cooperative. We all worked together to try and solve the case."

Telford leaned back in his chair, considering their answers. "Alright, one last question then. Was there anything happening on the lunar settlement that you would deem to be beyond the remit of the mission parameters?"

"I'm sorry, but aren't you a Doctor?" Vince asked. "And correct me if I'm wrong, but this isn't a debriefing, is it?"

Telford smiled thinly. "No, it's not a debriefing, but I do have an interest in the well-being of everyone who returns from the lunar settlement. It's not uncommon for people to experience some level of stress or anxiety after spending an extended period of time on the moon, and I just want to make sure that you both are doing alright."

Vince didn't buy it. He had a feeling that Telford was trying to gather more information from them than he was letting on.

"We appreciate your concern, Doctor," he said. "But we're both fine. We're ready to move on to the debriefing now."

Telford nodded and sighed, standing up from his chair. "Very well. I'll let the debriefing team know that you're ready for them." He gave them a polite smile before leaving the room, closing the door behind him.

Vince let out a sigh of relief once Telford was gone. "That was odd," he said to Eleanor. "I don't think he was just a Doctor checking on our well-being."

Eleanor nodded in agreement. "I got the same feeling. Do you think he's trying to gather information about what we found up there?"

"It's possible," Vince said. "But I don't think we gave him anything that he could use against us or the team."

They sat in silence for a few minutes, waiting for the debriefing team to arrive and wondering what was going to happen to them next. Vince couldn't help but feel a sense of unease. He had a feeling that their mission wasn't over yet, and that there were still more secrets to uncover.

"Hello Detective, Mrs Whittaker," a voice came along with the opening of the door and in stepped the unmistakable Dr Mendez herself. She was alone, which seemed strange, but Vince had been expecting a 'team' and not a singular person.

"Dr Mendez," Vince exclaimed, standing up and offering the Doctor a hand to shake, which she did.

"Welcome back to Earth," Mendez said, her tone polite but cool. "I hope your mission was a success."

"We believe we have solved the case," Vince said, watching Mendez carefully for any signs of guilt or deception.

"That's good to hear," Mendez said, nodding slightly. "I'd like to hear more about your investigation, if you don't mind."

Vince hesitated for a moment, wondering how much, and what exactly he was going to say to Mendez. He knew that they needed to tread carefully. "Of course, straight to business of course. We'd be happy to share what we found."

Mendez motioned for them to take a seat, and Vince and Eleanor sat back down across from her.

"During the course of my investigation, I took my usual approach to solving a case. That is to say that although this case was certainly different to any other that I have worked in the past, the similarities of investigations are always obvious."

Mendez nodded.

"First, I assessed the relationships between the crew members and tried to ascertain a possible motive for one of the key suspects to have committed such a deed. These, as you are aware, were Grace Thompson, Priya Nair, Leo Martinez and the Captain himself."

"And you found a motive?"

Vince shook his head. "The community up in the lunar settlement is a testament to human kindness and camaraderie. I can only salute you for your selection of such a diverse and wonderful team, Doctor."

"Thank you," Mendez replied. "But I'm sorry I don't quite understand. If everyone is so friendly up there, then how did you solve the case?"

"Well to be clear," Vince said. "They're friendly, but they're still human. But that's not the point. What I believed to have happened is nothing short of an accident, plain and simple. Dr Whittaker had a disagreement with Lead Scientist Dr Nair about searching new areas and decided to sneak out to see what he could find for himself. He suffered a tear to his spacesuit and lost his oxygen before he could make it back to within communications range."

"But that doesn't..." Dr Mendez started, then changed whatever it was that she was going to say. "Do you know what he was looking for on his own?"

Vince noticed the almost imperceptible flash of the Doctor's gaze to Eleanor as she asked the question. For all that Mendez knew, these two women were truly the only two people in the entire universe that knew what Whittaker was looking for. And that was exactly how Vince wanted it to remain.

"He told Dr Nair that he thought he'd found an irregularity in some of his tests, that perhaps there was a large cave system that he would like to explore. Dr Nair told him that there was plenty to explore closer to the settlement, and that the seismic scans? - you'll have to forgive me; I'm no scientist – could often be fooled by the composition and density of the ground. It doesn't really matter, my investigation concluded that all of this was one big accident, and I am happy to be able to report to you no findings of foul play on my end."

"Adrian wasn't exactly the best at taking orders..." Eleanor added. "He did tell me that he wanted to go and explore more of the lunar surface, but I never imagined that he was going to go and try to do it alone..."

Again, everyone around the table knew that what Eleanor had said was a fabrication, but Vince didn't want to let on to Mendez that he was in on this. It was also apparent that Mendez didn't want to spill the beans that she too had knowledge of the telephone conversations between Eleanor and her late husband.

"I can't imagine how difficult this all must be for you, Mrs Whittaker," Mendez said with a genuine look of sadness. "Do let me know if there is anything that I can do to make any of this a little easier for you."

Eleanor smiled back at Dr Whittaker. "Thank you, I really appreciate it," she said.

"So is there anything else going on up there on my little world?" Mendez said with a half-smile.

"Not really," Vince managed to reply casually. "Some minor technical issues that Ms Thompson has been sorting, I believe you know about the communications issue?"

"It is rather annoying, but I'm sure that Grace is the person for the job," Mendez replied. "I just feel so isolated being all the way down here, sometimes I feel like I'm missing out on a lot of the good stuff, you know?"

Vince nodded. "It really is like a whole different world up there. But like you say, I'm sure the right people are in all the right places, after all, that's your job, isn't it?"

"It is," Mendez replied. "But at what point does one think that perhaps *they* are the best person for the job?"

Vince raised an eyebrow at the question. "What do you mean, Doctor?"

Mendez leaned forward slightly. "I mean, at what point does one start to think that perhaps they could do a better job than the people they're overseeing? That perhaps they have a better understanding of the situation and the people involved?"

Vince's eyes narrowed. "Are you implying that there's something wrong with the way the mission is being run?"

Mendez held up her hands in a placating gesture. "No, no, not at all. I just... sometimes I get the feeling that there's more going on up there than I'm aware of. That there are secrets being kept from me."

Vince felt a chill run down his spine. Was Dr Mendez onto them? Did she suspect that they knew more than they were letting on? Again, he reminded himself that he needed to tread carefully.

"I can assure you, Doctor, that everything is running smoothly up there. The crew is doing an excellent job, and I'm sure you've all made some significant breakthroughs and discoveries."

Mendez looked at him sceptically. "I hope that's true, Detective. Because if there's something going on up there that I'm not aware of, I will find out. And believe me, you don't want to be on my bad side."

Vince felt a wave of unease wash over him at Mendez's quick change of expression, but he did his best to remain calm. He could only hope that Eleanor would follow suit.

"That reminds me actually," Vince said, changing the subject. "One of the scientists up there, Bill, he asked me to bring these mineral samples down for you." And with those words, Vince had begun to weave their plan. He couldn't take it back now and he could only hope that Mendez would fall for it. He reached into his pocket and retrieved the small, sealed parcel of diamonds and placed them on the table for Mendez to take. "I hope they'll shed some light on the lunar surface for you."

Mendez looked at the parcel on the table with a blank expression on her face. She didn't move for so long that Vince wondered if she had known what they were up to, but eventually she seemed to come to some internal decision and picked up the parcel.

"Sometimes it's more efficient on the power systems to run tests on mineral samples down here on Earth. I'll make sure these get to the right department for cataloguing," Mendez said.

Vince couldn't help but notice that Mendez's pupils had almost completely dilated, and as she spoke, her wide eyes didn't leave the parcel. It seemed that their ruse had been successful, and Mendez had been blinded to what was happening before her, by the promise of riches.

"I thought so, there had been some power issues up there too, remember I called you to ask about the battery capacity?" Vince asked.

"Oh yes... I recall," Mendez replied, not entirely present in the conversation any longer.

Dr Mendez then abruptly stood up and slapped her thighs. "Well Detective, Mrs Whittaker, if there's anything else I can help you with then please don't hesitate to call me, otherwise it has been a pleasure, but I must get back to my work." Then she quickly turned around and exited the room without another word.

And that was it. All they had to do was wait and allow Mendez the opportunity to keep the diamonds, and to try to contact Bill to arrange for more shipments.

Eventually, Dr Telford re-entered the room and cleared the pair to leave. It was all a bit of an anti-climax for Vince, who had been expecting some big Sci-Fi-esque decontamination procedure, though all that happened was that they were escorted to the front gates and told that they could wait for a taxi there.

"What do you think will happen next?" Eleanor asked as they waited.

"I have no idea," Vince replied. "But I promise that I'll do everything I can to ensure Mendez doesn't get away with what she's done."

Chapter 26: Caught Red Handed

Vince knew that he couldn't co-ordinate with the lunar settlement in his accusation of Dr Mendez. He also had no idea, and no way of knowing what was happening within the inner workings of the lunar mission, so catching Mendez was going to be a very difficult task. What if she hadn't yet done anything with the diamonds? What if she had a change of heart? Or even what if she hadn't tried to contact Bill again yet?

Vince could only assume that two days was enough and that any longer would run the risk of their communications error being found out for what it was.

In the meantime, Vince had prepared his full and detailed account and summary of what he had found out on the lunar surface, though he did leave out some of the more incriminating details of what he found during his investigation. For example, he had no desire to speak about Grace's tampering, Leo's extra-curricular activities, Dr Nair's physical confrontation with Whittaker, or the Captain's constant meddling. He of course, spoke about Bill, Jane and Doctor Mendez's involvement in the diamonds and their subsequent smuggling operation.

Vince was just finalising his report, when his phone rang, startling him back into the world around him.

"Hello?" he asked into the receiver.

"Detective?" the voice returned. It was clearly Dr Mendez and Vince froze. He hadn't expected the Doctor to call, and the timing was so perfect that he couldn't help but instantly feel as though he was being watched. He eventually mustered the wherewithal to answer.

"Dr Mendez, how are you?" he managed.

"I'm fine, thank you for asking," Mendez said in a level tone. "I wonder if you could come to my office, I have a few questions that I think you may be able to help me with."

"Of course, Doctor," Vince replied as casually as he could. Please, send a car, tell me when and I'll be right there."

Mendez gave him the details and Vince quickly jotted them down before hanging up. He stood in silence for a long while, just looking at his phone and trying to process exactly what it was that Mendez could want. As far as he could see it, there were only two options: one: that she knew about either Bill and the plan to take her down, or two: she really did want to talk some more about the mission. Either way he couldn't refuse her, but he could do a few things to protect himself before he left.

Turning back to his computer, he picked up the summary he'd been working on and dragged it into an email, addressing it to the chief of police and a few other contacts he'd made during his career. He wanted to make sure that there was a record of everything they had found on the lunar surface, just in case anything happened to him or Eleanor. He also wanted to make sure that their investigation was on record, so that if anything did go wrong, the authorities would have all the information they needed to take down whoever was responsible. Then he clicked the send button, and his email was away into the ether.

Vince took a deep breath, trying to steady his nerves. He thought about just sending the police in to meet Mendez and be done with it, but he couldn't shake the feeling that without him, this whole gambit wasn't going to pan out as they had planned. He hoped that nothing had happened on the lunar surface that would change their planning, but again he couldn't be sure.

Vince didn't hear anything back from his email before the car arrived to transport him to Mendez's office and as he walked in, again she was the only person in the room. To his surprise, she greeted him with a warm smile and an outstretched hand, which he shook.

"Thank you for coming in to see me, Detective," Mendez said. "There are just a few things that I wanted to talk with you about with regards to your time on the lunar settlement. I'm sorry but when we spoke last, I was a little flustered as you can imagine."

Vince nodded. "Of course, anything you need. What did you want to aske specifically?"

"Well," Mendez said slowly. "I wanted to ask about Grace Thompson."

Vince was taken aback; this wasn't something he'd been expecting.

"Ms Thompson," Mendez continued, "Well, let me just say it. The rolling blackouts, the small issues that the habs have encountered. The fact that you yourself called to ask about the battery capacity on the lunar surface... would you have any reason to suspect that Ms Thompson has been causing issues in an attempt to sabotage our mission?"

Vince felt his heart race as he processed Mendez's question. He had to be careful; he couldn't let on that he knew anything about Grace's actions. He decided to play dumb for now and see where this conversation was going.

"I can assure you, Doctor, that Ms Thompson is one of the most dedicated and competent engineers I have ever met," Vince replied, keeping his tone neutral. "Of course, there have been some technical issues on the lunar surface, but I don't think that's indicative of any sabotage. I think it's just the nature of the job."

Mendez nodded thoughtfully. "I see. Well, I suppose it was just a thought that occurred to me. It's just that the timing of some of these issues is a little suspicious. Plus, the communication system is still malfunctioning, and it was my understanding that it would be a short-term situation."

Vince nodded. "I'm afraid I can't really comment, Doctor. But... is there anything else you wanted to ask me?" Vince asked, hoping to steer the conversation away from Grace.

Mendez looked at him for a moment before speaking. "Why did you call me to ask about the battery capacity?" she asked.

"Well, forgive me if I overstepped, but I wanted to ensure for my own peace of mind, that the settlement and the habs were stable. As you can imagine, not having left the Earth's atmosphere before I was a little uncomfortable having my life placed in the hands of total strangers," Vince lied.

Mendez nodded slowly. "Of course…" she trailed off. "But still, the battery capacity was good, yet the settlement still experienced rolling blackouts."

Vince shrugged. "As I said before, there have been some technical issues. The battery capacity might have been good, but there could've been other factors that can come into play, such as unexpected power surges or mechanical failures. I'm no engineer, but in my experience, there things are never black and white, are they?"

Mendez seemed to accept his explanation, but Vince could tell that she was still suspicious. He tried to maintain a calm and professional demeanour, even though his heart was racing. He couldn't afford to let his guard down, not even for a moment.

"I suppose you could be right," Mendez exhaled. "I apologise for bringing you down here just for that."

"It's no problem," Vince said.

"I have another question," Mendez said, apparently coming to some internal conclusion. "The scientist who gave you the package for me, did you speak to him at all?"

Vince felt the vein on his neck begin to pulsate. Mendez was asking about Bill, and he had no idea how he was going to get through this next section of the conversation.

"Only briefly…" Vince said, trying to downplay the importance of the question. "Why do you ask?"

"No reason really," Mendez replied. "Just on the few occasions that I have spoken to Mr Palmer, he doesn't seem to be himself. I know it's different communicating via text rather than on the phone or in person, but I just can't put my finger on it."

Then it hit Vince. Something that he hadn't thought about: what if Mendez and Bill had devised a code, such as a single word that they must say to each other if a situation arose like the one they'd manufactured? He felt his palms turn instantly wet.

"Yes... sometimes people do act differently when what they say is being recorded..." Vince said. "But tell me, you know Mr Palmer personally?"

"Of course, I know all of the crew personally. How else would I be able to choose each member of the expedition and be sure that they are not only capable but will also fit in with the rest of the crew?"

"Then tell me, what made Mr Palmer fit in with the rest of the crew?" Vince asked, but immediately regretted his question. He was asking too much about Bill.

Mendez looked at Vince curiously. "What do you mean, Detective? Are you insinuating that there's something off about Bill?"

Vince quickly tried to backtrack. "No, not at all, Doctor. I'm just trying to get a better understanding of the crew dynamics and how you selected them for the mission. Call it a personal curiosity."

Mendez's expression softened slightly. "I understand that, Detective. And to answer your question, Bill is an expert in his field and has a great deal of experience in similar missions back here on Earth. He's also a team player and has shown great leadership skills that could be transferrable to the lunar surface."

Vince nodded at the incredibly textbook answer, feeling relieved that he had managed to steer the conversation away from anything incriminating. He knew that he needed to be more careful with his questioning and not give away any hints about what he already knew.

"Could I share something with you, Detective?" Mendez asked.

"Of course," Vince replied.

Then the most unexpected thing happened. Mendez reached into her pocket and placed the same package on the table that Vince had given her, purportedly from Bill up on the lunar settlement. Vince watched in silence as Mendez unfolded the package to reveal the sparkling diamonds that had been contained within.

"What...?" Vince managed to ask with genuine shock.

"Do you know what these are?" Mendez asked.

Vince nodded. "They're surely diamonds, are they not?" he said, not taking his eyes from the stones. He could only imagine what they were worth. "But how?"

"Mr Palmer came across a cave filled with these stones. And when I say filled, I mean filled. These samples were sent down to me for testing, which I thank you for your assistance with."

"But why didn't they simply come down with the other samples in transport containers?" Vince asked.

Vince was now completely off balance. The fact that Mendez had not only brought up the issue of the diamonds but also the fact that she still had them wasn't something that he'd been expecting. Quickly he began thinking through all the information that he'd been given about Mendez, wondering if they'd made a mistake anywhere.

Mendez stared at Vince for a long moment before she continued. "Is there something you need to tell me, or are we going to continue this charade, Detective?" Mendez asked.

Vince opened his mouth to reply, then closed it again quickly.

"Listen Detective," Mendez said with a wide smile. "I want to know what you did with the real diamonds, how and when you managed to switch them out, who you're working with, and I want you to give me back my diamonds right god damn now."

"What...?" was all that Vince managed to say while he urged his mind to catch up to the situation. "I don't..."

Mendez picked up the open package and threw it on the ground, standing up and bearing down on Vince menacingly.

"White sapphires? I know they look nice and all but even a few basic tests prove them to be a cheap facsimile of the diamonds I was waiting for! My diamonds!"

"I..." Vince said. "White sapphires?" Then it clicked. Mendez had tested the diamonds, and found that they were in reality not diamonds, but a far less valuable mineral.

Vince's mind raced as he tried to come up with an explanation. How had this happened? Had someone switched the diamonds on him? Had they been fake all along? He knew he had to be careful with his words, but he also knew he couldn't lie to Mendez.

"Doctor Mendez, I swear to you, I had no idea," Vince said, trying to remain calm. "I was just given the package and asked to hand it to you. I didn't know what was in there and I certainly didn't swap anything out."

Vince's mind immediately switched to Eleanor and he wondered if there was any way that she could've switched out the package, or the contents. In fact, even the Captain could've done so. The pool of suspects had just blown wide open once again.

Then Vince began to laugh. It was a chuckle at first, then evolved into a long, drawling laugh.

"So you're telling me that you arranged for the largest diamond heist in all of human history, had these precious gems transported across space... and when you opened the parcel, all you would find would be a fake? I'm sorry Doctor, but this is all just too much."

Mendez looked at Vince with a mix of confusion and anger. "What are you talking about, Detective? This is not a laughing matter! I want my diamonds and I want them now!"

Vince composed himself and replied, "I understand that, Doctor, and I'm not laughing about the situation. It's just that it seems so ludicrous that someone would go through all this trouble just to switch out the diamonds for fakes."

Mendez crossed her arms and glared at Vince. "Then talk it through with me, Detective. How do you explain the fact that these diamonds are fake?"

Vince took a deep breath and tried to think clearly. "I don't have an explanation at the moment, Doctor. But I can assure you that I had no knowledge of any fake diamonds being swapped in. It could literally have been anyone who I came into contact with over the last few days. It could even have happened after I gave them to you!"

Mendez's expression softened slightly. "I see what you're saying, Detective and I apologise for my earlier outburst. It's just that these diamonds were incredibly valuable, and their disappearance could jeopardise everything."

"I'm sorry Doctor, but by 'everything', do you mean your plan to continuously smuggle diamonds back down to Earth for your own personal gain?"

Vince's question was met with a stunned silence. Mendez's eyes widened, and her mouth hung open in shock.

"What are you talking about, Detective?" she finally managed to ask.

"I'm talking about the fact that we both know these diamonds weren't just a one-time thing," Vince said, his tone firm. "We both know that you planned on smuggling diamonds down to Earth with the aid of your new recruit, Bill Palmer. And I'm willing to bet that you even told him that he should do what he 'needed to do' to make it all happen."

Mendez's expression hardened once again. "You have no proof of that," she spat out.

Vince shrugged. "Maybe not. But I do know that you had motive and opportunity. I know that you fast-tracked Mr Palmer onto the mission, and I know that you overheard Dr Whittaker telling his wife that he'd found the cave filled with them. What all of this does, is that it makes you the prime suspect in this case."

Mendez glared at Vince, clearly seething with anger. "I have no idea what you're talking about," she said through gritted teeth. Then she softened into a smile. "And you have no proof. You have no evidence of any of this, and thanks to whoever switched out the diamonds, you don't even have motive. Who wants white sapphires anyway?"

Vince maintained his calm composure, despite the rising tension in the room. "Maybe not, Doctor, but there's something you don't yet know: Bill died up there on the moon. He tried to kill both myself and Eleanor, and succeeded in killing another scientist in the search for the diamonds and their cave. The person that I would wager money on who you have been communicating with, has been the team up there in the settlement. That makes you an accomplice at best, Doctor, and a murderer at worst."

Mendez's face paled as Vince's words sunk in. "What... what are you saying? Bill is dead?" she asked in a shocked voice. "But..."

Vince nodded grimly. "Yes, he is. And we know that he was working with someone down here on Earth. Someone who had access to the lunar settlement's communication system. You, Doctor."

Mendez's eyes widened in horror. "No, that's not possible. I would never... no!"

"You had the motive and the opportunity, Doctor. And I've heard everything that I need to make my own judgements."

Mendez stared at Vince for a long moment, then slumped back into her chair. "I don't know what to say," she said quietly. "I didn't realise it had gone this far... that people had died. I was just trying to secure my own financial future, but I never wanted anyone to get hurt."

Vince regarded her with a mixture of pity and disgust. "Well, Doctor, it looks like you're going to have to answer for your actions now. And believe me, there will be consequences."

Then suddenly there was a loud knock at the door.

"And it seems like our time here is up, Doctor," Vince said, standing up. "You can come in," he said loudly.

When the door opened, in stepped three uniformed police officers, who seemed to stand still, awaiting Vince's instruction.

"Dr Mendez has confessed her involvement to me," Vince said. "I believe that you can now escort her to the station for questioning."

The officers then moved forward and Mendez stood up, her expression resigned. "I understand," she said quietly. "I'll cooperate fully."

As the officers led Mendez out of the room, Vince couldn't help but feel a sense of relief. The case could finally be closed, and he was satisfied that justice would eventually be served.

Epilogue

As the news reports flooded the airwaves and filled the pages of newspapers, the world was left in shock at the events that had taken place over the last few months on the lunar settlement.

The headlines screamed of a diamond smuggling plot, orchestrated by Dr Mendez, the lead scientist on the lunar mission. According to the reports, Mendez had fast-tracked fellow scientist Bill Palmer onto the mission, knowing full well that he would be able to assist her in her plan to smuggle diamonds back to Earth.

The reports stated that the diamonds were discovered by Dr Whittaker, but his death was deemed a simple accident, and the diamonds were left untouched until Bill discovered them. It was then that Dr Mendez began communicating with Bill, instructing him on how to smuggle the diamonds back to Earth without raising suspicion.

But it all fell apart when Bill was killed during an attempt on Vince Callahan and Eleanor Whittaker's lives, killing fellow scientist Jane McDonald in the process. The news reports stated that Bill had gone rogue and was working alone, but many still questioned whether Dr Mendez had played a role in his actions, or perhaps even outright ordered the man to kill in pursuit of their riches.

As the investigation unfolded, and in a rather fascinating twist, it was eventually revealed that the diamonds were not diamonds at all, but rather white sapphires. It would have been a crushing blow to Dr Mendez's plan, as the sapphires were worth only a fraction of what the diamonds would have been worth.

The news reports went on to describe the fallout from the events, including the arrest of Dr Mendez as the remaining suspect from the LSI. They also detailed the impact that the diamond smuggling plot could have had on the world's diamond industry, with prices potentially forced down as consumers questioned the validity of their purchases and the supply of the precious gems.

In the end, the world was left to wonder how something so audacious and dangerous could have been planned and executed under the watchful eyes of the world's scientific community. And while some may never know the full truth, the events on the moon will be remembered for generations to come as a cautionary tale of the lengths some will go to for personal gain, and greed.

Vince sat back in his chair. He knew that he had made a difference with his investigation, but the fact that lives had been lost, and that the 'diamonds' turned out to be something entirely different, left a sour taste in his mouth.

The world would never be the same again, and the cost had seemed just too high.

As he sat in his office, surrounded by the evidence and files from the case, Vince couldn't help but wonder what the future would hold for space exploration and the search for valuable resources on other planets. He knew that there would always be people like Dr Mendez and Bill Palmer, willing to do whatever it took to get what they wanted, no matter the consequences.

But he also knew that there were good people out there, people like the pioneers on the surface of the moon, who had offered their lives to the mission, and were dedicated to pushing the boundaries of human knowledge and making the world a better place. He knew that he had to continue to fight for justice and to protect those who were vulnerable to the greed and ambition of others.

As he packed up his files and prepared to leave, Vince couldn't help but feel a sense of relief. The case was over, the criminals were caught, and justice had been served. But he also knew that there would always be more cases to solve, more people to protect, and more stories to tell.

As he left the room, turning the light off and closing the door behind him, Vince thought about the lessons that he had learned during the course of the case. He knew that he had to trust his instincts, no matter how crazy they seemed. He knew that he had to work tirelessly to uncover the truth, no matter how difficult it may be. And he knew that he had to stand up for what was right, no matter the cost.

For Vince, the case of Dr Adrian Whittaker's death was just another chapter in his ongoing quest for justice and truth. And as he let his mind shut down, he couldn't help but wonder what other mysteries lay waiting to be uncovered, what other secrets lay hidden among the stars.

The team that Vince had met on the lunar settlement had remained within their roles because Vince had kept his word and decided not to include their various slight wrongdoings in his final report. Dr Mendez, however, was not so lucky. She was ultimately convicted on multiple charges, including conspiracy to commit fraud and murder, and was sentenced to life in prison. Her downfall became a cautionary tale for scientists and researchers everywhere, a reminder that the pursuit of personal gain should never come at the expense of the greater good.

Vince had met with Eleanor just once since the conclusion of the case against Mendez, though it was casual and did not last very long. They spoke over a coffee in a local café and Vince made sure to ask how things were going with Helen, and it seemed that no matter what happened in the world, some things were simply constants, destined never to change.

~The End~

A Thankyou

Again, your investment of your own time and money is always well appreciated and again, I ask that you **rate** and **review** everything that you read – and not just this book, so that lesser-known authors can grow their audience and gain the credibility that they deserve for their hard work.

Also, check out my website, it's usually kept up to date with current works, reviews and a few extra little bits. You'll find it at:

www.davidlingard.com

Thank you